"THE SHOOTING?" LIZ REPEATED.
"What does that have to do with anything?"

"Well…" Simone bit her lip. "Don't freak out or anything, but there's this… theory going around that the Sparrow Hills Shooter was gunning for cheerleaders at the dance."

"What? Why?"

"Because Nikki was a cheerleader. And so was Adrienne."

Liz blinked. "Adrienne Pirolli?" She remembered that name from Allie's notes. "She got shot in the arm, right? I didn't know she was a cheerleader."

"Yeah, well, she was. And now people think it's dangerous to be a cheerleader." Simone sat down on a bench and crossed her arms, looking annoyed.

"But why?" Liz said. "The shooter's dead. Why do they think it's still dangerous?"

"Oh. Well," Simone looked troubled. "There's this other rumor going around. That the shooter's not dead."

Liz stared at her. "They don't think Brock's dead?"

"No. I mean…they don't think Brock's the shooter."

NEAR OCCASIONS
John Paul 2 High Book Five

Christian M. Frank

NEAR OCCASIONS

John Paul 2 High

Book Five

CHESTERTON PRESS
FRONT ROYAL, VIRGINIA

To Oona and Ronin,
and to my friend Ryan
who wrote this book
in an alternate reality - A.

To Alice - J.

Cover design by Regina Doman. Photo from Spiering Photography. Interior images from iStockphoto.com, Regina Doman, and Spiering Photography.

Chesterton Press
P.O. Box 949
Front Royal, VA 22630
www.chestertonpress.com

Summary: Liz &J.P. just wanna have fun at their small private school, running a prank war and investigating a closed police case. But danger is near, and actions have consequences.
ISBN: 978-0-9899411-6-7

Printed in the United States of America

www.ChestertonPress.com

I am God.

The boy stepped on the shovel and pushed. It bit into the rocky ground. He heaved out a clump of soil, threw it to the side, and plunged the shovel into the ground again.

The plan did it. The plan—my plan—it's made me God.

And it truly had, in a sense. His will had become reality. The supposedly powerful ones—the cops, the FBI, the TV stations—they all did his bidding. He wanted to be dead to them, and so they pronounced him dead.

Heh. Just like the 'real' God.

The boy continued to work on the hole, widening it, deepening it. This was how he had achieved godhood: he was patient. He was careful. And he didn't make mistakes.

And now he had his reward. He'd made history. He'd become the first school shooter to survive the encounter—to get away with it, in fact. He'd changed lives from on high, and nothing had stopped him.

And now it was over. And he could walk away, forever God to those lives he had touched. Mysterious.

Unseen.

Unseen...

With a dull metallic clank, the shovel struck a rock. The boy looked down at it. He struck the rock again. *Clank.*

Nobody even *knew* what he'd done. *She* didn't know.

He took a deep breath, lifted the shovel high, and slammed it down on the rock as hard as he could. *Clank.*

The boy let out a string of obscenities that echoed through the empty woods, slamming the shovel down again and again. His rage had come out of nowhere; he didn't understand it and he didn't care to. A voice in the back of his mind urged him to calm down; someone might hear.

But he knew no one would. He was too deep in the woods. He had made sure. Because he never made mistakes.

And nobody would ever know.

She would never know.

Who cares? It's over. You won. Walk away.

He pulled himself out of the pit, walked a short distance away, and pulled something out from behind a tree: a heavy canvas sack. Dark liquid dripped out from one corner.

He looked down at the sack for a moment, then kicked it savagely, so that it tumbled into the pit. *Walk away.* That was the plan.

What good is God without worshipers?

She had never been part of the original plan, but now she was all he thought of: horrified, astonished, awestruck, trembling before him.

He wanted her to worship him. He needed her to worship him.

But she worshiped someone else now.

He had seen her posts, knew she was in deep with John Paul 2 High now. This school—was like a family, like a shell around her. Like a walnut shell. He needed to break it, crack it open, destroy it. He already had an idea how to do it, but it would require skill. Improvisation. He would need to make things happen without anyone seeing his fingerprints.

There was a movement from the bottom of the pit. A sound—a pitiful dog's whimper.

The boy smiled slightly. *Still alive?*

He closed his eyes and imagined the dog was her. He dug his shovel into the pile of dirt.

He started filling in the hole.

1

NO PROBLEM

"You can do this," Liz Simonelli whispered to her ankle as she wrapped it in turn after turn of Ace bandage. "You can do it, ankle. Don't make me mess this up."

Her ankle winced.

"Aw, come on," Liz muttered. "Don't be that way. It's been two weeks since you sprained, and it wasn't even my fault. I don't even *remember* spraining you."

She glanced around the locker room, making sure nobody was there. Liz didn't think talking to body parts would be accepted by the social strata she was trying to infiltrate.

She finished wrapping her ankle and checked herself out in the mirror. She was surprised by how well her 8th grade cheerleading uniform fit her for someone who was nearly sixteen, and about to start her second year at John Paul 2 High.

Her second year to be dealing with weird Catholic school problems, on top of all the typical drama queens, the chest-pounding gorillas, the geeks, the nerds, and the oh-so-holier-than-thou. And that was just in the original attending group of six, plus Liz.

Now there were going to be 21 students in the school. *God only knows what a new crop of losers and freaks is going to bring.* She took a step back to get a better look at herself in her old uniform. *I really can't believe I still fit in this thing.*

You've gotten taller. We used to be the same height.

The Liz in the mirror blinked. The thought, or memory, or whatever, had popped into her head out of nowhere. She was in the woods and Brian Burke, her friend from school, was hugging her, and she was saying how much taller he had gotten…

She grimaced. That didn't seem right. Not right at all. *Is that a real memory, or my imagination? Why would I imagine THAT?* But then, when it came to remembering the events of a few weeks ago, she was never clear on what was what. GHB had a way of doing that, especially when you weren't ready for it. Especially when it was forced on you. *Never thought I'd be someone who needed to know the symptoms of a date rape drug…*

She shook her head. *Focus.*

She went over her plan again to schmooze Tara Paulson and Simone Clearwater, the two captains of the Sparrow Hills cheer squad. They were older girls, and pretty. But the team was so shorthanded that they were willing to try out anybody—even an outsider with a gimpy leg.

At least I look good. She ran her fingers through her gold, curly hair. Good enough, anyway. The hair was a new addition. Normal Liz had dirty blonde hair, straight and mousy and blah. But cool Cheerleader Liz needed more glamorous hair. A dye and a perm did the trick. She smirked. Now she didn't look half-bad…

You're the prettiest girl here. Hands down.

The Liz in the mirror looked annoyed. Now where had that come from? Brian saying she was pretty? Brian didn't even like her. He was all gooshy over some other girl, Mary Summers. Whom Liz hated.

That memory couldn't be real. Because in this memory she felt happy and excited, like she could fly. It was a powerful, intoxicating feeling. It was dangerous. She shook her head. It had to be a daydream. A crazy, girly, stupid daydream.

But maybe it's not. Maybe it really happened. Your memory's all messed up from those drugs those jerks Hank and Bickerstaff put in you. It could have happened, right?

She looked gloomily into the mirror one more time. *Uh huh. Sure, Liz. Brian likes Mary, remember? Mary's an eight. That's what you told him: everyone has a number. "She's an eight," you said, "and you're a three."*

"And what number are you?" he'd asked.

I told him I didn't have a number.

But I do. Zero.

It was a hard truth, but it was still the truth. Liz considered herself a realist. Sometimes you have to tell the truth, no matter how hard it is. Her dad had told her that once. Accept it, acknowledge it, and move on.

She pulled her curls back and tied them into a ponytail. *It's go time. Let's do this, ankle.*

I came to look at cheerleaders and chew bubble gum, John Paul Flynn thought. *And I'm all out of bubble gum. Not that I ever had any.*

But the point is: cheerleaders.

John Paul Flynn (or J.P., as everyone knew him) liked cheerleaders—the female kind, anyway. And since there were no cheerleaders at his own school, John Paul 2 High (named after the same pope J.P. had been named for), he was headed for the nearest place that did have them, Sparrow Hills.

It was an easy decision to make, to spend time at the public school football practice today, watching the lovely ladies practicing on the sidelines while the guys sweated it out on the field. Sparrow Hills was less than a half mile from John Paul 2 High—close enough that J.P. could actually hear the whistles and the shouts of football practice. The two schools were separated only by some woods that took about five minutes to walk through. Anyway, football practice meant (maybe) cheerleading practice, too. And J.P. was bored. He got bored easily.

School hadn't started at John Paul 2 High, but the first day was tomorrow and his mom was setting up her classroom. J.P. had finished cleaning the room, and it was either watch cheerleaders or play the same boring games on his phone. Not a hard decision.

When J.P. arrived at Sparrow Hills, though, he was disappointed. No cheerleaders—only football players. *Oh man. The girls must be practicing somewhere else.* He sat down on one of the bleachers. J.P. wasn't really into sports, but he figured maybe he'd stick around for a while anyway, since some JP2HS students were playing on the team this year: George (junior, sort of the school leader), Athan (freshman, kind of a show-off), and Joey (freshman, Liz's younger brother, a loudmouth, but not so bad otherwise).

The Sparrow Hills football team was sort of a big deal. As the team executed a flawless play, J.P. remembered hearing somewhere that Sparrow Hills had won a string of championship games over the last few years, and had one of the best high school football teams around. The way this quarterback was passing, he could believe it.

A whistle blew and the team members scattered for a water break. He glanced beside him as a boy almost as tall as he was but much more muscular sat down on the same bleacher. He was dressed in a jersey and at first J.P. thought he saw his own last name on it: FLYNN—no. It wasn't that, it was FLYNT. J.P. gulped, and got to his feet. The boy looked at him; his eyes had a somewhat vacant expression and he looked like a thug. Which he was.

7

"Hey," said the thuggish kid. "Don't I know you from somewhere?"

J.P. swallowed again. *Only because you and your two friends beat me into a pulp last year.* He wondered if Neil Flynt would recognize him.

"Oh yeah!" Flynt said, and J.P. cringed. "You're from JP2 High, aren't you?"

"Um…yeah," J.P. said. "So uh, hey, what are you doing here? I didn't know you were on the football team—I thought you were a wrestler like Tyler—"

J.P. caught himself. He had forgotten: Tyler Getz was dead.

He tried again. "Um, yeah. I'm uh, sorry about Tyler. I'm sure he was a—uh—a nicer guy than he seemed. To me, at least."

Flynt cracked a smile. "Who are you kidding? Tyler wasn't a nice guy. Neither was I," he added. "We did some dumb stuff last year. Sorry about that."

"Yeah," J.P. said. "And I'm sorry about…"

Flynt looked at him with surprising quickness and J.P. suddenly remembered the worse part of the business. Flynt's buddy Brock had been responsible for the shooting rampage at Sparrow Hills last year. The police had found him three months later, dead. He'd committed suicide, just like every other school shooter.

Gosh, what must that be like to have a buddy who went ballistic and went on a shooting spree? Bet no one else wants to talk to him now! Wait, is that why he's up here alone instead of palling around with the other football players? Is that why he's talking to me in the first place?

All this went through J.P.'s mind in a flash.

"Don't say you're sorry about Brock, because you're not," Flynt growled. "No one's sorry he's dead. They all think he was the Sparrow Hills Shooter."

"Well, wasn't he?"

Now Flynt looked around him, and to J.P.'s surprise, he seemed to be a little pale. He got up and came over to J.P., and sat down close to him. When he spoke again, it was nearly a whisper. "That's what everyone else thinks. They think the case is closed and we're all safe now. But I don't think so."

"Why not?"

Flynt spread his hands and looked helpless. "I don't have any proof, but I just don't think it was him! He was a really good guy! I mean he could be a jerk sometimes, but he wasn't a killer. I'm sure Brock didn't do the shooting, but everyone's blaming him, and now he's dead. And then Tyler suddenly dies, just when it looks like he was getting better."

J.P. felt his scalp prickling. "What do you mean?"

Again, Flynt looked around, and then said in a low voice, "I was with Tyler the day he died. And it didn't happen the way the papers said it did."

Liz walked into the gym with barely a catch in her stride. The gym was full of girls stretching, going through routines, and mostly just sitting and chatting.

She spotted thin, black-haired Tara and sandy blonde Simone and ran up to them. "Hey guys!" she sang out. "Tara! Simone! It's so good to see you!"

"Liz!" Tara embraced Liz. "How are you? You feeling better?"

"Oh, sure, whatevs!" Liz said, exuding confidence with a casual toss of her head that made her golden curls bounce in a cute way (she hoped).

"Are you sure? We heard you were in the hospital—"

"It was only overnight," Liz said, not quite truthfully. It had been more like two days.

"Hmm." A redheaded girl sitting behind Tara and Simone gave a delicate, haughty sniff. "Who's this?"

"Liz Simonelli." Liz offered her hand. "Hi."

Red glanced at Liz's hand coolly, and said nothing.

Tara rolled her eyes. "Liz, this is Madison Williams. Maddie, this is—"

"Yeah, I got her name," the redhead said. "You're another one from that super-conservative Catholic school down the road." Madison tossed her hair disdainfully. Liz found herself impressed, despite herself. This girl was clearly a *master* at hair tossing. There was so much utter contempt in that hair toss. It spoke volumes. Nasty, nasty volumes. "Tara and Simone pack the squad with holy rollers now whenever they get a chance. First Nikki, then June Wolsey. Humph. Pretty soon I'll be the only reasonable one left on this jinxed squad."

"Hey!" Tara protested. "June earned her way on the squad!"

"Yeah, well, how about her?" Madison said, indicating Liz.

"She's getting over a sprain! How do you expect—"

9

"No, it's okay," Liz broke in. She smiled coolly. "It's fine. You want to see my stuff?"

Madison's eyes narrowed. *Ooh. She does a good icy stare too.* "Yes," she said. "I would. Do a couple high kicks."

Liz shrugged, and kicked one leg up in the air, above head level. She'd been practicing all week.

"How about a half-Russian?"

Liz took a deep breath and jumped into the air, her good leg kicking up and touching her outstretched hand.

"How about a couple full Russians?"

"Maddie!" Tara said.

"No problem." Liz took another deep breath, took a few steps back, and then leapt up, kicking out both legs in a mid-air split, her arms stretched out. *No Problem.*

Then she landed. And her ankle said *Problem!* in an unmistakable way.

She looked up and smiled brightly. "No problem, Maddie."

Madison didn't smile back. "Only my friends call me Maddie," she said. She walked away, toward another group of girls.

Liz headed over to the bleachers and sat down, hoping that no one could tell anything was amiss. *Nothing is amiss. I just did a full Russian on a sprained ankle. Therefore, I am in pain. This is expected. Wow. Ouch.*

That had gone pretty well. Madison was going to be a jerk, but Liz was pretty sure she could handle it.

But what had Maddie meant about the squad being jinxed?

Not thinking about it, Liz told herself sternly. *This is your ticket out of John Paul 2 High, and you're going to take it.*

J.P.'s eyes widened. "You're serious?" he said. "You think someone… you know… did Tyler in?"

Flynt nodded. "They said it was an injury from weight lifting, but I know that isn't true. We weren't even lifting when it happened." He dropped his head and stared at his big hands.

"Well?" J.P. encouraged after a few moments.

"It's tough to talk about, you know?" Flynt rubbed his eyes. "You know, Tyler survived the shooting and he was really starting to feel better. We were working out at the gym together. I had to drive him because the doctors wouldn't sign the forms so he could get his license back. They said he was too weak in the stomach to brake a car without hurting himself. So stupid. I mean, at the gym he could press, like, 180 pounds! The guy was making a comeback!" Now there were practically tears in Flynt's eyes. "Then Tyler said he had to go take a leak. And so he went off. Then I heard him shouting in the bathroom, like he was in pain, and when I ran in, I heard a door slam. And there was Tyler, rolling around on the floor holding his sides, like someone had just kicked him in the gut—and I ran out and yelled for someone to call 911, then I went back and… and… he was dead."

His shoulders began to heave. "Tyler was a… survivor. And he never had his… comeback."

"Um, well," J.P. felt less scared now, and more embarrassed. It was weird seeing a big, tough football player cry. "Maybe he shouldn't have been pumping iron again. I mean, if the doctor said he couldn't drive."

"Yeah, well the doctors are WRONG!" shouted Flynt angrily, then he seemed to get a hold of himself.

"You want to know what I really think?" he whispered. "I think that someone shot Brock, and framed him as the shooter, and that same someone killed Tyler, too. And I think I'm being friggin' stalked by someone." He looked around, and again, he looked really scared. "Look, kid, I know the three of us weren't the nicest guys around. We beat up a lot of people. You know what they say, about how some people snap and then take revenge? I think someone's doing that. They got Brock and Tyler. I'm next."

"Look," J.P. said, "I'm… I'm really sorry about Tyler, but you know, the police are sure Brock did it. I mean, you're safe. It's all over."

"It's not over!" Flynt almost shouted. "Someone else did it, I'm telling you! I bet they tried to take out Tyler that night at the dance. They screwed it up, but obviously that mistake's been corrected now. Then they got Brock and pinned it on him. Whoever it is, is really, really good. Smart, and… and dangerous."

There was a shout from below, and J.P. looked down to see the Coach was hollering in their direction.

"Flynt!" he yelled. "Are you on this team or not?"

"Sorry Coach!" Flynt yelled, and lumbered to his feet. But he glanced back at J.P. "Thanks for listening."

"No problem," J.P. said.

11

"Alright," Flynt said. "But I mean it, be careful. And tell Allie to be careful too."

J.P. gave Flynt a startled look. Allie Weaver was another one of his classmates—blonde and pretty. She had used to go to Sparrow Hills—and she had used to date Tyler Getz. But that was all ancient history now.

"Why isn't Allie safe?" he said.

"Nobody's safe," Flynt whispered. "Nobody."

He ambled down the bleachers, as another football player wearing a helmet and pads passed him. He had blue eyes and dark eyebrows and seemed vaguely familiar. The player glanced at Flynt's retreating back and then at J.P., and grinned. "Dude, Flynt telling you his conspiracy theories again?" he asked, and shook his head. "Poor guy's had a rough time of it. He's a little cracked."

"Sounds like it," J.P. said, and couldn't help feeling a little chilled.

"Powell!" yelled the coach.

"Seriously, don't let him get to you, though," the football player slapped J.P. on the shoulder as he passed. "What was he talking about this time? JFK?"

"Only the Sparrow Hill Shooter," J.P. said.

The player froze, as though he had been shot. When he turned back to J.P., there was an unreadable expression on his face. Dark, and kind of empty.

"Don't believe everything you hear," he said. "There are some pretty vicious rumors out there."

And he leapt down the bleachers two at a time, *bang bang bang bang.*

Looks like it's going to be a very interesting year, J.P. thought.

2

CAR TROUBLE

It was the first day of school. Liz sat in the driver's seat of her mom's Honda Pilot and pushed her new curls out of her face with her fingers, trying to remember. She put the shifter knob to "drive" and turned the keys. Nothing. *Why won't this work?*

"Don't shift until you've turned the key," her mother said from the passenger seat.

Liz felt like talking back, but bit her tongue. It was too early in the morning for another fight with her mother. She put it back in park, turned the key and felt a satisfying *thruuuummm* as the engine turned over.

"We're not leaving without Joey," her mother said.

"I know, Mom," said Liz, and rolled down the window. "Yo, Little Bro! Let's get a move on!" she shouted, and gave two short blasts on the car horn.

"Liz!" said Mrs. Simonelli sharply. "Let's be a little more ladylike. Besides, horns are for emergencies only."

Liz drummed her fingers impatiently on the wheel. She swept her eyes over the street, watching for traffic like a good driver should… no Joey. She read the sign stapled to the telephone pole outside their house, a notice for a lost dog. Brown coat, mixed breed, named Boone… still no Joey. She picked up one of her dad's work shirts left in the back seat of the car and read the laundry label. Cold wash, no bleach, tumble dry, blah blah blah.

Finally! Joey emerged from the front door with his backpack slung over his broad shoulder. He stumped toward the car before he stopped, then turned and went back to the house.

"Aw, c'mon, Joey," Liz shouted. "Shake a leg!" Liz liked expressions like "shake a leg."

"Just making sure I locked the door," Joey shouted back. He fumbled with the lock.

"Can we be done with the shouting, please?" said her mom.

"What, you're a teacher and you wanna be late for the first day of school?" retorted Liz. Joey got into the back of the car. "Hokay, time to get this show on the road," said Liz. She checked for traffic, and rolled back onto the road. Then she shifted into first gear.

"You're in first gear, Liz," said her mom.

"I know, Mom," said Liz tightly. She rolled down the street for a few seconds, then shifted into second.

"Liz, this is an *automatic*." Her mother rolled her eyes. "You don't have to shift through every gear. Just put it in 'D.'"

"If you're not supposed to use any of the lower gears, why did the car makers put them there?" Liz retorted. She liked driving this way. She had liked it ever since last spring, when her father had first started teaching her to drive in the church parking lot. *I wish we had a stick shift for you to learn on*, he had said. *Every driver should learn how to drive stick. Driving an automatic's hardly driving at all.* He had said it in an offhand way, but Liz took it to heart, and deeply regretted that she didn't have a stick shift to practice on. Then she discovered that she could sort of drive the Pilot like a stick if she shifted her way through the gears. Her dad had thought it was funny. Her mom hadn't.

Liz stopped at a red light and shifted into neutral.

"Oh, please, Liz!" her mom yelled, putting down her tablet. "Just put the car in drive and leave it there!"

"It's not hurting the car," said Liz.

"I just want to look over this material for science class before we get to the school," said her mom. "So please stop fooling around with the gear shift and just drive."

"I *am* driving," said Liz. "This is just how I drive. Relax, okay?"

The light changed, they started down the road again, and Liz's thoughts returned to last spring. That had been the last time she felt she could talk with her dad. Soon after that, things became complicated between them. When they were working on the school over the summer, he had blamed her for an incident that had nearly burned down the building—an incident that was completely not her fault.

14

They were only about a mile from the school now. They were approaching a stop sign, and since it was only going to be a quick stop, Liz downshifted into first gear instead of neutral.

"Liz!" her mom barked, slapping her tablet down on her lap. "How many times do I have to keep telling you to stop monkeying around with the gear shift!"

"Don't yell at me when I'm driving!" Liz yelled.

"Put the car in gear and leave it alone!"

"Fine!" Liz checked the intersection and took her foot off the brake. She gave the Pilot a little gas and angrily jammed the shifter up to the second highest gear—

Ka-chunk!

The Pilot gave a horrible shudder and died in the middle of the intersection.

An icy wash of fear ran down every nerve of Liz's body. *Oh no! I killed the car! I killed the car! I killed—*

"Liz!" said her mom. "What did you do? What did you do?"

I killed the car! I shifted into reverse while the car was going forward! I killed the flipping car! Dad's going to tear my head off for this!

In a panic, Liz turned the ignition. Nothing. She tried again. Nothing. The car wouldn't start! *I can't believe I killed the car! Please no, please no, please no!* How much would it cost to replace a car like this? Under $10,000? Over? Liz had no idea.

"Liz! We're stopped in the middle of the intersection!"

"I know, Mom!"

"I told you not to monkey around with the gear shift!"

"This wouldn't have happened if you hadn't been shouting at me!"

"This wouldn't have happened *if you'd just left the car in drive like you're supposed to!*"

A sedan drove up to the intersection on Liz's right. *Oh, great, just what I need.* She continued to futilely turn the ignition.

The sedan stopped, and waited patiently for the intersection to clear. Liz continued to crank the ignition and prayed for a miracle.

"Liz! We have to get out of—"

"I know!" *Oh, please let me not have killed the car, please no, please no…*

The sedan gave a short, annoyed little beep.

From the back seat, Joey said, "The car's in reverse."

"I know it's in reverse!" cried Liz, on the verge of tears. "That's why the engine conked out."

"You can't turn the ignition while it's in reverse," said Joey.

Liz looked at the gear shift, momentarily dumbfounded.

She shifted into park, and holding her breath, turned the ignition once more…

Thruuuummm…

The Pilot started as though nothing was wrong. Liz felt the panic drain away. "Thank you, Joey. Thank you thank you thank you…"

She saw Joey shrug in the rear view mirror. "Sure. No problem."

Liz put the car in drive and started forward just as the sedan started forward as well. So she braked to let the other car around her, but just then the sedan braked too, apparently to let Liz have the right of way. Liz hesitated, then moved ahead—and so did the sedan. So Liz braked. And the sedan braked.

"What are you waiting for?" Her mom said in frustration. "Get out of the intersection!"

Fine. I don't care if we have a head-on collision. Liz stepped on the gas and roared forward. *Anything's better than being stuck here with my mom.*

This year is NOT off to a good start.

The group of freshman kids gathered around the school doors had no idea they were being watched.

They have no idea of what's in store. No idea what I have planned for them. They won't know what's going on until it's already happening. Until it's too late. And that's when I'm at my best.

I'm hidden. I'm silent. I crouch in the shadows, taking aim, stalking my prey with the skill of a hunting cat…

… no, that's not right. Like a ninja… no… like a hunting cat, trained in the deadly ninja arts, and with a cloak of invisibility.

And a can of diet soda, shook up real good. Which reminds me…

"GRENADE!"

The group of freshmen all turned in surprise as a can flew through the air and landed with a *PFFFFFFF* in front of them. Soda foam sprayed from the partially-popped top. Some of it sprayed on one of the girls, who shrieked.

Perfect. Three... two... one...

"Look out! I'll save you!"

J.P. sprinted out from behind a parked car, burst into the middle of the group, and belly-flopped onto the fizzing can, ignoring the pain from his rough landing. He curled himself around the can, yelling, "Get clear! Get clear! Tell my mother I love her!"

For a moment he lay there, eyes scrunched closed. One of the girls, Jacinta Summers, giggled. J.P. opened one eye and glanced around. As he'd hoped, everyone in the small crowd was staring at him, looking either amused or confused (or in the soda-sprayed Kristy Vogel's case, annoyed). Joey Simonelli, Liz's round-faced younger brother could barely contain his mirth.

Slowly, J.P. got to his feet, his tie and white school shirt stained with soda and grass. He looked intently at the nearly empty can.

"Huh. It was a dud. Thank God for small miracles." He picked the can up, downed the rest of its contents, and handed the empty can to the always-acting-cool Kevin Snyder, whose gawky face looked both disdainful and confused. "Make sure this gets to Bomb Disposal. Which is in Costain's office. In his top desk drawer."

"Wha... really?" Kevin stammered.

"DON'T... question me, private," J.P. scowled. "Unless you want to find your locker filled with a different 'fun' liquid every day from now until graduation. It's a little game I call 'Sticky Surprise', and it's very popular with everyone but the victim. Bleach, motor oil, ketchup. Anything goes, really."

He spun around with a flourish and walked away, feeling triumphant.

"Who was that brave red-haired man?" he heard Joey say dramatically. "He saved our lives!" J.P. sauntered off around the side of the building as if nothing had happened, only stopping to rub his aching knee when he was sure no one was looking. He knew it was going to be stiff and sore for a little while.

But it was for a good cause. Totally worth it.

A moment later Joey came running around the corner, huffing and puffing and still chortling. "Aw man! That was great, J.P.! You should have seen Kristy after you left. She was all like, 'he could have ruined my uniform!' and I was all like 'get over it!' and then she was like—"

"Yep, yep. I get it. I hear ya." J.P. gave his knee one last squeeze and straightened up. "Kristy doesn't have a sense of humor. That, I expected. The important thing is, did Jacinta like it?" Jacinta Summer's willowy figure, blonde hair, and laughing blue eyes had been on his mind a lot lately. She was cute, and fun, and laughed easily: all of his favorite qualities in a girl.

"Oh yeah! She kept trying not to laugh at Kristy, but the more Kristy kept whining, the more Jacinta kept laughing! It was so funny!" Joey couldn't hold it in anymore; he burst out into loud guffaws, trying to talk in between snorts.

"Alright, alright little trooper." J.P. patted Joey on the back. "Take a breath. Can't have you dying on me. I'm gonna go try to find your sister. Are you going to make it?"

"Ye—yeah. Sure… I'll be… okay," Joey panted, finally having caught his breath. He waved J.P. on. "I think I saw her go behind the school."

"Thanks. Let me know if Jacinta says anything about how awesomely awesome I am. I did save her life, after all." J.P. headed off around the back of the school.

Liz stood at the edge of the woods looking at the school building. She had spent the entire past year wishing the school would fail and shut down. But that was never gonna happen now. They had spent the summer fixing the place up, and now there were all these new kids.

New kids. She had met most of them over the summer work camp, but this was the first time she'd seen them all dressed up in the school's black and white uniforms, like they belonged here. Now the parking lot was full to bursting, and the newbies were *everywhere*, milling around

18

the front doors, boys kicking around a soccer ball on the lawn, girls gossiping intently on the picnic benches, new faces and new names and new parents...

This year was going to be *very* different. John Paul 2 High was going to be a *real* school, and who would run it? The newbies! Just look at them! Standing around like they *owned* the place! Who did these newbies think they were? Who were these dudes kicking a soccer ball, like *they* decided that soccer was going to be JP2HS's sport? Who were these girls sitting around the picnic bench like *they* decided what was going to be the inside dish?

Liz's eyes narrowed. *They need to know who's in charge. This may be a new school. But I'm old school.*

"Liz!" a happy, familiar voice said behind her.

Liz winced, and turned to see Celia Costain, the principal's oldest daughter and the school's biggest fan, running up to her, her long, curly dark hair bouncing behind her.

"So good to see you! Did you get my email about the Bible study?"

"Yeah, no—what?"

"The Bible study me and Allie are running!" Celia said, her brown eyes very earnest. It would have been easier to hate Celia if she wasn't so doggone nice about everything. "There's a lot of kids at the school this year, Liz, and I really think it's important for us to help them fit in. So, George and I decided that we're going to do a Bible study over lunch every Tuesday, and invite the freshmen to join us. He and Brian are going to do one for the boys, and Allie and I will do one for the girls. You can help, too, if you want!"

"Um...no, that's not really my thing."

Celia shrugged. "Well, could you help me out by reaching out to the new kids, helping them feel part of a community?"

"Part of what? This is a school, not a community!"

"Well, it should be *both*," Celia said. "And don't forget about the secret meeting on Friday." Her eyes strayed over Liz's shoulder. "Hey! Could you go and talk to Isabel? I think she has a hard time fitting in." Celia was already walking away. "Thanks, Liz!" she said over her shoulder.

Liz stalked around the side of the school building. *School hasn't started, and I already have a job.*

Naturally, the first person she saw was Mary Summers. Mary was tall, pretty, and the only other girl in Liz's sophomore class of four, and could probably have any boy she wanted. She could flip her hair pretty masterfully too.

"Liz! Good to see you again!" Mary said in a fake voice. Or maybe it wasn't fake? Liz wasn't interested in knowing. "Hey, I wanted to talk to you about something…"

"Not now," Liz said brusquely. "Busy." She turned and went the opposite way. She kept surveying the crowd, and spotted Isabel Reyes, her target. The freshman girl she was supposed to be nice to. *Trust Celia to guilt me into anything.* Isabel was excitable, Hispanic, and always seemed to have messy hair. Liz was coming up with something imaginary and friendly to say to Isabel, who was coming up the walk, when she saw that Isabel Reyes was carrying a guitar.

Isabel was Charismatic, or a "Kare-O" as Liz liked to call them. Celia and the Costains were kinda Kare-O too, but at least they were pretty low-key about it. But here was Isabel Reyes, at JP2HS, with a guitar. Liz knew exactly why a Kare-O would be carrying a guitar. To play Kare-O music and get everyone else to sing along.

A disturbing thought occurred to Liz. Allie had been going to that evangelical church over the summer. She was a Kare-O now, too. And she and Isabel might convince others to join their ilk. What if Allie and Isabel turned JP2HS into a Kare-O school, with everyone praying with their hands palm up over their heads, Matt Maher songs on their playlists, and guitars, guitars, guitars everywhere? Liz tried to picture herself before a college admissions guy, or a job guy, trying to explain how she possibly could have gotten a good education at a Kare-O school. *I was there before the Kare-Os took control!* she imagined herself pleading.

But in her imagination, there could be no mercy: Maybe she did attend JP2HS when it still had a decent reputation as a regular Catholic school. But if it went Kare-O, that was going to go on her *permanent record.*

Liz could not let this enormity stand. Isabel Reyes *must be stopped.*

But she would need help. Then she heard someone behind her and smiled slightly. Without turning, she said, "Oh, hi, J.P."

J.P. stood up and scowled. "How do you DO that?" He shook his head in exasperation as he stood up from his crouch. "You weren't even *looking* at me."

Liz turned to face him, rather pleased with herself. "Maybe I've developed eyes in the back of my head. Or I could just be channeling my natural paranoia."

J.P. leaned next to her against the same tree. "Yeah, well, it's not paranoia if people *are* really trying to kill you."

Liz felt ill.

"Oh … sorry," J.P. said sheepishly. "I forgot people really *were* trying to kill you."

"Don't worry about it," Liz sighed, and looked down at her injured ankle. "The dumbest part is, I don't even remember anything about it. I have some vague memories of Brian, and that jerkface Hank, and lying on the floor. A little bit about the ambulance. Allie was there, I think." She snorted and shook her head. "Maybe me and Allie should start a club. The Bad People With Guns Tried To Kill Us club."

Now J.P. was looking over his shoulder a bit nervously.

"What's wrong? Hoping to join our club?" she couldn't help asking.

"Naah," said J.P. "Nothing really…Oh yeah! I'm supposed to remind you not to forget the meeting we're all having on Friday at lunch."

Liz shrugged. "Okay. Reminded." She turned her attention back to Isabel. Better a challenge than the half-memories of bad things that she couldn't sort out.

"Sssso—what are you thinking about?"

"Plans for this year," Liz said. "All these newbies. They have to be taught a lesson. Taught who this school *really* belongs to."

J.P. squinted and nodded. "I see your problem."

"And the best way to teach them is: prank war. Want to help me out with it?"

J.P. smiled. "You're preaching to the choir, Lizzy. Preaching. To. The. Choir."

Liz stuck her hand out and spit on it. "Shake on it then, partner. This year we're gonna rock this joint till it splits. Give everybody something to think about that doesn't have anything to do with guns or God or Bibles."

J.P. spit on his own hand, took hers, and shook it once. "Little lady," he said in his best old prospector accent, "you got yo'self a deal."

3

UNICORN BINDER

"No, I'm not interested in talking about it any further; I've said all I plan to say to the press. No, I'm sorry. Good-bye." Mr. Costain flipped his phone shut and sat down heavily in his office chair. "Well J.P., what can I do for you?"

J.P. looked at him quizzically. "Aren't you going to call me Mr. Flynn?"

Mr. Costain looked at his watch. "School doesn't officially start for another couple of minutes, so until then, you can just be J.P."

"Sounds great, Dan," J.P. said with a smile.

"Don't push it."

"No, sir. Not me. Never." J.P. glanced around the office, on a private reconnaissance mission. "Uh… my mom asked me for the key to the janitorial closet."

"Okay, hold on." While Mr. Costain rifled through his desk drawer, J.P. thought about the annoying media microscope they'd all been under, off and on since last June. Everyone in the town of Sparrow Hills had grown used to the presence of the press after the events at the high school. This past summer, when a former town inspector and his son tried to make a land grab and burn down the school, even little John Paul 2 High had made the news—at least, the local news. By now, it was all really, really boring to J.P.

Finally Mr. Costain pulled a key out of his drawer and handed it to J.P. just as Mrs. Simonelli came in.

"Dan, I've got to talk to you," she began. As J.P. left, he heard her say, "Rosemary Summers is complaining about our science textbooks again. Nothing seems to satisfy her!" J.P. paused to listen.

"Well, she seems very committed to the school," Mr. Costain said.

"She seems very committed to making the school over in her image!" Liz's mother snapped. "I know what people like her do: they're always causing problems! They come here with high expectations…"

"And perhaps that's good for us," Mr. Costain said quietly. "It can spur us on to do better. We have to look at the positive side here. Otherwise, how else can we foster *agape*?"

J.P. wasn't sure what that last word meant. *A guppy? A puppy? What? Are we going to be fostering puppies now?*

Ah well. He had seen enough of Mrs. Summers during work camp to know that she was bossy and annoying. J.P. was willing to forgive her that because her two daughters were both cute. *Bossy mom, cute girls. There're always trade-offs, aren't there?*

When Liz opened her locker, she was greeted by her old tool belt that she had angrily thrown in there on the day when her dad fired her. Seeing it reminded her of the injustice of that firing, and the anger that she felt that day came back to her for the thousandth time.

He should have believed me when I said the school fire wasn't my fault, Liz seethed in her mind.

"Hey, Liz!" It was Allie, a few lockers down, waving.

"Hey, Allie," Liz said in a guarded tone. She had never felt that close to Allie Weaver, who was everything Liz wasn't: glamorous, popular, and very, very pretty without even trying.

Allie came over and pulled Liz into a hug, which Liz returned awkwardly. "How are you?" she said. She looked genuinely concerned about Liz. This was a first.

"Um…fine," Liz said warily. "Is something wrong?"

"No! Nothing!" Allie said quickly—a little too quickly. "By the way, I LOVE your hair! That perm looks great!"

Liz shut her locker door and turned to Allie, watching as her kinda-sorta friend went back to rifling through her locker. Then she saw Allie pull a strangely familiar binder out of her locker.

"By the way," the older blonde girl said as she put the binder on top of her other books, "I'm supposed to remind you about the meeting…"

"Gaaaah!" said Liz, annoyed. "Yes! I know! The meeting at the grotto on Friday. I remember!" She stared at the binder, wondering why it seemed familiar. There was a cartoony unicorn, and a child's handwriting scrawled across it.

"Oh, come on," said Allie. "You *have* to be there to show the new freshmen how things are. And like Celia said, we're trying to build community…"

"Yeah. Showing the freshmen…" Liz said automatically. She remembered! The day of the first fire…over the summer… everyone had been evacuated from the building. But Liz had seen Allie run back to the building and coming out with…

"…so that's what we're going to be saying. And look, I know it might seem silly to you," Allie was still talking, "but Seal has been working so hard and it would mean so much to her if we would all get behind her and—"

"Oh yes, of course! I'll be there for Celia!" said Liz rapidly, and then without pausing to take a breath, she continued, "Hey! Here's a funny question! What's with that unicorn binder?"

Allie glanced at it. "Oh! I just brought that to the school to—well, I was bringing it to the cemetery to leave on Nikki's grave after school. It was a present from her, and it kind of symbolizes—"

"So what's inside it?" Liz cut her off. "Your diary?"

Allie held the binder to her chest defensively. "Nothing important."

"You sure? Because that's the *exact same binder* you came running in here for when the school was on fire."

"I didn't risk my life! The building was only *partly* on fire." Allie protested.

"Come on, what's in the binder?"

Allie blushed. "Oh, fine," she muttered. "If you really care that much, I was doing my own stupid little investigation of the shooter over the summer, before they found out it was Brock."

"Really?" said Liz, surprised. "You've been gathering evidence? Can I see it?"

"No," Allie said firmly. "The shooter's been caught. It's over."

"C'mon. What's it gonna hurt?"

"Just forget about it, okay?" Allie snapped, finally losing her temper. "Look, I don't want to go through that again. It's not… healthy for me. Okay?"

"Okay, okay," Liz said. "I was just curious. Geez." The bell rang for the start of school, and Allie hurried off.

Liz followed her quietly. She watched as Allie went down a side hall to a garbage can, opened the unicorn binder, unclasped the three rings, dumped all the contents into the trash, and walked away.

As soon as Allie was safely out of sight, Liz raced over to the garbage can. She reached in greedily, grabbing up the loose pile of papers, notecards, clippings, and other odds and ends. When she realized there was nothing else in the can except what Allie had just thrown away, Liz quickly pulled out the plastic liner, puffed the air out, tied it, ran back to her own locker, and stuffed it in. "So you've been doing an investigation, Allie?" she said to no one in particular. "Interesting. Verrrrry interesting."

She started as Brian Burke rounded the corner. As soon as he saw her, a concerned expression creased his face, and she didn't want another fake hug. Pretending that she was really anxious to get into class, she hurried right past him.

J.P. looked around the room as he walked in the door. First class of the new year was theology. Just like last year, the entire school took the humanities classes together. Which meant that everyone had to cram into one classroom; and that meant that for the first time, a classroom at JP2HS actually looked full.

And just like last year, Mr. Costain was teaching theology, history, and literature. For the first few minutes of class, he explained why he taught all three classes, so that he could draw attention to the connections between the different subjects, so that the students would get the big picture, blah blah, and a bunch of other reasons which J.P. didn't pay attention to at all.

"This semester we're going to do a little something different for theology class," Mr. Costain said, walking up to the board. "We're going to focus on Love."

J.P. perked up in his chair, and instinctively started looking at the girls. Some of them looked interested, but others, like Mr. Costain's beautiful daughter Miranda, looked bored. J.P. needed to entertain them.

At the back of the class sat James Kosalinski, the school's only senior, fat and sneering. J.P. already knew from experience that trying to entertain James was a lost cause.

"Hey Mr. C," he said, raising his hand. "Can we call you the Love Doctor?" Some of the girls snickered.

"I don't have a doctorate, Mr. Flynn," Mr. Costain said evenly. "I have a Master's. You may call me the Love Master. That is all. Now, our first question: What is love?"

"Baby don't hurt me?"

The classroom erupted into laughter. *Good!*

"That's enough, Mr. Flynn." Mr. Costain waited for them to settle down. "Seriously, what does the word 'love' mean? Who here loves ice cream? Raise your hands."

Slowly, most everyone's hands went up.

"Now raise your hands if you love fried chicken."

Some hands went down.

"Who here loves their parents?"

Most of the hands came up, but not all. Mr. Costain smiled slightly. "In case you're wondering—yes, I will tell your parents if you— there you go," he finished as everyone's hand quickly went up.

"Now, who here feels the same way about their parents as they do about fried chicken?" Everyone's hand went down. J.P. was tempted to keep his up, but he was actually kind of curious now.

Mr. Costain nodded. "You see? The word 'love' is kind of hard to define, isn't it? There have been whole books written about how to define it. And we're going to be reading one of them." He held up a slim paperback. "This one, right here—*The Four Loves*, by C.S. Lewis. I

27

have copies for all of you." He pointed to a cardboard box on his desk. "Celia, George, please hand them out."

As the books were passed out to the packed classroom, Mr. Costain started writing on the board:

$$\text{Storge} \qquad \text{Philia}$$
$$\text{Eros} \qquad \text{Agape}$$

"These are the four loves," he said, pointing to the board. "Four of the most powerful forces in the world. They all come from God. God is Love, and when we learn about these loves, we'll learn a little about God, too. We're going to study them all this year—yes, Mr. Wilson?"

"I mean…you hear that," Mitch stammered. Outside of class Mitch was a talker, but he appeared nervous now. "You hear that love is…really powerful and stuff. But isn't that just… you know, something people say? Like, it's just a feeling."

"I think you should hold off on that thought until later on," Mr. Costain said. "Love isn't 'just a feeling', and it's much more powerful, in its fullness, than anything else out there. These loves—" He tapped the board, "dominate the life of every human being. These are forces that bind us together, or tear us apart. Let's start here," Mr. Costain said, pointing to the board. "Each of these names a different type of love. The first one, Storge," (he pronounced it *store-jay*) "means love for home, family, and the familiar things in life. *Philia* means the love of friendship. *Eros* means the love between a man and a woman. And *Agape* is the love of God, and the love between those who love Him and are part of His Body."

The classroom was silent for a moment. Then, slowly, one of the freshman girls raised her hand—a skinny girl with freckles and red hair.

"Yes, Agnes?" Mr. Costain said.

"When we said we loved ice cream …" Agnes hesitated. "Would that really be an important force?"

"Oh, absolutely," Mr. Costain nodded. "That fits into *Storge*. Very important," his expression was very serious, but there was a slight smile to go along with it.

Agnes looked unsure. "But … why?"

"Why? Imagine a life without ice cream!"

A few nervous laughs rang out, but most of the class looked as if they didn't know whether Mr. Costain was joking or not.

"Love is always important," Mr. Costain said briskly, and wrote IMPORTANT on the board. "Otherwise it wouldn't be love. Then we might call it mere infatuation. So if your attraction to something is lasting, than it's truly a type of love. But there are other characteristics of love. For example—what if we loved ice cream too much? What if we ate gallons of it every day?"

"We'd get fat?" Miranda said, raising her hand lazily.

"You'd die!" Jacinta said. "You'd get diabetes or something!"

"Yes," Mr. Costain nodded as some of the girls giggled. "*Dangerous*. In fact, loving anything or anyone too much can be dangerous. So that's another characteristic of love." He wrote DANGEROUS on the board.

"Mr. Costain?" Josephine Grantham waved her hand frantically. "That's not right. Not *all* love is dangerous—I mean, you have 'Agape' up there, that's God's love, right? So it can't be dangerous!"

"On the contrary, Miss Grantham," Mr. Costain said. "In my view, *Agape* is the most dangerous love of all."

There was silence, except for a loud snort from James.

"But that's a mystery, the biggest mystery of all—and a subject for another day," Mr. Costain continued. "For today's class, we're going to focus of the first love: *Storge*." Mr. Costain underlined the word. "Now, you all said you loved your parents, but let's be honest. I'm sure that none of you jump out of your bed every morning really excited about loving your parents, right?" He smiled slightly. "We're just your boring parents. *Storge* is not exciting. It's probably how you feel about this school." J.P. saw Liz roll her eyes.

"Then how is it *love*?" Allie said from the first row. She looked a little frustrated.

"*Storge* is the first love." Mr. Costain said. "It's basic to everyone, everywhere, at any age, and can be directed toward anything at all. It's affection. It can be a quiet sort of love, but still very powerful. You've heard the phrase 'you don't know what you have 'til it's gone'? Well, that's a sentiment aimed partly at *Storge*—we grow familiar, and then complacent, and finally we take it for granted, so that we go the whole day without really being thankful for the things that make life good…"

J.P. was about to raise his hand, when he saw Miranda Costain looking at her nails and frowning. She had dark curly hair pulled back into a ponytail, blue eyes with long lashes, and perfectly bored eyebrows.

As if sensing someone was looking at her, Miranda glanced at him, and sneaked him a tiny pert smile.

He forgot what was going on around him, and even forgot the question he had going to ask Mr. Costain--about the last love, that was supposed to be the biggest mystery.

4

LOCKERS AND DESKS

Liz opened her locker, shaking her head. *Man, that was a long class. Four loves? More like four stupid Greek words that don't make any sense. I don't even like my mom. What does that make us?* The next class of the day was Mrs. Flynn's class, math. Liz's worst subject ever.

"So what did you think of that?" she heard Allie say.

Liz looked up. Allie was closing her locker door, and James was kneeling and shoving books into his backpack. George was at his own locker a few feet away.

"What did I think?" James muttered, shoving his copy of *The Four Loves* into his backpack with one fat hand and standing up. "Hm. It was interesting. But I don't know if we should be studying C.S. Lewis's works. He's not even *Catholic.* Then again, Mr. Costain has always been unorthodox…"

Uh, oh. Liz had just noticed George looking annoyed.

"…so I'm not surprised he idolizes Protestants," James went on. "In any case, I'm not so sure this 'four loves' talk is really about theology—"

"Like you know any better," George said, coming toward the pair. "And you should stop that."

James heaved an exaggerated sigh. "Oh, wonderful." He turned to George, smiling unpleasantly. "Stop what, Georgie?"

"Stop bad-mouthing Mr. Costain!" George walked up to James, eyes narrowed. George was muscular and James was heavy, but the two boys were the same height. "Do you have any idea how much he's sacrificed for this school?"

"Oh, of course. St. Dan Costain of Sparrow Hills." James said scornfully. "I'm not allowed to disagree with the Blessed One, am I?"

George slammed his locker. "He knows more about theology than you do. Why don't you just trust him?"

31

James' lip curled. "Because I know more about theology than you do. Independent thinking and such. You should try it some time. Or maybe just thinking, period."

"And so, on with the insults. That's all you know how to do, isn't it?" George smiled tightly. "Insult. Mock. You never have anything positive to say. That's why nobody likes you. Nobody wants you here."

Liz was surprised—not because George and James were butting heads; they had been doing that all last year—but at how George was matching James in nastiness this time around.

James' eyes blazed with anger. "I know how to do a lot of things, Georgie," he said in a soft, dangerous voice. "You have no idea. Maybe someday I'll show you."

"Oh, you want to do something? Huh?" George took a step forward, fists clenched. "Great! Let's go!"

Here it comes, Liz thought. She was scared, but interested. She'd been waiting for the day when the two oldest male students would finally duke it out.

"Fight!" J.P. crowed. "Fight, fight!"

"Okay, stop!" Suddenly Allie had stepped between them, hands outstretched. But to Liz's amazement, she was looking from one to the other in fury. "Both of you!"

This was also new. When Allie first came to the school, she had never stopped George and James from fighting.

George gritted his teeth. "Allie, he—"

"You are just as bad as he is!" Allie turned on George. "You're both idiots!" She glanced at James. "You both claim to be Catholics, you both tell me you're serious about it, but whenever you're together, you start acting like ten-year olds!"

"Alison!" James looked affronted. "I am not the one acting childish here!"

"Guys, what happened?" Celia asked as she hurried up. *Of course,* thought Liz, *here comes the Great Peacemaker.*

"Nothing, Seal," Allie said in a hard voice. "Just the usual idiocy from our two idiots here."

George pointed at James. "He was insulting your—"

"George here butted in on a private conversation," Allie snapped. "And then James started with the stupid insults. And now they want to go outside and start punching each other. Because that's what Jesus wants, right guys?"

George and, to Liz's surprise, James both looked a little mortified at that, but neither backed down.

"Oh…okay." Celia sighed. "Come on, George." She tugged at George's arm. "Come over here."

George's eyes darted to Celia for a moment. His fists unclenched.

"Yes, walk away, Georgie," James sneered. "Go ahead."

George's eyes blazed again—but before he could make a move, Allie had jumped in between them again. "James," she said imperiously. "Come with me. I want to talk to you, alone, right now."

She fixed her eyes on him. James glared back at her, looking angrier than ever—but something seemed to hold him back. "Miss Weaver," he growled. "I am not going to—"

"Yes," Allie said firmly. "You are. Now come on." She grabbed his arm. "Let's go."

James, looking furious and frustrated, allowed himself to be led away by Allie. Liz gaped. *I thought she hated him! And I thought he hated her as much as he hates everyone else!* This was a surprising turn of events. Last year, Allie had always referred to James as Creepy Boy. And she had dated George. *Boy, things have turned around.*

"Man," J.P. said. "I *really* thought they were gonna fight that time."

"Yeah," Liz murmured. "Me too. Well, it's bound to happen one of these days."

Lunch period arrived at last. Since it was a nice day, all the students went outside to eat at the new picnic tables that they had helped install over the summer. But J.P. had to stay inside. He had been "volunteered" by his mom to move old desks out of one classroom and into the cafeteria where they would be stored for the semester.

After twelve desks, he was sweaty, sore, and not even half way done. He looked at the clock on the cafeteria wall and knew he wouldn't finish in time. *Wonder if anyone else is done lunch and could help me out?*

"George!" he shouted into the empty cafeteria. "Brian? Joey! Where the heck is everybody?"

"Who's shouting?" A boy carrying two paint cans came into the cafeteria from the outside door. J.P. recognized Athanasius Courchraine, called Athan for short. Athan's long hair was back in a ponytail, and he was followed by a gaggle of girls (including Jacinta Summers, J.P. couldn't help but notice) and a couple of other freshmen boys, including Joey. They carried dropcloths and paintbrushes.

"What's going on?" J.P. asked, watching as Athan set the paint cans down near the wall on the opposite side of the large room.

Athan said, "Priming the wall. Mr. Costain said over the summer that I could paint some stuff in here, so that's what I'm doing. We're going to have an artist's club."

"But we haven't decided exactly what we're painting yet," said Isabel Reyes, brushing some hair out of her face.

"Oh." He noticed Jacinta Summers was holding a yellow balloon with a few spiral rainbow ribbons on it. He called to her, "What's with the balloon?"

"It's my birthday," Jacinta said, her cheeks a little pink. "Isabel gave it to me."

"Birthday, huh?" J.P. gave Jacinta his most winning smile. "Well, then, happy birthday. Mine's in a couple weeks. Maybe we can go to the SpeedEMart down on the corner and get some birthday slushees."

Jacinta laughed. She was really cute when she smiled. "Thanks, but I don't think my mom would let me," she said. "I better see what Athan needs me to do." The freshmen were spreading a dropcloth under a section of wall. Athan cracked a can of primer, and led the group in painting part of the wall white.

J.P. was left all alone again. Feeling bored, tired, and somewhat annoyed, he picked up a desk and placed it on top of another. They were designed to be stacked that way, with the bottom of one desk-

and-chair set fitting neatly into the top of another. *I'm never gonna get this done on time. But I suppose I could stack 'em until it's time to go.*

He stacked a third, a fourth, then a fifth. He was barely tall enough to do it. Then he looked up at the ceiling, which was higher here than any other place in the school, and back at the desks. And smiled.

It took the others two more desks to notice what he was doing. By that point J.P. had maxed out the number of desks he could stack while he was standing on another desk. The giant stack leaned a little to the right; he tugged it straight and stood back to examine his handiwork.

"Wow, that's tall!" he heard a girl behind him exclaim. J.P. kept his grin a secret as he stepped down from his desk-stool. He wasn't feeling tired anymore. He turned to take in his audience, and saw that three new girls had just walked in. One was Miranda Costain.

Miranda was even cuter than Jacinta. No, not cute: hot. She was wearing a green babydoll T now, her school uniform shirt slung over her shoulder. Her hair was dark brown and curly, and her arched eyebrows were elegant, disdainful, and cool. Seeing the stacked desks, she leaned against the propped-open metal door next to her followers, Vivian and Kristy, and raised her eyebrows in a way that said, *interesting; but now what?*

I'll show you 'now what', J.P. thought, and he hefted another desk onto the pile. Girls like Miranda wanted to be *impressed*. They wanted to see crazy and reckless. Good thing those were J.P.'s specialties. *Climbing all the way up there should make a first impression.* He stood on a desk, and tossed another desk onto the stack. He barely made it.

Miranda called to him, "Looks like you reached the limit."

He met her eyes. "I don't believe in limits."

Miranda had to smile at that, and J.P. knew he had her attention.

At that moment, Joey jostled against Jacinta with an open paint can, and she yelped. "Hey—!" She let go of her balloon, and it shot up to the ceiling and bumped there, out of reach, between the wall and J.P.'s desk stack.

35

J.P., Miranda and everyone else looked up at the balloon bobbing around fifteen feet above—and then Athan jumped up and headed straight for the desks. "I got it."

Oh no, J.P. thought, panicked. *He's going to ruin my bit. He's going to climb my desks first!*

But Athan didn't. Not at first. No, he first pulled himself up on top of the propped-open entry door with one quick motion, and balanced on top. Then he sprang onto the middle of the desk stack. The stack began to lean over, getting an "Ooooh!" from everyone, but Athan smartly directed it against the wall, and the top desks hit the wall and stayed there, making a very steep stair near the hovering balloon. Athan quickly clambered up the desks, grabbed the balloon, and wrapped it around his wrist. The desks started to wobble, but Athan had already dropped to the floor, landed on his feet, tucked into a roll, and came up right in front of Jacinta. The entire movement was over in less than fifteen seconds.

"Yours, right?" he asked, deadpan, unwrapping the balloon and handing it over. He then walked away, apparently oblivious to her startled, open-mouthed stare, and resumed his priming.

Miranda blinked, cocked her head to the side, and threw Jacinta a look that said, *can you believe what we just saw?* Jacinta shrugged and shook her head.

The other boys finally found their voices. "Dude. Chris, did you see that?" Joey said to the other boy. "DUDE!" They both ran over to Athan. Joey yelled, "You *have* to show me how to do that!"

Only Isabel wasn't impressed. "You could have been killed! That was dumb!" J.P. was inclined to agree with her.

"You kidding? That was the coolest thing I ever saw!" Chris gushed. "Are you a parkour guy or something?"

"I took a couple classes when I was younger, but nothing special," Athan said. He kept painting away, as if he hadn't just done some amazing, athletic, totally cool and risky stunt, just to rescue a stupid balloon.

This kid can't be for real, J.P. thought dejectedly. *No one can be that good at something and not know it.* Except apparently, Athan could.

J.P. stared up at the desks, for the first time realizing that he'd probably have to *un*stack them too. So much for impressing Jacinta and Miranda.

And Miranda and her friends were leaving. *Maybe she wasn't as impressed as she seemed. At least* she's *not all hot for Athan now.* Then J.P. noticed Athan looking out from his little throng of admirers, towards Miranda's retreating back. He frowned in disappointment.

That little jerk! J.P. fumed. *He* was *showing off. He did it all to impress Miranda!*

Liz found J.P. alone in the cafeteria. He was red-faced and sweaty, and trying to pull apart a desk that was stuck on top of another desk.

"J.P.! You'll never guess what I found!" Liz ran toward him clutching a garbage bag of papers to her chest. "Get a load of this!" Proudly she dumped the contents of the bag onto the desk J.P. was standing in front of.

J.P. stared at the disorganized pile. "Crumpled-up papers! Just what I always wanted."

"I don't know for sure if there's anything here," said Liz, flipping through the mess. "I haven't gone through any of it yet. But there's a lot of it, so there's plenty of potential. This could be huge!" She started sifting through the sheets of paper. They were all out of order, and several of them were flagged with post-its sticking out like bookmarks, making it awkward to adjust into a neat stack.

"Oh, I have no doubt there's *plenty* of potential there. I mean, the recycling possibilities alone! Paper airplanes! Spitballs!"

Liz smacked him on the head. "Shut up and listen! Don't you see what this is?"

"Um… actually, no."

"Allie's notes! On the shooter!" said Liz, still rifling through the papers. "Here, look! This one's a map of the shooter's movements the night of the dance." She showed J.P. a piece of paper that had a printout of a satellite view of Sparrow Hills and the surrounding wooded area. A red marker line traced a path from the gymnasium roof through the woods. Liz's eyes were drawn to the spot on the path where Allie had drawn a blue 'x' in marker. It was at the spot Liz and Celia had been in the woods when they encountered the shadowy, hulking figure they later found out was the shooter fleeing the crime.

"Whoa. This is intense!" J.P. exclaimed, scanning through more pages. "She was pretty serious about this. Why'd she let you borrow her notes?"

"Welllllll…" said Liz. "She didn't exactly *let* me borrow them."

"You stole all this from her?!"

"No! It's not stealing! She threw them in the trash!" said Liz quickly in a whisper. "That makes them public domain. I have salvage rights!"

"Well… If she threw this all in the trash… I guess that makes it morally okay, then!" said J.P. happily. "Let's check 'em out."

At that precise moment, Liz heard the sound of a door opening behind her. Thinking quickly, she swept everything back into the trash bag, then turned to see who had come in.

"Hello, guys," said George. Liz knew he almost always had to play policeman for the rest of the school. Now he looked suspicious. "What are you two up to?"

"Oh, just plotting how to destroy JP2HS!" Liz said brightly. "Kidding! Just kidding! J.P., are you going to help me throw out this trash or what?"

The first day of school ended with a not-completely-unexpected Safety Class, which was mind-numbingly boring to J.P. Given the excitement over the past school year and summer, the adults went predictably on and on about extinguishers and electricity and emergency numbers and stranger danger and never play with fire and poison control and radiation detectors (or was it radon? J.P. didn't know or care) and keeping an eye on any suspicious non-students hanging around your school and What To Do If You Come Face To Face With A Maniac With A Gun.

J.P. raised his hand.

"Yes, J.P.?" Mr. Costain said warily.

"Can we dedicate an hour of our school day to some kind of wicked kung fu class or something? Because then if some guy pulls a gun, we'd be all like 'woooYAAAHHHH!' and kick it out of his hands, and then there'd be this mad fist fight, and—"

Athan spoke up. "You would never actually kick a gun out of someone's hands. That's stupid."

"Oh yeah? What, are you some kind of martial arts master or something?" J.P. said. *He probably is. Jerk.*

"Gentlemen—" Mr. Costain started.

"I'm not a master," Athan said stiffly, "but it's just common sense. If you're close enough to kick a gun, you're close enough to grab it."

"Oh, come on," J.P. argued, "no one's arms are as long as their legs. Except maybe yours, Mr. Stubby Pants. Or is it Mr. Gorilla Arms?"

Mr. Costain cleared his throat. "Mr. Flynn, I said—"

"At that range the difference in arms and legs doesn't really matter," Athan said, clearly ignoring both J.P.'s taunt and Mr. Costain, "but you have more control with your hands. If you'd just *think* about it for a minute instead of yammering on and on—"

"Athanasius!" It wasn't Mr. Costain this time, but another man standing in the doorway. He was well-dressed, short and rather thin, and had his wavy dark hair slicked back along his scalp. He had the same light olive-colored skin as Athan, the same chiseled cheeks and jawline, and he wore a slight beard that would make him appear rakish if he weren't decidedly stern.

Athan shrank in his chair, looking embarrassed. "Sorry, Dad," he mumbled.

J.P. smirked at him for a second until he heard his mother say, "And what about you, J.P.?"

"Oh. Uh, sorry." J.P. sat still and tried to keep from smiling. He got in trouble all the time so that was no big deal, but seeing Athan smacked down was a real treat.

"Ah," Mr. Costain said, "That'll do it for the meeting. J.P., Athan, you two can stay behind and clean up the classroom. Now we'll close with a prayer…"

After everyone else left the room, the two boys went about their assigned task, J.P. sullen and Athan resigned. "So what's your dad do? End meetings for a living? Bet he's always in demand," J.P. said. He didn't like talking to Athan, but he liked silence even less.

"He's a lawyer," Athan said, not looking up from his sweeping. "A criminal defense lawyer, specializing in juvenile crime and crimes against kids."

"So what's he doing here?"

"Probably to help with the school discipline. You know, arrange for prosecuting school bullies and loudmouths…"

"Ha ha ha," snarled J.P. But all the same, he wondered.

It must have shown on his face, because Athan said, "Nah, he's just here to look over some legal documents. Free legal advice for the school. He does that sort of thing all the time for people he knows." He continued to clean up the room briskly, and J.P. couldn't think of what else to say.

5

GROTTO MEETING

It was Friday morning, and J.P. was just putting the finishing touches on the freshman boys' lockers. They were all in a row: Athanasius Courchraine, Christopher Manzzini, Joey Simonelli, Kevin Snyder, Mitch Wilson, and Paul Wolczak. He had, naturally, started with Paul's locker and saved the worst treatment for Athan. Since he had copied the master locker key early last year, it was a cinch to pull it off.

By the time he had finished, no one else had arrived, so he decided to do the girls' lockers for good measure. Liz was supposed to do it, but the Simonellis were always running late. He yanked the huge bag of packing peanuts down the hall to where the girls' lockers started.

Filling the top section of each locker with packing peanuts was harder than it looked, but he managed it in record time. There were more girls: the new sticker labels read: Vivian Andros, Agnes Burns, Miranda Costain, Mary Rose Fogle, Josephine Grantham, Isabel Reyes, Jacinta Summer, Kristy Vogel.

He was just sweeping up the spare peanuts with a broom when he heard the Costains arriving. He looked around for a place to hide the broom—the sight of J.P. working would definitely look suspicious.

Too late! Mr. Costain walked briskly down the hallway. J.P. let his shoulders slump and yelled in an off-handed way, "I'm done with the hallways, Mom!" Then he went off to see if there was anything interesting going on in the parking lot.

He found Jacinta and Kristy talking about a movie, and debated about whether or not he should interrupt their conversation by vaulting over the picnic table. But then he thought that they might compare him unfavorably to Athan, so he slouched away.

Eventually he ended up in his homeroom. He had his math homework to finish, for his mom's class. He pulled out the worksheet from yesterday and started filling it with random numbers, paying more attention to the sounds from the hallways as people started opening their lockers.

He heard a locker bang open and an "Eeep!" from Jacinta and an exclamation from Kristy. *The fun has begun.*

It was awesome. He heard laughter, loud complaints, and above all wonderment on who had done this. Josephine was mad: the "Styrofoam peanuts from hell," as she termed them, stuck to her wool skirt.

Then he started hearing exclamations from the boys. *Their* lockers had a fine line of toothpaste along the edge, ensuring that their hands, sleeves, and books were all squishy with minty fresh goodness. Athan had gotten a whole tube's worth in his locker.

When the uproar got loud, J.P. walked innocently out into the hallway and looked around. He was pleased to see Athan grimly stalking towards the men's room with toothpaste smeared all over his math textbook.

"What's going on?" he asked Joey.

"Someone pranked all the freshmen!" Joey said. "This is so fun!"

There was a bit of a chaos in the hallway with toothpaste and packing peanuts everywhere. Celia was on it, getting a broom and yelling for help cleaning up.

Liz Simonelli strode through the crowd to J.P. She wasn't grinning, but her eyes were laughing.

"Good beginning, Japes," she said. "That's a nice way to start the war."

PRANKS, Liz wrote firmly in all caps on a fresh page in her notebook, and then underlined it twice. She needed to think of something to top J.P.—something clever. She glanced around, making sure nobody was close enough to see what she was doing—but although the classroom was starting to get crowded, no one was sitting near her.

Every school day at John Paul 2 High started with a rosary, but it never seemed to start on time. Now that everyone was cleaning up the hallway from J.P.'s opening salvo, it was no big surprise that the rosary was delayed.

She tapped the notebook with her pencil, and then wrote *NO ANIMALS.* They had done animals last year, crickets and cows. This year it had to be different.

SHAVING CREAM
LOCKER RAIDS?

"Hi, Liz."

Liz looked up to see Brian Burke. And instantly, three horrible things happened:

1) Her face felt hot, which meant she was *blushing*.

2) She clutched her notebook to her chest like a frightened 12-year-old girl.

3) She made a sound that could only be described as "eep!"

Brian blinked. "Excuse me?"

"Eeeyeah, heh heh, hi," came out of Liz's mouth. "What's up, Burke? Sooooo… what's up?"

"Uh, nothing." Now Brian was *grinning*, like he thought Liz was making a *joke*, and now something was happening in her chest—palpitations? Was she having a heart attack? *This isn't a* joke, *Burke, I could be* dying, she wanted to say, but she couldn't say *anything*. She could only sit there blushing like a friggin' *girl*, watching his lips move and dimly realizing that he had just asked her a question.

"What?" she said. Or, more accurately, squeaked.

"I said, what were you writing?"

Liz hesitated, then handed the notebook over. She couldn't think of a good excuse not to. Brian wasn't a snitch. Brian had known about all their pranks last year and had never ratted them out—good golly, had he actually gotten *taller* in the last two weeks? Good golly, was she actually thinking *good golly?* What was *wrong* with her?

Brian scanned her notes and chuckled. "Uh, oh. So there's more to come."

Then, to her horror-slash-joy-slash-total-confusion, he sat down in the desk next to her.

"I haven't talked to you since you've left the hospital," Brian said matter-of-factly. "What's up?"

43

"What? Oh, right," Liz said. "Sorry, I've just been busy with… stuff." She thought of everything she had been doing since she had left the hospital, two days after the Day of Bickerstaff. Physical therapy on her ankle. Keeping up her relationship with Tara and Simone. Grinding through the summer schoolwork her mother insisted on giving her, then, after she got on the cheer squad, practice, practice. And somehow in all that mess, there was never time to talk to Brian. Why? Most of the summer they had been so close…

"How's your ankle?"

"Fine."

"And how do you feel?" Brian looked concerned. "I mean, you were pretty upset when I told you what happened with Bickerstaff. Do you still not remember anything?"

"Not really," she said. "The last thing I remember was hitting you with the water balloon." For some reason she felt ashamed at the memory. *Why? He totally deserved it… didn't he?*

Brian cleared his throat. "Yes. I remember that too."

"But I guess that's okay," Liz added. She had an idea. "Because you know, you told me everything that happened, so I don't *have* to remember. Right?" She snuck a glance at him. For some reason it was hard to look at him, but she had to now. She had to see his reaction.

To her dismay, she saw his jaw tighten slightly, and his eyes dart up and to the right. "Yeah," he said, looking away. "Everything I can remember."

He's lying.

Liz looked down at her lap, her heart pounding a little harder. *Easy now. You can't be sure.* But she *was* sure. Brian was definitely not telling her something. *What? And why?*

"Hey, Brian!"

Brian and Liz both looked up. *Oh. Great.*

Mary Summers walked up and sat down on a desk on the other side of Brian. "How are you doing?" she said brightly, tossing her long brown hair to one side. At least she wasn't as good at hair tossing as Madison.

Liz glanced at Brian and was happy to see that he looked extremely uncomfortable. And with good reason; Mary Summers was the girl that Brian had a bit of a crush on this past summer—a crush that had ended badly. Liz didn't know the details, but she knew Brian was angry about it, and definitely didn't want to see Mary anymore. Which Liz didn't mind either.

"Hi, Mary," Liz said in a perfectly friendly voice. "Are you enjoying school so far?"

"Oh, hi, Liz, yeah," Mary said after doing a very unconvincing double take and screwing her mouth up into an equally unconvincing smile. She immediately said to Brian, "Look, Brian, I've been thinking about…you know."

"Yes," Brian said stiffly. "I know."

Wish I *did*, thought Liz.

"And I just wanted to… well—"

"All right everyone!" Mr. Costain had walked into the classroom. "Time for the rosary!"

A minute later everyone had started reciting Hail Marys, and Liz finally had a chance to think. Why would Burke lie to her? It wasn't like him to do that. Brian was a very truthful person. It was one of the things Liz liked about him, and one of the reasons that she had never lied to him. Not once. She *had* to be honest with Burke, because he was always honest with her—until now.

"Holy Mary, mother of God, pray for us sinners, now and at the hour of our death…"

Liz glanced at Brian. His eyes were closed, his lips moving—he was actually *praying*, because he was really serious about that sort of thing. He was such a decent guy.

So why would a decent guy lie?

Brian had told her that she had met him in the woods, and they had argued, and she had run away from him and twisted her ankle, and then he had carried her to the school, where Hank had ambushed her, and Bickerstaff had tried to shoot her, yada yada yada. But whatever Brian was *not* telling her had to have happened when they were alone. In the woods. She had the oddest feeling that they hadn't just argued there. That they had hugged, and he had said she was beautiful.

She scowled. *Those are NOT memories, idiot. Those are daydreams, and you KNOW it. There's no WAY that really happened.*

"... Blessed art thou among women, and blessed is the fruit..."

Had she... had she told him the truth? The awful, awful truth?

That she kinda dug him? That there were a billion things about him that she just thought were neat? Like how thin and wiry he was...how he stroked his chin sometimes as if he had a beard...how he sometimes sounded like a mustachio-ed, monocle-ed gentleman from the 19th century, with his harrumphing and *what-fors*... Other people might find those things annoying, but Liz didn't. Liz thought they were neat.

She liked them.

What she liked even more, though, was how fundamentally *good* he was. He was straight up. He was a mensch. He was always honest. He wasn't like her. And that's what she liked. She could trust him. She loved talking to him. She loved having him around. And she didn't really like sharing him with anyone else—although she would never dream of saying that out loud.

But she must have. It explained everything. She had confessed her Like to him, and he had probably freaked out—*Liz likes me, oh no! Horror!* But now—oh happy chance!—she had managed to get her memory wiped, and he could just pretend it never happened! How marvelous for *him*.

No. That couldn't be it. She didn't want to believe it.

It couldn't be true, because Brian was good. She wouldn't be in Like with him if he wasn't. He wouldn't be so dishonorable. It must be something else.

At least, Liz desperately hoped so. She had a very good reason for keeping all this stuff to herself. If Brian ever knew how she felt about him—and these stupid feelings had gotten worse the more she knew him—their friendship would be over.

What were they going to do, date? Impossible. She couldn't date Brian Burke. She had her reputation to think of. And besides, he *wouldn't* date her. Not old, ordinary, nondescript Liz, his ol' buddy that he felt comfortable with because she wasn't hot enough to look at… sometimes she wanted to stab him with a tomato stake. He could be *so* insensitive…

"… *Glory be to the Father, and to the Son, and to the Holy Spirit…*"

And that's why she had been mad at him for so long. But she wasn't now. Now she felt giddy and nervous and supremely happy, like she had discovered a great and glorious secret, a secret she couldn't tell anyone… a secret that would change her whole life and paint the whole world in brilliant colors.

She didn't trust this feeling. It told impossible stories. It told her that something *wonderful* had happened out in the woods. Like something out of a fairy tale. Like (she cringed to even think this) her *dreams had come true.*

She needed to know the truth. She needed to ask him what had happened, and not stop until she got an honest answer.

She poked Brian's arm with one finger. "Hey," she whispered.

He looked annoyed.

She grinned despite herself. She really did love to irritate Burke. "I know you're praying," she whispered. "I got to ask you something after rosary. Okay?"

He gave her a terse nod. That was enough for her.

When the rosary ended (finally), everyone got up and started talking. Brian turned to Liz with an annoyed/amused look. "So? What did you want to—?"

"Hey, Brian, can we talk now?" said the familiar, annoying breathy voice.

Brian turned to Mary Summers, looking both nervous and annoyed. "Um, Mary, I need to—"

"It's really important," Mary said, looking anxious. "In private. Just a few seconds. *Please*, Brian."

A look came across Brian's face that Liz had learned to utterly loathe that summer: that goofy, entranced look. "Um, sure," he said. For a moment he glanced back at Liz, looking vaguely apologetic, but

47

then Mary whisked him away, and he was following her out of the gym like a puppy dog, and Liz was left sitting there like a freaking goober.

Okay. No big deal. I'll get a chance to ask him later. But something inside of her didn't think so. That same something wanted to tomato-stake Mary Summers now. Even more than usual.

It was lunch time. Time for the big meeting. J.P. took a slow, meandering pace through the woods. He was probably already late for the meeting, but he didn't care. He needed time to erase his sour mood. The day had started off so well with Miranda and her friends. But then… *Athan.* What an annoyance.

All week, Athan had been showing off, in small, subtle ways. First was the desks thing, of course, and the whole "Look at me, I'm an *artist!*" nonsense. Yesterday he had led the day's opening prayer in Greek, and earlier today J.P. had caught him tutoring Vivian Andros in geography. *As if he actually knows the names of all the countries in the Middle East. Nobody knows stuff like that, except college professors and terrorists and Brian.* Even worse, Miranda had been following along from the next seat over.

Athan was definitely the kind of person J.P. just couldn't stand—a know-nothing con artist who pretended he was sooooo smart and cool, and somehow got people to fall for it. Athan was messing everything up. He didn't know his place.

J.P. swore a vow to himself: *I will never, ever let Athan Cork-whatever overshadow me.*

As the youngest of ten kids, J.P. had already spent the vast majority of his life in the shadow of somebody or other. He also had to sit by and watch his older brothers and sisters get celebrated for passing an important test, or graduating, or getting married. At almost 16, J.P. hadn't really achieved anything worth celebrating yet; by the time he did, there wouldn't be anyone at home except his parents to congratulate him.

By the time he had been enrolled in JP2HS, J.P. was desperate for the attention, and he knew how to get it: make people laugh. It was his one great gift. Sometimes it even happened when he wasn't trying; like when his voice cracked or he made a weird face or he said something stupid. That was okay. *Any* opportunity was a good opportunity.

Everything was fine at the school until now, he thought, sitting up. He stared at an anthill near his foot, and watched as the little ants climbed in and out, some carrying their little loads, others building up the dirt hill grain by grain. *We were like that last year*, he thought. Everyone had fit in somewhere; everyone had a "thing." George was the leader. Allie and Brian pulled double duty, she as both Catholic noob and hot chick, he as token black guy and resident super-genius. Celia was the nice, helpful one, Liz was the sporty cynic. James did a great job as the Obnoxious Weird Snob No One Liked.

And J.P. was the Comedian. The cool guy. The one you could count on for flash. For show. For crazy stunts and off-the-wall unpredictability.

But then Athan had to come along, with his artsy-fartsy notebooks and his show pony ninja flips and his stupid girlie haircut. And where did *that* fit in? The last thing the school needed was a Guy Who Could Do Everything.

Or a Guy Who Had It All And Made The Rest Of Us Look Pathetic.

Or the Sensitive Serious Guy Who Wooed All The Ladies (Especially The Ones J.P. Liked).

J.P. sighed and headed to the meeting, feeling worse than when he'd started.

He could hear Helpful Celia giving a speech before he could see anybody; he could just imagine Leader George standing authoritatively on one side, and Genius Brian nodding along supportively on the other. When he arrived it was just as he imagined, plus there was Attentive Allie seemingly hanging on every word, Annoyed James doing the exact opposite, and Lackadaisical Liz hanging out on one side, looking bored.

All the new students together made a small crowd. Even though it had only been a few days, little groups had already started to form, particularly amongst the girls. Miranda was clearly the leader of one group that included her sidekicks Kristy and Vivian, as well as a few admiring boys, including Mitch and Kevin. The short, stout and opinionated Josephine Grantham led another group of girls. And then there were unaffiliated students, like Mary and Jacinta and Isabel and several boys that J.P. didn't know. All the upperclassmen were standing together in front of the new students, so J.P. chose a place off to the side, next to James.

"What's happened so far?" he whispered.

"Shut up," James hissed back. "They're talking about the night of the shooting." He looked... weird. Weirder than usual. Nervous, maybe.

"Anyway, it was a big deal for us," Celia was saying. "I think I speak for all of us when I say that it was our toughest time together, ever. It wasn't even our school, but somehow we were all there. God brought us all where He needed us to be. What I think we're saying is that we all learned a lot from all the stuff that happened. And the most important thing is that we need to stick together. We're not just a school, we're a family."

Everyone seemed to be nodding and listening quietly, except James.

Celia raised her voice. "The night of the shooting at the dance, all of us here agreed to something really important, something we thought would help to keep us strong, like a family." She took a deep breath. "We all agreed to not date anyone at our school, ever. At least, not while we're enrolled here."

There was some mumbling from the crowd. A boy J.P. had never seen before spoke up from the back row. "So dating is against the rules here?"

"No, Paul," Celia said, "it's just an agreement we all made at the end of last year. When you date in a small environment like ours, there's too much that can go wrong. One bad break-up can ruin everything. We're all too close; we all know each other. Does that make sense?"

More confused mumbling, louder this time.

George stepped up again. "Here's the thing," he said sharply, "we need to stay united. Dating in a place like this isn't uniting; it's dividing. So we want everyone here to agree to the same rules, and stand by them. Maybe when the school grows we can change things, but right now this is the way it's got to be. You all understand?"

Isabel raised her hand. "I agree."

"Me too," Agnes chimed in.

Next to raise his hand was Athan. "I get that it's kind of extreme, but I see why it's a good idea right now. I agree too."

Huh, J.P. thought. *Maybe he isn't interested in Miranda after all.*

Whatever Athan's intentions toward Miranda were, he had swayed many of the others. Now other hands were going up. The girls seemed more eager about it than the boys, but there were no holdouts, not even Kevin.

The only ones who didn't move were Miranda and her two friends. Miranda crossed her arms with a scowl; Vivian and Kristy both looked at her uncertainly.

"Great," Celia said. "Then if we're all agreed—"

"We're *not* all agreed." Miranda said loudly.

Celia sighed. "Miranda—"

"This might have made sense when there were seven of you, but now there's all of *us*. And we weren't there when you prudes formed this little plan—"

"That's why we're asking you—"

"Asking? Sounds more like demanding," Miranda said, giving George an annoyed look. "Besides, what's all this about not wanting cliques? You guys are all standing up there, while the rest of us are all over here."

"Wait a minute, Miranda," George said, "That's not what this is about at all."

"I wasn't *talking* to you, George," Miranda snapped, and turned back to Celia. "You're the one who brought the 'family rules' into this, but just because dad runs the school, that doesn't make this place our house. You just want no dating at the school because Dad won't let us date at home."

Now the murmurs were back again. *She kinda has a point*, J.P. thought.

"Well," Miranda said, raising her voice a bit and looking around at the others as she spoke, "who put you in charge here, Celia? Was it Dad? Because I don't remember him saying anything like that to *me*."

Celia looked frustrated now. "Oh, stop it, Miranda—"

Miranda tossed her head and put her arms around Kristy and Vivian. "You may think you're kings and queens of the hill up there, but you're not. And we're not going to agree to your stupid, childish rules."

There was an uncomfortable silence.

"Hey, Miranda?" Jacinta Summers said, "It's not childish."

Miranda glared at Jacinta, but Jacinta only smiled. "No, I'm serious!" she said earnestly. "I think Celia just wants what's best for the school. She's not trying to boss us around."

"Oh, you don't know what she's like at home," Miranda fumed. "Playing the perfect daughter who does just what Mom and Dad say."

"Oh, well, I fight with my sister all the time too," Jacinta said lightly. "But that doesn't mean it's not a good idea. I'd rather be friends with everyone than spend all my time worrying about who likes who. Wouldn't you?"

Miranda didn't look like she agreed, but it didn't matter. Jacinta had already killed her little rebellion—the mumbling had stopped, and even Kristy and Vivian looked like they were ready to cave in.

Oh well, J.P. thought. *Rest in Peace, J.P.'s love life.*

And after everybody else started back toward the school, Miranda approached Celia away from the others. J.P. happened to be behind them, and could hear every word.

"I don't care what everyone *pretended* to agree to today," Miranda hissed at her sister, before stalking off to join her friends. *"This. Isn't. Over."*

6

WEIRD SCIENCE

Well, that's that, Liz thought as she sat in her mom's science class that afternoon. *No dating. Heh. Like I care.* She didn't mind joining the no-dating pledge; it was a good way to equalize the 10s and the 8s and all the other numbers. No dating meant that all girls got an equal shot at not having boyfriends. Besides, her last relationship, freshman year, had ended with some mace in the face, after her boyfriend—Rich Rogers—had almost raped her. So she was okay with being single.

She stifled a yawn. Last year, she had referred to science class as Sleepy Time With Mom, since her mother spent most of last year's science class lecturing at them from a textbook. "This year we're taking a more hands-on approach," her mom was saying. *Uh, oh. No more Sleepy Time?* "We're going to do projects too, and you'll be working together quite a bit."

Work together? Liz glanced at the other three kids in the room with her—Brian, J.P. and Mary. There were a lot of freshmen, but their class—the sophomores—was still tiny.

"We'll start with life sciences," her mom continued, and picked up her jacket. "Follow me, and bring your books."

As they walked down the hallway, Liz closed in on Brian. "Hey," she said quietly. "So…we still need to talk."

"Um…yes," Brian said, pushing open the door to the cafeteria and walking through. "We do." He glanced back down the hallway, looking nervous.

"What's wrong?" Liz said.

"Shhh!" Brian said, glancing at Mary, who was talking to Mrs. Simonelli about creation science: one of Mrs. Summer's champion causes. Liz smiled inwardly. *So he's nervous around Mary. This is good.*

They went into the woods that bordered the square lawn behind the school building. It wasn't long before Mary caught up to them. "Hey, Brian!" she called. "Wait up!"

Liz scowled at Mary. *Why don't you just leave him alone? Can't you see how nervous you're making him?* "Brian," she said, keeping her voice calm. "Remember, I still need to ask you something—"

"Sorry!" Mary was there, a little more breathless than usual. "What do you think she'll make us do?" she asked Brian, gesturing at Liz's mom. "Dig up worms and bugs or something?" She giggled and sidled up to him.

"That doesn't sound like *my mom*," Liz said, sidling up to Brian from the other side. "Why don't you ask *me* about what *my mom* might do?"

"Because I wasn't *asking* you." Mary took another step closer to Brian, so that their shoulders were nearly touching. Brian stepped back, looking alarmed.

Liz grinned. "Well, I'm *answering* you," she said triumphantly, leaning an elbow on Brian's shoulder. She had meant it to look cool and casual, but thanks to Brian being taller it actually felt uncomfortable. "And quit crowding in on my pal."

Mary scowled. "Looks like *you're* crowding in on him." She made a move to push Liz's elbow off Brian's shoulder.

"Quit it!" Liz jumped back, throwing Brian off balance by accident—at the same time, Mary's hand hit Brian's shoulder. He stumbled, lost his balance and fell on the wet grass. "Ow!"

"Hey!" Liz's mom, already at the edge of the woods, gave them all a stern look. "Quit fooling around and get over here! That means you, young lady!"

As Liz tramped away across the school's back yard, she saw J.P. pull Brian up with a disgusted look. "Man, how did it come to this?" he said. "Two girls fighting over you?"

Liz clenched her teeth. *I wasn't fighting over him. All I want to do is ask him a simple question. If only Mary would leave him alone for three seconds!*

"All right kids," her mom said as they gathered underneath a large tree. "Look around. How many forms of life do you see? Liz?"

Liz looked around. "Um…trees?"

Her mom looked disappointed, unsurprisingly. "That's nice Liz, but what kind of trees? Anyone know what tree this is, for example?" She pointed upwards at the branches above their heads.

Brian raised his hand. "That's an oak tree. You can tell by the leaves."

"Very good. What other forms of life can you see besides trees? Mary?"

"Um… grass?" Mary said.

"Very good, Mary," her mom said, and Liz scowled. *Really, mom?*

Mrs. Simonelli handed each of them a paper grocery bag. "Now for the next ten minutes we're going to have a little competition. I want you four to pair up and walk through these woods, and find samples of different species. The pair that brings back the most samples wins. Plant, animal, it doesn't matter."

"Hey, Burke!" Liz said loudly, interrupting her mom before she lost her chance to claim Brian. "Wanna be my partner?"

"Liz!" Her mom said reprovingly. "There's no need to shout! So… Liz and Brian on one team, Mary and J.P. on the other. Well, go ahead, and take your textbooks with you. I'll be waiting here for you."

Mary scowled as she walked away with J.P. Liz turned triumphantly to Brian. "Well, whaddya say, partner? Ready to catch some bugs and leaves?"

Brian stuck his hands in his pockets. "Sure," he said glumly. "Whatever."

Liz's good mood vanished. '*Whatever'?* She thought as they walked into the woods. *Whatever? What does that mean? Would he rather be with Mary after all? Then why did he look so nervous before? And why do I feel so nervous all of a sudden? It's freakin' Burke here, Lizzy. Get a grip.*

"So you want to split up?" Brian said.

"What?" Liz squeaked. *Great! Back to squeaking again!*

"You know, to cover more ground," Brian said. "We're sure to find more kinds of trees and such that way."

"Oh!" Liz said, and was relieved to find that her voice was back to normal. "Um... no. I'd rather, you know... stay together."

Brian shrugged, and didn't seem to notice (thought Liz couldn't imagine how he'd missed it) that she had started blushing. "Okay. We'd better get cracking then. Here's a maple leaf." He pulled a leaf off a nearby branch and handed it to Liz. "I think I see some birch trees over there. Come on."

They spent a few minutes gathering samples. Mostly it was Brian who pointed out different plants, mosses, or bugs and Liz who got them. That suited Liz fine; it gave her time to think. Or at least to calm down a bit. *All right. How do I ask him? I should be subtle. Smooth.*

"So," she said, bringing a bit of brown moss to Brian that she'd peeled off a slimy rock, "you remember the last time we were in the woods? Because, heh, I sure don't." She immediately felt like facepalming herself. *Real smooth, Liz.*

"Um, sure," Brian said, and once again she saw that nervous look. She tried again. "Brian—"

"Liz," he said, pulling up suddenly to face her. "I have to ask you something." He looked serious. "I know we just made that promise about not dating anyone from the school, and you know I take that really seriously, but..."

Liz blinked, and for some reason she couldn't breathe quite right. "Yes?" she said faintly.

"Would it be okay with you if...?"

A grin broke out on her face. "Go on, if what?"

"If... well, if Mary and I sort of hung out more?"

Liz blinked again, confused. "What?"

"We wouldn't be dating or anything," Brian said hastily. "I mean, we've all just promised not to date. It's just that Mary feels that well... she and I dating nearly ruined our friendship and she'd like us to be friends again. And I agree—I can't keep being annoyed with her—not when there's only four of us in our class. But I don't want it to seem to you as though we're cheating on our promise."

Liz stood there. And just stared at him.

"So, well, um, what do you think?" Brian stammered after few more uncomfortable seconds. "I know you don't like Mary, and I know things between you and me got a little weird over the summer…"

"Weird?" Liz said. To her relief her voice sounded perfectly normal. That's the way it should sound, right? It wasn't like Brian was being unreasonable. He just didn't want to hate Mary anymore. Right?

So why did she now want to hate *him*? And her?

"Well, you know, maybe it would be a little awkward," she said in a perfectly normal voice. "But no big deal."

"Are you sure?" Brian said. And suddenly Liz knew that he was asking sincerely. That he really would do what she asked him.

And that meant there was only one thing she could say.

"Burke," she smiled easily, reaching out and patting him on the shoulder, "don't stress about me. Seriously. We're friends. I can't say it's a great idea, but I can say it won't make me not be your friend. If you want to date Mary, or pretend-date Mary, or whatever, go for it."

"We're not dating," Brian mumbled. "That's not what this is. Liz, are you *sure* you're okay with this?"

"Sure I'm sure." Liz kept grinning. Her face still felt kind of wooden, but she knew, being an actress, that she didn't *look* wooden. "Now come on, let's find some more bugs."

She turned away, and pointedly (but not too pointedly) started examining a bush. Still numb. No secret happiness. No more jitters. No more excitement. Zero feelings. *Zero.*

It was only later, after class when she saw Brian whisper something to Mary and saw her laughing and hugging him, that Liz realized that she hated Brian Burke with the heat of a thousand suns.

This is a stupid school, she thought, not for the first time. *Can't wait to get back to cheerleading practice at Sparrow Hills. This place stinks, all the way through.*

57

J.P. had made faint attempts to charm Mary, but it was clear she wasn't really interested: she was paying more attention to the back of Brian's head as he and Liz trudged through the woods. This miffed J.P. *Why does she even like him? I mean, Brian's nice, but come on! She's way better looking than him.*

As they were heading back into school, Mary broke away and ran up to Brian. Whatever they were talking about, the hug Mary gave Brian looked a lot like a Public Display of Affection (something that had been banned at St. Lucy's and was technically not allowed at JP2HS). J.P. was struck by the hypocrisy of it. He knew that Brian had liked Mary, and it was obvious that Mary liked him. What was going on? Had they made a secret pact to date? *Naah, Brian would never do that… Would he?*

He looked at Liz, and saw her face, and knew he wasn't imagining this. *Low blow, Burke,* he thought.

"Hey, Liz!" he shouted, and Liz stalked over to him.

"Check this out. It's still here."

He pointed to the rear corner of the school where there was a clump of bushes.

"What?" she said, suddenly interested.

"Our secret weapon for the prank war," he said in a hushed voice, leading her over. He plunged his arms shoulder-deep, almost sticking his face in, and came up with a ratty old gray hose, a little thicker than the green ones.

"Artillery for our cause," J.P. said. "This is a classic. Nothing says 'hey, summer's not over yet!' like a blast from an industrial strength hose running the kinds of high water pressure these old buildings were allowed to carry. Remember this baby?"

"How could I forget ol' Hosey?" she said with a grin. "And I can think of several people who deserve a face-full of him right now."

"Let's do another round of 'surprises' for the freshmen after school's done," he suggested. Since they were teachers' kids, there was usually at least an hour to kill after school while their parents had meetings and worked on curriculum.

58

"Why just do the freshmen?" Then Liz shook her head. "No, can't. Got cheerleading practice at Sparrow Hills."

"What! You're cheerleading this year? At Sparrow Hills? Can I come?"

"Um. No."

"Awww."

He thrust his hands in his pockets, pretending to be disappointed. But honestly he was, a little. Everyone seemed to be doing Cool Stuff at Sparrow Hills. Jerkface Athan. Possibly-Two-Faced Brian. And now Liz. *I gotta get a life*, he thought to himself. *Maybe I'll just go down to football practice again. Anything's better than staying here.*

7

DEADLY RUMORS

Football practice was in full swing by the time J.P. arrived. As he walked over to the stands, he was surprised when one of the players gave him a thumbs-up. He'd returned it before he realized it was Flynt the goon. He had almost forgotten that crazy conversation. But he remembered now—and he remembered the stolen notes Liz had shown him.

"Hey, Flynt," he said.

"Whassup?"

"Not much. Hey, I just wanted to let you know that... I'm looking at... that thing we talked about. Me and a friend of mine. We're on the case."

"Really?" Flynt looked impressed. "Cool!"

He saluted and jogged away. J.P. went up to the stands, feeling a little pleased with himself. *I've got to introduce him to Liz.* He sat down near a group of football players to watch the practice. Joey and George were both sitting on the bench, but Athan, much to J.P.'s surprise, was on the field.

When Athan's turn to catch came up, J.P. leaned forward, hoping Athan would drop the ball and look like an idiot. But Athan shot off the line faster than any of the other players, and grabbed the ball out of the air without breaking stride.

"Woo! Did you see that?" One of the guys in the group of players next to J.P. said. "That kid is *fast*."

"*Pfft*," J.P. scoffed. *If they only knew what a jerk he was...*

"What, you think he wasn't fast?" the same boy said, turning to J.P. He had a hooked nose and a buzz cut which, combined with his pads, made him intimidating.

"Who, Athan? Oh... uh... he's fast," J.P. said, trying to think up something cool to say. "For a lame... uh... lame person. Who is lame."

The other boys stared at him.

60

"He also… um… can't paint worth a crap."

"What? Paint?" The three boys looked at each other, confused, then looked back at J.P. "What are you talking about?"

"Aaand… and he's a stalker too," J.P. said, ignoring the question and trying not to sound nervous.

"Stalker?" Hook Nose said. "That little receiver guy?"

"Oh yeah," J.P. said. "Hiding behind corners, lurking in the bushes, all that stuff."

"How do *you* know?" asked one of the other players, an enormous black kid, almost as round as he was tall.

"I've seen him do it, that's how," J.P. said.

"How? Is he stalking you?" asked the third boy, a skinny Italian-looking kid with dark hair.

"Well, you know," J.P. said, seeing an opportunity and leaning in closer. "Let's just say he's the kind of guy who likes to watch wrestling practice when he gets a chance." He felt bad saying it at first, until he remembered how Athan had embarrassed him in the cafeteria.

Hook Nose smirked. "Is that so?" He turned to the other guys. "Guess we'll have to watch our backs then."

"Oh, don't worry," J.P. said, "Athan will do that for you."

All three of the other guys laughed. "You're funny," said Hook Nose, and stuck out his hand. "I'm Dylan. My friends call me Dyl. This here is Fatty, and this is X."

"Hang on, I'm confused," J.P. said. Which one of you is Fatty?"

The big black guy snorted with laughter, and the other two grinned.

J.P. grinned back. "My name's J.P. But some people call me Japes, or Johnny P., or—" he almost said 'Jay-Pee-Enator', but caught himself at the last second. "—or just J.P." he finished.

"Well, J.P.," Dyl said, "you're a funny guy."

"Yeah, that's what Flynt said too."

Dyl looked surprised. "You know Neil Flynt, huh?" he asked.

"Sure," J.P. said. "We're tight. We…" He had no idea what Flynt actually did. "You know, do stuff together. Hang out."

Dyl looked J.P. up and down. "I don't suppose you'd want to help out the team this year, would you J.P.?"

J.P. tried very hard not to let his mouth hang open. *Me? On the team? Miranda will be so impressed!* "Sure. I'd love to! What do you need me to do?"

Dyl turned to consult in whispers with Fatty and X for a moment, then said, "Can you do any gymnastics or anything? How are you at falling down and stuff?"

"Sure!" J.P. said. *Of course, falling down would be important in football—I guess.* J.P. had been tackled by his brothers ever since he could stand. And his older brother Sean had taken judo classes for a while, and taught J.P. how to hit the ground in a way that reduced the impact.

"Oh, I fall down good. Watch this!" He went over to the grass beside the bleachers, took a couple steps to build up, then jumped as high as he could and landed laid out on his stomach. The three boys groaned in sympathy; but J.P. got up right away, dove forward through a partial somersault in the air, and landed on his back. More groans from his new friends, and a gasp from some other bystander.

Now for the finale. J.P. made to get up again, but purposely let his foot slip out from under him and hit the ground on his side. "Oops!" He got up on all fours, then let his hands and feet both slip out together. "I can't…" he stood part way and fell again, "seem to…" he tripped to his right, "get up…" he fell forward and ended up in a handstand, awkwardly hand-walking over to the fence while the crowd laughed and clapped.

He stopped his hand-walk with his feet drooping over the top of the fence, his hair hanging down to the sidewalk, and his shirt falling down over his face. "Say, guys?" he said, letting his voice crack and speaking loudly enough so everyone could hear him, "can you give me a hand here?"

Really loud laughing now. *A crowd! I love crowds!* He straightened his legs and rolled right-side up, standing with the momentum. Rolling on the concrete did hurt his shoulder a little, but he didn't care; he had them applauding now. "Thank you, thank you!" he said with a bow and a little flourish, "I'm here all week."

Dyl clapped him on the back. "Well, you're hired," he said with a smile. "You'll make a great mascot."

"Mascot, sure! Wait, *mascot?*"

"Yeah! You know, keeping up morale on and off the field? All that stuff. You said you were tight with Flynt, right? He was in with last year's mascot, too. We were kind of worried cuz no one came along who could, you know, fill the position. But if you and Flynt are buds, that's perfect. You're good with people, you're fast, and you can do all the tumbling and clown stuff."

J.P. couldn't think of what to say. A whistle blew.

"Hey, we got to go," said Dyl. "It's our turn to drill. But talk to Brad about the mascot stuff. He can get it for you. Tell him you're Flynt's friend and you shouldn't have any trouble. And thanks again for taking the job! You're gonna do great, man!"

Yeah. Mascot. Miranda will looooove that. Still, he was feeling pretty good after all the laughs and applause. Soon he was imagining riling up the crowd, dancing in the end zone, taunting the opposing players, hanging out with the cheerleaders… *This might actually be really awesome. I'm going to be the coolest mascot ever!*

*B*eat *'em!"* Liz yelled, then clapped her hands twice and took a step to the right.

"Bust 'em!" Clap twice, step to the left.

"WE're the SPAR-row Hawks we're-gonna-crush-them…" she knelt down, straightened up, threw her arms out, nodded twice—

Coach Fusco, a brown-haired woman in her 40's, blew on her whistle and waved her arms. "Stop, stop!" With a disgruntled murmur, Liz and the rest of the squad—about sixteen or so girls—stopped the routine.

"What's wrong now?" one of the girls whined.

63

"Wrong?" Coach Fusco looked exasperated. "You were totally late, Jessica. Like, really late. You were out of sync with everyone else. You all got to start over."

There was a chorus of groans, which Coach Fusco waved off. "You're only as good as your worst teammate," she lectured them. "If anyone makes a mistake, *that's* what people are gonna notice."

In the locker room after practice, Liz pulled her sweatpants down over the ankle cast and pressed down on it experimentally. She felt a twinge. *It's getting worse. Maybe I should get this thing looked at by the docs again.* That would be the sensible thing to do.

But then, if Liz were the kind of person to do the sensible thing, she probably wouldn't have hurt her ankle in the first place. She put more and more weight on the foot, adjusting herself to the pain. *See? (Ouch!) No problem. A doctor would probably tell me (ouch!) to use crutches or something. I don't (ouch!) have time for that.*

"You think I need to practice more?" said a loud, angry voice. "Really, Simone?"

The locker room quieted down. Everyone looked to the door where Jessica was standing with Simone and Tara. She looked furious.

"I didn't say that," Simone said hastily. "I just said if you wanted to practice more, I'd be happy to—"

"Yeah right, like I'm going to spend more time here!" Jessica shot back. "If I'm doing so bad, maybe I'll just quit! I'm risking my life just being here!" She shouldered her bag and ran out of the locker room.

"Jessica, wait!" Tara ran after her.

Simone just stood there open-mouthed, until she noticed everyone was looking at her. "What?" she said, irritated.

"She's got a point, you know," one of the girls said.

"Gabby," Simone said warningly, "shut up."

Tara came back in, looking troubled. "What's going on?" she said.

"Gabby's making trouble," Simone snapped. "She's trying to scare people with stupid rumors."

"Stupid?" Gabby said indignantly. "Look at the facts!"

"I know the facts, but it doesn't matter. He's dead now, so it doesn't matter."

Another girl snorted. "Yeah right, you really think… look, everyone knows he's still out there."

The locker room exploded with voices. "That's right!" Gabby said. "You all know he's still out there! The police are still asking questions!"

"Hey, hey, hey!" Liz walked right in the middle of the group and waved her arms "Hey! What are you guys talking about?"

Gabby gasped. "You didn't tell her, Simone? She's practically on the hit list, going to that private school."

"Tell me what?" Liz said, baffled. Simone and Tara both looked startled and (Liz thought) a bit guilty.

"Liz," Simone said after a moment. "Grab your bag. We need to talk."

Liz followed Simone out of the locker room. "What's up?" she said. "What were they talking about back there?"

"Let's go somewhere where we can't be overheard," Simone said. They walked down the hall and out a door that led them to the side of the school, overlooking the football field, full of players practicing. Simone took a deep breath. "Look, Liz, you're good at cheering, and that's why I let you on."

"Um…right."

"I mean, Madison's full of it. I wouldn't just let anyone on the squad."

"Yeah, I guess," Liz said after a moment, trying to decide if she should be offended or not.

Simone looked crestfallen. "Look, Liz, the truth is that we're hurting. We used to be way better than this. Half those girls there are straight from JV. No one wants to join the cheer squad this year, ever since the shooting."

"The shooting?" Liz repeated, "What does that have to do with the cheer sqaud?"

"Well…" Simone bit her lip. "Don't freak out or anything, but there's this… theory going around that the Sparrow Hills Shooter was gunning for cheerleaders at the dance."

"What? Why?"

"Because Nikki was a cheerleader. And so was Adrienne."

Liz blinked. "Adrienne Pirolli?" She remembered that name from Allie's notes. "She got shot in the arm, right? I didn't know she was a cheerleader."

"Yeah, well, she was. And now people think it's dangerous to be a cheerleader." Simone sat down on a bench and crossed her arms, looking annoyed.

"But why?" Liz said. "The shooter's dead. Why do they think it's still dangerous?"

"Oh. Well," Simone looked troubled. "There's this other rumor going around. That the shooter's not dead."

Liz stared at her. "They don't think Brock's dead?"

"No. I mean…they don't think Brock's the shooter."

J.P. jogged around the field. *Gotta find Brad… Gotta find Brad and ask him about mascot stuff—which one is Brad again?*

But J.P. was lucky. Someone yelled, "Nice going, Brad!" and J.P. saw a tall muscular guy in a helmet with "POWELL" emblazoned on the back look up with a wave of acknowledgement. J.P. recognized him— he was the player with blue eyes who had told him Flynt was crazy.

"Hey, you're one of those JP2 kids," Brad said. "You were here before, talking to Flynt."

"Um…right," J.P. said.

"Do you know you're bleeding?"

"Huh?" J.P. looked down at his elbow, which was smeared in blood and gravel. He must have cut it during his accidental mascot audition. "That reminds me," he said, turning to the quarterback, "You're Brad, right?"

"Yeah, that's me. You're… uh…"

66

"Name's J.P. I'm supposed to talk to you about getting a mascot uniform."

"A mascot uniform?" Brad asked, puzzled.

"Yep," J.P. said proudly. "Dyl said to get the uniform from you. He said to tell you I'm Flynt's friend—but you already knew that."

Brad's eyes narrowed. He looked J.P. up and down appraisingly, as if sizing him up. J.P. couldn't imagine why. *It's just a mascot job.* "Is that a problem?" he asked. "I mean if you don't need me—"

"No, that's not it," Brad said, looking around at the people nearby. Was he looking for someone? Finally he smiled. "Well, if Dyl says you're the guy for the job, that's good enough for me. So did Flynt explain what the mascot does around here?"

"Sure," J.P. said glibly. He didn't really understand the question, but he knew enough to not say no. "I assume there's a lot of hanging around the bleachers, working the home team crowd, stuff like that?"

"Yeah, that's where everybody will be looking for you," Brad said, although it seemed like he had more to say. He didn't say anything though, and J.P. started to feel weird. He also noticed Brad kept looking up into the stands. "You looking for somebody?" he asked.

"Huh? Oh, nobody in particular," Brad said.

"Soooo then… mascot gear?" J.P. said, sounding a little too chipper. "I've got to get practicing. Go team, and… uh… all that. Right?"

"Sure," said Brad, "sure. Uh, sorry. I'm just kind of distracted."

"Yeah, I noticed. Anything I can help you with?"

Brad looked at him funny, then chuckled. "You want to *help* me? You barely know me, man." J.P. could feel his face turning red, and it must have been, because Brad said, "No, it's not bad. It's just… usually when people want to help me, it means they want something, y'know?"

"Oh. Well, I don't want anything from you. Except a mascot uniform. And all that comes with a mascot uniform. You know. Mascot stuff. For mascotting. You ever notice how if you say that word enough, it stops seeming like a real word? 'Mascot'. 'Massscot.' 'Mas—' Sorry. I'll shut up now."

"You're a little weird, you know that?" Brad said, amused. "I guess that's good for a… for that thing you're doing for us. Oh, thanks a lot. Now I can't stop thinking about how weird that word is."

"Hey, any time you need someone to bring the weird, I'm your guy."

"Riiiiight," Brad drawled. "Well, here's the thing: I can give you the practice mascot costume right now, after practice. But the game mascot costume isn't ready yet. Got it?"

"Yeah! Got it!" J.P. said jauntily. "No, wait. I don't. There's *two* mascot costumes?"

"Yes," Brad said. "And the game costume is the one you want. It's got all the stuff. Got it?"

"Okay," J.P. shrugged. "Sure. Anything else?"

"Yes," Brad said with a hint of impatience. "Once I get everything, we got to meet so I can hand it over to you. Probably won't be till next week. So where do you want to meet?"

"Well, you know, I go to school down the road, so any time you want to come down, we can meet in the parking lot or something," he said. "Just don't be… you know, obvious. I don't want anyone there to know." *I don't even know if Miranda likes* football; *I doubt she'd be happy dating a football clown.*

Brad smiled knowingly. "Yeah, I thought as much. Don't worry, I can be discreet. Do you have a car? I can park next to you and move it from trunk to trunk without anyone else seeing."

"Yeah," J.P. said. "It's a dark blue BMW. Last year's model. Can't miss it. Just let me know before you come." *So I can swipe my mom's car keys before you get there.*

Brad grinned. "Well, alright then, man." He pointed up at the school. "The practice mascot costume's in the closet next to the locker room doors; go grab it. And I'll come by sometime next week in a silver Chevy. I'll pretend I'm there to see someone else."

"Sounds great," J.P. said enthusiastically. "When I see you pull up I'll come out and unlock the trunk, and you can stick it in there."

Out on the field, the football team was gathering together in a giant circle. "I got to get back," Brad said. "But thanks, man. This is gonna be great. You're gonna have a good time."

Liz stared out at the football field. *Brock… not the shooter.* She had a queasy feeling in her stomach as Allie's words flashed through her mind: *I don't want to go through that again. It's not healthy for me.*

No. It couldn't be possible. "Simone," she said, "why would anyone think that?"

Simone sighed. "Well…mostly because of Ginger."

"Who?"

"Ginger Josslyn. We were all friends with her. Remember her? She was at your capture-the-flag party—I think she was hanging out a lot with Brian's family."

"Oh yeah." Liz remembered her now. Tall, built like a model, really pretty. Jealousy-inducing.

"Well," continued Simone, "she's super-convinced that it's not Brock. She had all these theories…she's pretty smart too, so we almost believed her—"

"Where is she?" Liz cut in. "Can I talk to her?"

"Now look," Simone said, annoyed. "I don't want you to stir up trouble—"

At that moment, there was a sound of a door opening, followed by a burst of angry voices. They turned around to see a man in a red windbreaker and a red baseball cap exiting the building through the same door they had used. He had a thick neck, a muscled build and greying goatee, and looked vaguely familiar to Liz. "I'm not talkin' about it anymore!" he shouted over his shoulder.

A second man came out the door—a small, thin man with glasses, mousy brown hair and a young, eager look, clutching a notebook in one hand. "Come on, coach!" he said. "Why not? There must be something else you remember—"

"No, there isn't!" the first man shouted, and suddenly Liz remembered where she had seen him—on the news, every time they covered local sports. "Hey, that's—" she whispered.

"Yeah, Coach Deperoy," Simone said in a hushed tone.

"Wonder what they're arguing about… let's hide!" Liz ducked behind the stone bench. Simone followed. They both peeked underneath the bench at the two men, who were about twenty feet away.

Liz felt like they were spying on a celebrity—which they kind of were. Everyone in town knew Coach Deperoy's name and face—he had been coach of the Sparrow Hills football team for years, and had led them to half a dozen state championships. He was the closest thing to a local legend their town had. At least one of Deperoy's protégés had gotten into the NFL. There had been rumors for years that they were going to put up a statue of him in the local park. Seeing him in person, on the other hand, was weird—especially since he was so agitated and annoyed.

"This isn't my first time talking about this, you know!" the coach yelled at the man with glasses.

"I just want to ask your players a few more questions," the man with glasses said. Liz noticed something round and shiny hanging on his belt. "We're just… pursuing some leads."

"I don't think so!" Coach Deperoy said, pointing at the man. "I don't think there's a 'we' here! I think it's just you, Detective!"

The other man's eager expression faded. "I don't know what you're talking about," he said. "I've been ordered—"

"No, you haven't been 'ordered' to do anything!" Coach Deperoy snapped. "After you came by last time, I called your Sergeant. Yeah, Sergeant Wozniak's an old friend of mine. He told me there is no ongoing investigation. He told me that the case was closed. So that makes me wonder what exactly you're doing here, Detective Irving?"

The man with glasses—Detective Irving—looked staggered. "I—" He licked his lips. "I just have a couple questions. They're important."

"Yeah, well, ask someone else!" Deperoy growled. "I'm done here! If you want to bother me or my players again, you better have a

70

warrant. Which I know you won't get." Without waiting for a reply, he stalked away and disappeared into the school, slamming the door for good measure.

"Wow!" Liz whispered. "That was epic!"

Simone gave her an incredulous look.

"Aw, c'mon. It was like something from a movie!"

"Just...Shhh!" Simone hissed back. "He'll hear us! Shhh! Shhh!"

"Stop shushing!" Liz said, a little louder. "Your shushing is too loud!"

"I'm shushing because you keep talking!"

"I'm talking because I gotta tell you to stop shushing!"

"It doesn't matter," said a dry voice above them. "I saw you when I first came out here."

Liz looked up. There was the man with glasses, looking down at them with a wry smile.

Feeling sheepish, Liz got up and Simone followed.

"I'm Detective Tom Irving," the man said, offering his hand. "But I guess you already heard that."

"Right," Liz said, shaking his hand. "So what are you detecting, anyway?"

"Yeah, what are you doing here?" Simone added.

"Look," he leaned in closer, "I don't suppose you girls heard recent rumors about the Sparrow Hills shooter?"

Liz and Simone glanced at each other.

"What kind of rumors?" Liz said.

"About him still being at large. Targeting anyone new. Anyone being followed, harassed, anything like that."

Simone was frowning. "Have you been asking other people about this?"

Detective Irving studied her face for a moment, his eyes narrowed. "You *have* heard something, haven't you?"

"Yeah, I have!" Simone snapped. "I've heard rumors about some cop asking people about the shooter and freaking people out, and I bet it was *you!* Thanks a lot! Half the girls on my squad have quit because of you! Come on Liz, let's go."

She tugged on Liz's arm, but Liz resisted. "Why do you think he's still at large?" she asked.

He gave her a shrewd, sizing-up look. "What's your name?" he said. "Liz Simonelli."

The detective's eyebrows shot up. "Aren't you the kid that tracked down Herman Bickerstaff?"

"Uh…yes! Yes, I am," Liz said, pleasantly surprised. She had talked to a bunch of cops after Bickerstaff's arrest, but none of them had given her credit for what she had done—until now. "Yeah, I was kind of investigating him, with some of my friends."

"Well, your guys did a better job than some of my guys," Irving muttered, then said, "To answer your question, Liz, I don't think anything, *officially.* I just have questions. It all seems…too convenient, don't you think? All the evidence we got. And the suspect dead. And we never found out who made the 911 call telling us about Brock's body. Look," Irving said as Simone started to object, "Take this." He pulled out his wallet and extracted a business card, "If you hear anything, give me a call. Just keep your eyes open, that's all I'm asking."

"*Well.*" Simone said with distaste after Irving had walked off. "So *that's* where these rumors are coming from. I hope he gets fired."

"Maybe he knows something we don't," Liz said, distracted. Her mind was racing. "Maybe he's onto something."

"Yeah, or maybe he just likes hanging around high school girls because he's a perv," Simone retorted. "Did you see how he was leering at us? Ugh. Let's go inside before he comes back and asks us out." She started to walk away.

Liz stared down at the card in her hand, then put it into her pocket. "Simone," she said. "Give me Ginger's number."

"No!" Simone walked back to her, waving her hands. "No, Liz, I'm not going to let these stupid rumors go any further."

Liz inhaled. "Look," she said. "I don't want to cause any trouble. It would just make me feel better if I talked to Ginger myself. Okay?"

Simone pursed her lips. "Promise not to tell her or anyone else here about Irving."

"Yeah, sure," Liz said, crossing her fingers.

Simone snorted. Then she pulled out her cell phone. "Fine. I'll text it to you. Tell Ginger I said hi."

8

ON THE CASE

Athan and his club were painting a mural of the twelve apostles on one wall in the cafeteria. J.P. hated it. No matter where you sat, the cafeteria smelled like paint.

"So," he said to Brian, "what's the deal with you and Mary?" He had noticed Brian and Mary hanging out a lot, sitting next to each other in class and talking together. "You guys are acting really tight lately—like you're dating."

"Are we?" Brian said, startled. "I hadn't realized."

"Yeah. So what's up? Last I heard you two were meeting together to talk at your parent's house over the summer. What happened there that changed everything?"

Brian looked around, his face red, and smiled. "I don't exactly know," he said, turning back to his lunch. "I kissed her."

J.P.'s eyes widened. "You? Kissed *Mary*?" Brian made a frantic "be quiet" motion with his hand, and J.P. lowered his voice. "How did you do it? What did *she* do? Did she slap you? Liz is *not* going to be happy about that." *Oops. Maybe shouldn't have said that last part. Too late now.*

"J.P.! Keep your voice down!" Brian whispered fiercely, then lowered his head closer to J.P.'s. "Don't joke about stuff like that with Liz. We're still friends, you know."

J.P. shrugged and pretended that it *was* just a joke. But he wasn't blind. He saw the way Liz had been looking at Brian, and how Brian wasn't looking that way back.

"Anyway," Brian continued, "Mary didn't slap me; she kissed me back. Then…it didn't feel right. I felt like I got too… you know."

"Uh huh. I do. Please, say no more. Really—No. More."

Embarrassed, Brian smiled gratefully. "Thanks. It feels strange talking about it like this."

J.P. grinned, patting him on the shoulder. "Yes. Yes it does. So you can feel free to stop any time."

"Right." Brian took a drink, set his soda down. "Anyhow, I didn't handle it as well as I could have. We argued and she left. But then on the first day of school, she came up to me and apologized, and…um… well, we're just being friends, getting to know each other and seeing where God leads us."

"Sure. You *would* both say it like that."

Brian looked at J.P. sternly. "Don't joke about it, man." He sighed. "Look, you know I've always thought God has a hand in my life. I know you think it sounds facetious…"

"If 'facetious' means cheezy, then yes I do."

"…but it doesn't make it any less true. It happens, just in ways we can't always see. This summer though, I feel like God let me see some of those ways. I don't know. It… it changed things for me."

The summer again. Always with the summer. And the Summers. Gah.

J.P. was weirded out. He didn't like discussing religion. It made him feel weird; much weirder than discussing the kissing of girls. He was really uncomfortable talking about God Stuff at all, to Brian or anyone. "Look, I *do* think God's… got my back, I guess. You know? I just don't get into the Kare-O, 'Jesus is my bestest friend everz!' stuff. It just… doesn't seem right. It seems…" He struggled for the right word. "Disrespectful, I guess."

"Huh." Brian grinned. "You sound like me three months ago."

J.P. sniffed, sulky. "Yeah, well, what happened to *you?*"

"Never mind." Brian stood up to take his trash to the can. "Don't worry. It'll happen to you someday."

"Not likely," J.P. said under his breath as his friend got up. He thought about following him, talking to him about Liz. But as much as it bugged him that their Threesome from last year seemed to be breaking apart, he refrained from saying anything. *Talking to Brian about Liz, or to Liz about Brian, seems to be a sure way to get my head bitten off.*

Dinner in the Simonelli household was an event. It took, at minimum, two hours to prepare. Unless it was Sunday dinner. Then it was at least four hours to prepare.

Sunday dinner was always held in the dining room. It was the only time Liz was allowed a shallow glass of wine with her meal. It was also the time that the Simonelli family discussed Important Family Matters.

And this particular Sunday dinner was the time that Mr. Simonelli dropped the bombshell on the family.

"So…the economy's pretty bad lately," he said.

"Yeah," said Liz. She was heaping a side of salad greens on her plate, next to a mound of stuffed pasta shells and homemade dinner rolls.

"Construction bids are slowing down," said her dad in an offhand manner.

"Yeah," said Liz, now slightly alarmed.

"And your mother, she's been doing extra work with the Courchraine's law firm," said Mr. Simonelli.

Liz passed the salad bowl to Joey and listened.

"So here's the good news: with the help of some buddies, I landed a big fat contract." Her dad leaned back in his chair as though receiving applause. None came, of course. He leaned forward again. Then he said, "The bad news, it's in New York. So I have to go away for a while."

"Oh," said Liz. She felt an odd little *nothing* inside. It reminded her of the *nothing* she had felt when Brian had told her about fake-dating Mary—only this *nothing* felt a bit sharper.

"I'm gonna be gone for a month at least," said her dad as he stabbed a few pasta shells onto his fork. He looked up. "Possibly two or three."

Liz said nothing. Neither did anyone else.

"Hey, hey!" Mr. Simonelli broke the silence. "This is *good* news! The economy's bad all over, but I'm still getting work, okay? So let's have a little celebration here." He twirled a pasta-laden fork in the air as he raised a glass of Pinot Noir. "I know you don't want me to go away, and I promise I won't be gone for any longer than necessary." He paused. "But I'm busting my butt to provide for youse alls, and a bad economy means nothing to me, okay?" Mr. Simonelli stopped twirling his fork and got suddenly serious. "Because you," he said, "are all. Going. To be. Provided for." He stabbed his fork in the air at every period for emphasis.

Liz had no doubt of that. She always knew that her dad would bend heaven and earth to support them. No, what worried her was how she and her mom could get along without dad there. Just by being there, he served as a balancing force between them.

"Anyway, sorry I had to ruin Sunday dinner with that, but it had to be said. So let's move on to new business. What's new to talk about?"

"How about Liz's algebra scores?" said Mom.

"Um, no, we don't need to talk about that," said Liz hastily.

"You barely passed algebra 1," her mom objected. "I don't know how you're going to pass algebra 2."

"Math is something you'll use the rest of your life," said her dad sagely. "Money's tight now, but this is important. Your mother and I have talked about making a small stipend for a little extra tutoring. Say ten to twenty dollars a week…"

Liz said nothing. She poked at her salad greens and stuffed pasta shells, trying not to think about a whole semester with her dad gone and her mother constantly riding her about math grades.

Liz sat on the living room couch, working on her mom's laptop while her dad and brother watched a football game and her mom graded papers on the dining room table.

Searching for 'math tutor' on the net had turned out plenty of results. None of them were free though, or even cheap. There were plenty of online programs, but her mom didn't want that. She wanted a living, breathing human being to teach Liz, and she didn't want to pay a lot of money either. In short, she wanted the impossible, or else she wanted to tutor Liz herself, and Liz did not want that. At all.

Her mind wandered to her conversation with Detective Irving.

I don't think anything officially, he had said. *I just have questions. It all seems… too convenient, don't you think?*

"Hm." Liz frowned at the laptop screen. Then she searched for the names 'Brandon Brock' and 'Sparrow Hills'.

News stories. Images of scenes from the shooting. Pictures of Brock—lots and lots of pictures. He didn't look very impressive, with his dull brown hair, watery eyes and weak chin. Was this really *the* guy?

The police seemed to think so, with the evidence they had. Liz had read the whole story just like everyone else. The rifle used in the shooting belonged to Brock. Brock had sent those crazy stalker emails to Allie—they had proved it from his laptop, somehow. And finally, most damningly, Brock had shot himself with his own pistol in the woods. He had committed suicide, just like most of the other school shooters. That's what school shooters did: kill a bunch of people for no reason and then kill themselves. It was hardly even news. The only reason the Sparrow Hills shooting had gotten so much attention was that Brock had delayed the 'kill-yourself' part for a month or two. But he had killed himself eventually. Just like he was supposed to…like it was scripted.

Liz decided she needed to make a phone call.

She locked herself in the upstairs bathroom, pulled out her phone and dialed Ginger Josslyn's number.

After only one ring, she heard a girl's voice. "Hello?"

"Hi, is this Ginger Josslyn?"

"Sure is. Who's this?"

"Hey," Liz decided to just tell the truth. "My name's Liz Simonelli. I'm a friend of Allie Weaver and," she gritted her teeth, "Brian Burke."

"Oh yeah! I remember you! You're the one who maced—"

"Rich Rogers, yeah." Liz rolled her eyes. That's the way everyone at Sparrow Hills knew her.

"Hey," Ginger exclaimed, "Didn't you get shot at or something over the summer? Are you okay?"

"Uh, yeah," Liz said, not bothering to correct Ginger's mistake. *Kidnapped, shot at… whatever.* "Anyway, I really wanted to talk to you about something."

She told Ginger how she had joined the cheerleading squad, and what Simone had told her about the rumor that Brandon Brock wasn't the shooter, that the shooter was still out there, and that he might be targeting cheerleaders.

"And then Simone mentioned that you had some theories about the shooter," Liz finished. "She almost made it sound like you knew something. So do you?"

"Do I…what?"

"Do you know that Brock wasn't the shooter?"

"Um…no." Ginger sighed. "Look, Liz, I'm sorry you got the wrong impression, but I don't really know any reason why Brandon couldn't have been the shooter. If the cops and the FBI say he was, then I guess he was. So you don't need to worry, okay?"

Liz wasn't worried. She was frustrated. *What were you hoping for, exactly? Isn't it* good *that Brock really was the shooter?*

"Look," she persisted, giving it one last shot, "why would you even think that Brock wasn't the shooter? Come on, there's got to be some reason."

"Well… I guess because I've known him since he was a kid."

"Really?"

"Yeah," Ginger said. "He used to hang out at my house. Him and Tyler Getz were friends with my cousin Neil since, like, forever. They were a regular bunch of brats, but not killers. Tyler was the ringleader; the other two followed him around like a couple of puppy dogs when they were kids. Brandon was always the dumbest of the three. He wasn't like… dark, you know? He was just a big, dumb jock and a bully. Even if he did go postal, why would he start by shooting Tyler?"

"Yeah, that doesn't really make sense," Liz said eagerly. "And plus, if he was so dumb, how would he avoid getting caught for so long?"

"Luck, I guess?"

"Luck?" Liz's annoyance returned. "Luck?" She didn't like that explanation. It was too easy.

Ginger sighed. "I gave up trying to explain it a while ago. I'm not the police; I don't know what they know. Maybe he was just obsessed with Allie. Tyler used to date Allie, after all. Brock could have been jealous."

"Huh." Liz had thought of that. But it didn't seem to fit. A flash of memory came up, brief but terribly vivid, of the shadow in the woods, a shadow of a bulky figure, and a harsh, cruel, delighted laugh…

"Look Liz, I hope you don't obsess about this. I've been there. We both need to let it go, for good. I mean come on—it has to be Brock, right? The police have evidence! They're convinced! All of them!"

"Right, right, sure. I still want to learn more about Brock though. Who else can I talk to?"

"Hm." Ginger sounded resigned. "Well, you could always talk to Megan. His sister."

"Brock had a sister?"

"Yeah, I knew her at school. She graduated a few years ago and she's still local. I think she works at that swanky restaurant downtown, *La Chinchilla's*."

"Okay, thanks. That's actually really helpful."

"Great! By the way, how's Brian doing?"

The question caught Liz off guard. "Um…uh…fine, I guess," she stammered. "How would *I* know?"

"Aren't you guys dating or something?"

"No," Liz said blankly. Then a thought occurred to her, both exciting and scary. "Wait, you were at that camp with Brian, weren't you? Did he say something about me?"

"Well, not exactly," Ginger said with a teasing tone. "I just got the impression that he was thinking about some girl while he was there."

"Oh," Liz said sourly. "That's not me."

"Oh. Are you sure? Because when I saw him at the party he was looking for—"

"I gotta go. Thanks again." She hung up the phone and bowed her head, breathing hard. Ever since their lovely conversation regarding Mary, Liz had tried not to talk to Brian, or think about him, or *feel* about him. It just made her angry, and sad. Really, really sad.

She flipped open her phone. Once she found the number for *La Chinchilla's* restaurant, she hit the call link and tried to drain all the swirling emotions she was feeling out of her voice.

"*La Chinchilla's*," a female voice said. "How can I help you?"

"Yeah, can I speak to Megan?"

"Um…Megan Brock?"

"Yeah, is she working tonight?"

There was a long pause. "No." The woman on the phone sounded nervous now. "No, we don't have anyone by that name working here."

Liz almost laughed at the obviousness of the lie. "Really? You just told me her last name. Are you sure?"

"Well." Now the woman's voice was cold. "I'm sorry, I can't help you. Good evening."

The line went dead. Liz stared down at her phone. *Huh. That was weird.*

9

GOOD HAIR SMELL

J.P. rarely paid much attention during class; he always managed to skate by somehow. He was much more interested in sitting in the back row and watching his friends.

He noticed the cold stares Liz gave Brian when he wasn't looking, and the occasional stolen glances of... *is that worry? Annoyance? Heck if I know...* from Brian to Liz when *she* wasn't looking. He noticed something strange going on between James and Allie. Two times J.P. had seen her approach James between classes, on *purpose*, and ask him questions. J.P. couldn't hear either conversation, but the first time James looked confused, and the second time he had actually gotten angry with Allie and given her a lecture on respecting his privacy (he pronounced it so it rhymed with "livery" or "snivelly"). She hadn't seemed fazed, though. J.P. wondered what it was all about.

Other than that, though, nothing really interesting happened at school, until one Wednesday afternoon. The last class of the day had just ended, and J.P. was heading for his locker. He turned the corner and stopped short.

Miranda Costain standing by his locker.

"Have you seen Celia?" she said lazily. "Oh, never mind. She's always around when we don't want her, isn't she?"

"Yes," J.P. said. "Yes she is." He didn't know what else to say. He didn't know what to think either, except *woohoo!* and *yes!* and *don't say anything stupid!*

Miranda shoved a book into her tote bag, dropped it on the floor, and leaned on the locker next to his. "So that your locker?"

"Yeah. Where's yours?" Of course he knew exactly where her locker was, but she didn't need to know that.

She waved a hand carelessly down the hall. "That way. My dad tried to assign all the new kids lockers near each other, and somehow mine ended near the main doors, where everyone can bother me. Typical."

J.P. shrugged, hoping he looked casual. Like he cared, but didn't care *too* much. "Well, this one next to mine is free, if you want it."

Miranda leaned in and opened the locker. She was so close he could smell her hair. It smelled like strawberries. He tried not to look like he was sniffing. But man, did she smell good. *Don't say that out loud, though. Don't say 'you smell good.' No matter how good it sounds in your head.*

"Yeah, maybe," Miranda said, then leaned back. J.P. wasn't sure what that meant. What was she even *doing* here? Was she hitting on him?

Miranda looked down the hall. J.P. grasped at the opportunity for conversation. "Waiting for someone?"

"Oh, just waiting for my dad to finish up principal stuff." She sniffed.

"Oh. Well… uh… I'm just… you know. Waiting on my mom." J.P. was suddenly on the verge of panic. *She doesn't want to talk about your mom, stupid!* Why couldn't he think of anything to say? Everything that came to mind was terrible. *I think you're beautiful. Do you want to go out sometime? You smell good—NO.*

He was about ready to just leave before he did something really embarrassing, when Athan came around the corner from the cafeteria.

"Hey," Athan said as he walked over to them, "does anyone want to help with the mural painting?" He said 'anyone', but he was looking right at Miranda when he said it. J.P. glowered.

"I did enough painting over the summer, thanks," Miranda said dismissively. "Didn't you?"

"No such thing as enough painting," Athan said with an easy grin. "Besides, this is a different kind of project. We're expanding our mural. Are you sure you don't want to help? I could really use someone with a good eye for color and design."

Oh, that is so totally not fair. How come he could come up with something cool to say? He's not cool!

But Miranda grabbed J.P.'s arm. "Thanks for the invite," she snapped, "but J.P. and I were just about to go for a walk. Come on sweetie, let's go."

J.P. dutifully walked away with her, cool and casual—but he would not have been more shocked if everybody had spontaneously broken into a song-and-dance routine about fluffy bunnies. She *was* hitting on him. Miranda Costain was *hitting* on him!

She stayed by his side all the way to the front doors. As they exited the building and headed across the grass, the logical portion of J.P.'s brain started noticing things. This all felt weird, and artificial, and— *SHUT UP.* The reckless part took over. He didn't care that this all felt unbelievable. He didn't care that he was worried about the inappropriate sniffing of hair. He didn't care that he was right in front of the school, and everyone would see them, dating rule be damned.

He was going to kiss Miranda.

Right there.

He would pull her to a stop, spin her to face him, and kiss her right on the lips. And nothing would stop him!

...except maybe if Mr. Costain or Celia jumped out from around the side of the building right then and said, "Ah-HA!"

Which, of course, they did.

Not so much jumped as walked, of course, and not so much said "Ah-HA!" as "Oh, Miranda, there you are." But it had the same effect. J.P. jumped back with a herky-jerky two-step and yanked his arm out of Miranda's.

All three Costains were staring at him. He was vaguely aware that he had shouted something like "AHHHoooo!" He could feel his heart like a rapid-fire machine gun his chest.

"Uh... sorry. There was a... um... bear. In the woods. It's gone now."

Three single Costain eyebrows on three different Costain faces were raised in his direction. *Do they know they're all doing that? That's kind of creepy if they don't. Also if they do.*

"There aren't any bears around here, Mr. Flynn," Mr. Costain said.

"Oh. Well, it might have been a... a big dog. Or a fox. Or a tree log. A tree log. A log, that was once a tree, that fell over. And now it looks like a bear. From a distance."

"Yes," Mr. Costain replied, "it must have been something like that." Now his eyebrow was accompanied by a slight smile.

"What are you and Miranda doing?" Celia asked. Her eyebrow was not amused.

"Just walking, not that it's any of your business," Miranda replied nonchalantly, but with a provocative little smirk.

Celia's eyes narrowed into slits. Miranda's eyes narrowed too. J.P. felt suddenly like he was in the old West. And it was high noon. And he was watching a showdown. No—that he was in the *middle* of an old showdown, in between the two shooters. And he was without a gun.

"Oh, we were just talking about… you know, history." He held up his textbook.

"Okay then," said Mr. Costain, seeming not to notice his daughters on the verge of killing each other with nothing more potent than sassy glances. "Miranda, it's time to get going. See you later, J.P." He walked away, followed by Celia.

"So I guess I'll see you tomorrow or whatever," Miranda said, turning to leave. "Thanks J.P.!"

"You're welcome," J.P. said quietly, watching her walk away with her father and sister.

The next day, Liz entered the cafeteria and looked around for a place to sit. Lunchtime was different now. Before, everyone ate at one table, except maybe James. Now there were five round tables, and students clustered in groups of six or eight. Liz noticed that Celia usually sat with the new freshmen, particularly Jacinta and Isabel. It was a typical welcome-ey, Celia-ish thing to do: trying to make the school one big happy family.

She saw J.P. and ran up to him. "Hey," she said. "Wanna plan the next prank? I was thinking something with water guns…"

But J.P. had his eyes locked on the table where Miranda was sitting with her gang. "Actually, I got other plans," he said, and started to walk away.

"Aw, come on," she said, grabbing his arm. "I got more than just that to talk about." She lowered her voice. "I got…you know…binder stuff."

"Binder stuff?" J.P. repeated, his eyes still on Miranda. "What do you—oh! I forgot to tell you—I met someone who thinks the shooter's still out there."

"What? Are you serious?" Liz felt staggered. "Tell me everything! You can't leave me hanging like this!"

"Yeah, well, it's no big deal. He's kind of a nut. I'll tell you the whole thing soon, I promise." He dashed away.

Liz watched J.P. go and sit next to Miranda, happy as a clam. She felt disgruntled. *Freaking boys.* For a second she considered joining them, but being around Miranda (who looked like a 9 but was just an 8 because she was too whiny) always brought out her worst side.

She went over to the emptiest table and sat down. The only other two people sitting there were James and Allie. It was weird; she would have expected those two to be arguing about something. But they weren't. Both were reading books and engrossed by them. They weren't paying the slightest bit of attention to each other, or to her.

Awww. I was hoping to see a fight. Well, lunch isn't over yet. Let's see what happens.

She opened her brown paper bag, and turned it upside down. A sandwich, a banana, and a can of soda fell out, the can clattering loudly on the table. She caught it before it could roll away.

James looked up, annoyed. "Quiet," he said huffily. "Little girls should be seen and not heard."

"Hey, this isn't the library," Liz said. "I don't need to be quiet. And besides," she added, "What kind of chauvinist attitude is that? Women should be seen and not heard?"

To her surprise, James looked flustered by this. "I didn't mean it like that!" he protested. "I meant *you*, not women in general! It was an attempt at humor."

"Oh, sure it was," Liz retorted. "We all know what you really think about girls—"

86

"Oh, hush, Liz," Allie said, turning a page of her book. "Stop stirring up trouble. James wasn't bothering me."

Allie continued to read. James stared at her with an odd expression—and then with a sudden jerky movement, he got up. "I have to go," he said stiffly. "Miss Weaver. Miss Simonelli."

He walked away, leaving Allie and Liz alone at the table. Allie frowned and turned a page of her book.

What's so great about that book? Liz thought. She peered at it, and then started in surprise.

"Allie," she said. "You're reading the Bible."

"Gee, ya think?" Allie said, still not looking up.

"Wait a sec." Liz was suddenly worried. "Is there some homework assignment I missed? Did Mr. Costain tell us to—?"

Allie made an exasperated sound and finally looked up. "Look, I read a bit of the Bible every day. It's something I started doing over the summer. Okay?"

"But why?"

"Well, why not?" Allie asked. "Word of God here," she said matter-of-factly, holding it up. "Question is, why aren't *you* reading it every day? Got it memorized already, do you?"

"No," Liz said, searching for a good excuse. "I read the Bible, too, sometimes."

"Outside of class?"

"Sometimes," Liz squirmed.

"Hah!" Allie scoffed, "you barely read it *in* class." She had a teasing expression on her face, but then it faded as she looked at Liz. "Is something wrong?"

"No."

"You look like something's bothering you."

Liz couldn't say what was really bothering her: that Allie Weaver, who was already older, prettier and more popular than her, was now holier as well—at least she was trying to be. The old Allie Weaver was shallow and ditzy, but at least she was fun to talk to sometimes. They could just gossip about makeup and boys, without things getting all... biblical.

"Hey," Allie said. "Sorry if I freaked you out."

"You didn't freak me out!" Liz snapped. "It's just that...um... I need a math tutor." It was the first thing that came into her head. "My mom says I got to get a tutor to get my grades up or she'll start teaching me herself. And I don't want *that*."

"Hmm." Allie tapped the table thoughtfully. "You know what? You should ask James."

"James?"

"Yeah. I've been with him in math class. He's really smart. And your mom loves him—all the teachers do. I bet he'd be a great tutor. And he's always looking to make extra money."

"How do *you* know that?"

"Because he told me." Allie opened her Bible again.

"You two talk about stuff like that?" Liz gave Allie an odd look. "I thought you hated James."

"I never *hated* him," Allie said defensively. "I just didn't get him. The trick with James is to never take what he says seriously. Then he becomes tolerable." She smiled slightly.

Liz snickered. "Sounds to me like you *like* him." Liz snickered.

"Right." Allie rolled her eyes. "Because I'm only allowed to either hate a boy, or be in love with him. Now *that's* not sexist."

"So you *don't* like him?"

Allie threw up her hands. "Omigosh, you are really annoying today. No, I don't *like* James. I don't hate him either. He's just my friend. Just like you're my friend. *Everyone* here's my friend."

"Oh, so you're just turning into Celia. Everybody's bestest pal!"

"Um, no," Allie said, sounding a bit like the old haughty Allie now. She paused, and sighed. "Look, not that it's any of your business, but I've sworn off dating *any* guys for the time being. Or even *pretending* to."

"Well, yeah, we all have, haven't we?"

"I would have stopped even if we hadn't made that promise. It just hasn't worked out for me." Allie eyed Liz. "Hasn't for you either, huh?"

"Well, um…"

"I'm sorry. That's none of *my* business." Allie reached across the table and patted Liz's hand. "But Liz, let's be honest—it's harder for girls like us."

"Girls like us?"

"You know. We've both had boyfriends. And if we wanted to, we could have them again. So it's harder for us to give up dating."

"No it's not!" Liz said quickly. "I mean… thanks and all, but you're totally wrong. I can't just *get* a boyfriend whenever I want."

"Oh, sure you can," Allie said, dismissing Liz's point with a wave of her hand. "You're smart, you're assertive, you're pretty—"

"Yeah, well, pretty isn't enough. I mean it's easy for you; you're *gorgeous*," Liz muttered.

Allie hesitated. "Well…you can be, too, if you want to be," she insisted. "Really, Liz. But the point is that you and me are the only girls here who actually *have* been in relationships. So if you ever want to talk about it, I'm here."

"Thanks," Liz said. "That's really… nice of you."

Allie smiled. "No problem." She went back to reading her Bible. "And talk to James about tutoring. He'll say yes, as long as you pay him."

Liz chewed on her sandwich thoughtfully. She appreciated Allie's gesture, but she felt a bit annoyed by it, too. *Talk about my problems to you? Yeah, right. You wouldn't understand. You can't.*

No matter what Allie thought, she and Liz were *not* equals. Allie never had the problem of being ignored. No boy ever called Allie *ordinary*. Allie was a *10*—the only 10 Liz had ever met. She had real power. Wrap-him-round-your-finger power. All the other numbers could flirt with boys, but it took work. And sometimes it meant degrading yourself (Liz could attest to that). But 10's didn't even *need* to flirt. Allie got boys to fall for her without even realizing it. Of course, she had problems: her parents were divorced, and her best friend had gotten killed. But Liz had never really, truly felt sorry for her. Do you feel sorry for the princess in a fairy tale? No. You don't. Princesses were always guaranteed a happy ending. It was different for the tavern wench. Liz always felt sorry for *her*.

Enough distractions, she thought. *I better go find James. And then talk to J.P.*

10

MATH AND MASCOTS

"So what do you think?" Liz asked, hunched over and shivering. Her school sweater wasn't warm enough. Fall was giving way to winter. She glanced up at the sky. *Looks like a storm is coming.*

She had found James outside, sitting on a rock by himself, reading the same book he had been reading at the lunch table with Allie. It had a picture of ghoulish nightmare creatures and the name "H.P. Lovecraft" on the cover.

James looked up at her with a crooked eye. "You said twenty bucks a week, right?"

"Right. And it'll only be about an hour on Mondays. An hour-and-a-half tops. I'm already falling behind, and it would be a big help."

"Isn't your mother a teacher?"

"Yes, you know she is," said Liz impatiently. "We don't get along. I need someone else to teach me."

James puffed his cheeks as he considered the offer. Liz felt a few drops of rain on her cheeks. *Here it comes.*

"C'mon, James. You're good at this math stuff and I suck. It's twenty dollars, easy money."

James shrugged his big shoulders, shifting his lumpy black raincoat around his bulky frame. "Where would we do this?"

"My house. Your house. Heck, the public library. Anywhere. I don't care. I just care about getting through algebra 2."

"The library," said James definitively. "And I get paid before each session."

"You got it," said Liz quickly, before James could change his mind. She put out her hand, and they shook on it.

Yes! One problem solved. "Okay, we'd better get inside before the storm hits."

She hurried inside as the wind started howling in earnest and soon there was the drumming of rain on the roof. When James finally stumped into class, he looked like a wet, mad cat. Liz couldn't help grinning.

Squaaaaawk!" J.P. shouted as he burst out of the locker room in his Sammy the Sparrow Hawk costume. The gym was empty: the football players and cheerleaders were outside practicing. J.P. wanted to practice his moves in secret. There was a pep rally on Saturday, and he wanted to be ready.

He waved manically, jumping up and down, squawking at random as he galloped down the gym. He made his way up to the top of the bleachers and looked around for a moment over the empty gym, imagining what it would look like packed with cheering fans.

He ran down the bleachers, wings spread. Then, taking off the big bulky Sparrow head, he started practicing his breakfalls. *Get up, fall down. Get up, fall down. No pain, no gain.*

He practiced rolling and standing up, rolling to the rear from a standing position, and even a handspring. His jump forward into a handstand was pretty good, but he ran out of strength mid-move. *Yikes. Not enough spring in the ol' handspring.* He picked himself up off the ground and started stretching. *Probably should have started with this.*

"Hey!"

J.P. looked up from his toe touch position. Flynt was jogging toward him, dressed in pads and a faded jersey.

"Oh, hey, Flynt," J.P. said, straightening up. He wondered if Flynt wanted to talk again about his the-shooter-is-still-alive theory. Unfortunately, J.P. had more important things to do just now, like pretending to be a giant cartoon bird. And maybe, just maybe, being Miranda's secret boyfriend. Hopefully he could be both of those things at once, as long as Miranda didn't find out.

"So what's with the getup?" Flynt said.

J.P. flexed. "Believe it or not, you are looking at the next Sammy the Sparrow Hawk."

Flynt let out a low whistle. "No way."

"Yup." J.P. couldn't help but preen a little. After some major practice time, he would be ready to blow everyone's minds at the first game. They wouldn't know what hit them. They'd be completely in *awe* of his skills. *And if Miranda doesn't think it's cool to be dressed up as a giant bird, I'll just find a girl who does.*

"You're doing all the mascot stuff?" Flynt asked, incredulous. "Like *all* of it?"

There was a shout and some of the cheerleaders jogged into the gym from practice. J.P. hastily put on his head. He wanted to remain anonymous for now.

"Yeah, sure," he said, his voice muffled. "Brad and I already talked about this."

"You sure you know what you're doing?"

"Of course I do," said J.P. loftily. "Just 'cuz I go to Catholic school doesn't mean I don't know what's what. Brad told me what my job is." He flapped wildly, jumped, and went sliding several feet across the smooth gym floor on his padded, fuzzy backside, all the way to the group of cheerleaders.

"Nice one," one girl said, hands on her hips. "What are you doing, anyway?"

He shrugged his shoulders, then shook his tail feather. She laughed.

Ahhh. Chicks dig the hawk! J.P. strutted around in front of the girls, puffing his chest out, flapping his wings and waving as the rest of the cheerleaders jogged in. He saw Liz bringing up the rear, going slowly, and he could tell her ankle must be hurting. But she didn't even look in his direction (he hadn't told her either).

Flynt stepped close to J.P. and spoke in a low voice while J.P. blew kisses after the cheer squad. "But it's not a game, you know. If you're not careful, it can be pretty dangerous."

"Tell me about it," J.P. mumbled under his breath, feeling the ache in his back from all his flips. "But no, you don't need to worry about me. I've actually been doing all this stuff for a while now. I mean not all the time, but for longer than you'd think. My brother basically taught me everything I need to know."

"Your brother? And, and... you already talked to Brad?"

"Yeah, I said I did, didn't I? He's good with it. He gave me this costume already, and he's giving me the game costume tomorrow at my school." J.P. hoped the game costume had some extra padding.

Flynt looked confused. "Ooookay," he finally said. "Well, I guess that's good enough for me." He walked away. "I'll get the word out that the mascot's back."

J.P. watched the clock impatiently. *Ten more seconds. Five. Four. Three. Two...one...*

"*Lunch!*" he shouted, hopping out of his seat in excitement. Unfortunately, the bell rang at the same time, so no one really noticed the outburst. He broke into a jog once he reached the hallway, brushing past Miranda, Kristy, and Vivian as they stepped out of the freshman math classroom.

"Hey, watch it!" Kristy called out testily. He turned and ran backwards for a few strides, flashing a flirty smile and a wave. Vivian rolled her eyes, but Miranda waved back and blew a kiss in his direction. *I'm making progress,* he concluded with a fist pump. *In your face, Athan!*

His victory was short-lived, though—in all the excitement he hadn't noticed Liz's backpack and tripped over it, crashing to the floor in front of her open locker. He heard some giggling behind him, but didn't turn around. *Let's just pretend that didn't happen.*

"Dang, that hurt," he grumbled, rubbing his now sore knee and glaring at the backpack. "Stupid bag."

"Don't blame your clumsiness on my bag," Liz stared down at him. "You were acting like an idiot just now."

"And I guess you'd be the expert on that, right?" He sighed when Liz's cocky grin disappeared. *Who knew she was so sensitive?* "Uh... I didn't mean it," he said, picking himself up off the floor.

"Whatever," Liz said, snatching her bag off the floor and shuffling off down the hall, head down.

"Later, Liz," he called after her. She held up a hand, more of a dismissal than a wave. *What's eating her?* He wondered, but then he

94

caught sight of Brian standing at the other end of the hall with Mary. Mary was oblivious, going on about something and clearly thinking Brian was listening. But Brian was staring at Liz, a slight but visible scowl on his lips, as she trudged through the small crowd of students. He kept staring until she disappeared into the ladies' room.

Suddenly J.P. remembered the reason he was in a hurry, and made for the front door of the school. Celia was just about to push it open, carrying her lunch bag and several books under her arm. Over her shoulder, J.P. saw a silver Chevy sedan parked next to his mom's BMW. *Oh dangit; Brad's here already. So much for keeping it quiet. But I do not want anyone to see me with this mascot gear yet!*

"Hey, Seal!" he said, sliding in front of her and blocking her way out the door. "Where are you going? Lunch room's that way."

"I thought I'd sit out on the steps. It's really nice outside," Celia said.

"You… uh… can't."

"Why not?" She was looking at him keenly.

"Ummm. Because…" *Think, man. Think.* "Because your dad is looking for you."

"Oh. He is? I should go find him then." She gave him an amused look. "You're up to something, aren't you? You're acting weird."

"Weird? Me? I'm being totally normal. Or as normal as a guy like me could be. Which probably isn't all that normal to other people. But it's J.P. normal."

"Mmmm… I guess you're right about that."

J.P. watched to make sure she really went back inside, then dashed out to the parking lot. Brad stepped out of his car, a curious look on his face. "Who was that?" he asked.

"No one," J.P. said distractedly, hitting the trunk button on his mom's key chain. "Let's get this over with before she comes back."

Brad chuckled and reached down to pop his trunk. "You were serious about not letting anyone find out about this."

"Serious as a heart attack, dude. Come on, come on. She'll be back any second."

Brad opened his trunk, revealing a big, fluffy, black-and red mascot costume, looking newer and more colorful than the one he currently had, along with a ratty old paper bag. Brad picked up the bag. "Let's get this in your trunk first, and then—"

"J.P.!" Celia ran back outside, accompanied—to his horror—by Miranda. "I need to talk to you!"

"Bah!" he said under his breath, "why must women *always* want my attention?"

"Most guys don't complain about that," Brad laughed. "Come on, let's go talk to them. It won't take long."

"No!" J.P. almost shouted. He pointed to his mom's trunk. "You, uh…put the stuff in there while I distract them."

Brad looked dubiously at the mess in the BMW trunk—books written by JP's dad that his parents carried around to sell at conventions, bags of clothes, a brown paper sack full of nails and screws of different sizes, a couple small tool kits, a single lace-up shoe, and a host of other junk. "Are you sure you want it in there?"

"Yeah yeah," J.P. said distractedly, putting on a broad smile for the Costain girls. "I know it's messy, but don't worry about that. I gotta go." Miranda was already walking towards him. J.P. hurried to intercept her.

"Miranda!" he said. "Ah… it's a beautiful day in the neighborhood!" He put an arm around her and walked up to Celia. "So… What did you want, Seal?"

Celia gave him the patented Costain Eyebrow Raise. "Have you been putting things in my dad's office?"

"What? Why would I do that?" he said in what he hoped was a convincingly disdainful manner.

Miranda snickered. J.P. put on his most guileless smile.

"John Paul Flynn, that smile says you're up to something." Celia looked both amused and exasperated. "So far Dad's found a bunch of empty soda cans crammed in his desk, a bunch of Muscle Fitness magazines taped over his window, a really old bag of crab chips in his lunch, and an entire cardboard box full of soy sauce packets in his office fridge where his bottled water normally goes."

"Uh…" J.P. tried to come up with something that didn't immediately sound suspicious. Fortunately for him, students started coming out of the cafeteria, pushing past them to get outside into the fall weather.

Miranda grabbed him and pulled him along with her. "Oh, leave him alone Celia," she called over her shoulder, "If he says he didn't do it, then he didn't do it."

"Did you do it?" Miranda asked surreptitiously as she dragged him to the picnic bench. "*Please* tell me you did it."

"Ehhh…" J.P. shrugged. "I can't say I didn't have *something* to do with it…"

Miranda giggled and squeezed his arm tighter. "I love it when you do stuff like that. Celia is SO uptight." She sat down at the table, pulling J.P. down next to her. "So," she said, "who's the guy by your mom's car?"

"Huh?" J.P. stared at her blankly for a few seconds before he remembered the whole reason he was out here. "Oh! Uh… that's… that's nobody. Just a friend of mine from the football team. You probably wouldn't know him."

"Nobody?!" said a voice. J.P. turned to see Kristy, with Vivian behind her. "That's Brad freaking Powell, quarterback of the freaking Sparrow Hills freaking football team!"

"*Eeeeeeee!*" Vivian squealed. "What is he doing here?"

"Never mind that," Kristy said, nearly hyperventilating, "*he's coming this way!*"

It was true. Brad had shut both trunks and was sauntering across the JP2HS lawn toward the picnic table. J.P. shot up off the bench and hurried over to Brad. "What are you doing?!" he whispered fiercely. "No one's supposed to be paying attention to you!"

"Relax," Brad said, handing J.P. his mom's keys. "I was just going to talk to George."

"Oh." It was Miranda; J.P. hadn't seen her get up to follow him. "Well, *that's* not very interesting."

"Yeah," Brad said absently, but he was scanning the grounds and not paying much attention to Miranda. "Sorry about that."

Miranda looked like she was about to say something but before she could, she was interrupted by Vivian and Kristy pushing up from behind her. "Oh wow, um, Brad," Kristy gushed, "it's like, SO nice to meet you."

"Hi, I'm Vivian," said Vivian, stepping in front of her friends, "but you can call me Vi," she said, tossing her head and batting her lashes as she held out her hand.

"So like, what are you doing here?" Kristy said, then suddenly flushed. "I mean, not that you're not welcome. You're ALWAYS welcome here, Brad!" More blushing. "I meant…"

"I'm mostly here to see J.P.," he said. "He's helping me out with some 'Hawks stuff. Right Japes?"

"Right. You know me," J.P. said. "Always trying to help out my friends."

The two girls stared at him like he was that Really Interesting Guy from that one beer commercial; even Miranda seemed impressed. J.P. stood a little taller and tried to look nonchalant.

"Well, it was nice meeting you. All of you," Brad said, glancing at Kristy and Miranda in turn.

"I'm Miranda, by the way—" she started, but Brad was already walking off, towing J.P. with him.

"Hey, man," Brad said under his breath when they had put some distance between themselves and the freshman girls, "run interference with 'em for me, will ya? I'm not really up for a fan club right now." He raised his voice. "Yo, Peterson!" George looked up from the picnic table where he was sitting with Athan, Joey, Celia, and some of the freshmen. Brad sauntered over, and Joey got up to bump knuckles with him. J.P. turned to see Miranda following; he grabbed her arm gently and spun her around, leading her back toward the table. Fortunately, Kristy and Vivian came along, going on and on about how Brad was so hot, and asking a million questions.

"Yes, yes," J.P. said, trying to answer them all at once. "Brad is my friend. Yes, I know I'm awesome. Yes, I'll make sure to talk about you next time I'm hanging out with the team. No, I'm not on the team.

Not—not that they didn't ask me. I just—well, it's kind of a secret. I'm like a secret weapon. No, I can't tell you. Because... because I just can't, that's why."

"So what *does* the varsity quarterback want with George?" Miranda asked when Kristy and Vivian had wandered off.

"You know," J.P. said, perplexed now that he was actually thinking about it, "I couldn't tell you. Something football-ey. He was really anxious to visit us at the school."

"Huh. Well, whatever," Miranda said. She talked on about something else, and J.P. glanced over his shoulder to make sure that the trunk of his mom's car was really and truly closed.

11

PHILIA

"Hey," Liz whispered to J.P. as they were sitting down the next day for theology class. "Over lunch, SpeedEMart run, okay?" J.P. nodded, and Liz felt better. *We really need to talk about investigation stuff. I need something else to think about.*

It was a cold afternoon. Liz was sitting in the far corner of the classroom, next to the outside wall, where the rows of windows offered a view of the woods that surrounded their school. The upper part of the windows were tinged with frost on the edges; the bottom halves were not. It was frigid outside; she could hear the furnace rumbling, and heat radiated up from the baseboards. The combination of the cold outside and the heat inside made her uncomfortable, but the discomfort had the good effect of keeping her focused.

"*Philia,*" Mr. Costain wrote another Greek word on the board. "We usually think of friendship as fun. It's a good thing. We all like having friends. It's a universal human need."

He turned back to the blackboard and started drawing. "But what *is* friendship, really? And what *isn't* it?" He stepped back so they could see:

"Let's say these two little guys are friends," he said, smiling slightly. "They hang. They talk. They do stuff together. That's friendship. Right?"

Several kids in the front row nodded. Liz was bored, though. She started a doodle of her own on her desk with a pencil.

"Right. Now, let's change things a bit," she heard Mr. Costain say, and then the scrape of chalk on blackboard. "Now—what do you think?"

There were some chuckles. Liz, looked up and saw the board had changed:

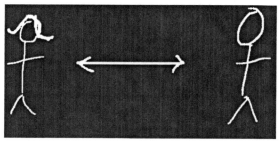

"What's different?" Mr. Costain said. "What's changed?"

Several hands went up. Mr. Costain pointed to one of them. "Yes, Miranda?"

"You made one of them a girl," Miranda said. For once, she sounded interested. "And you drew that arrow thingy between them."

"So what? What's the big deal?"

"Well, *obviously*, I mean …" Miranda stammered. "I mean, before they were friends, but now it's … you know."

"Now it's love," Mr. Costain finished. "Not just love, but *luuuuuuuuuve*. What we have here," he said, tapping the drawing, "is called *Eros*, and we are *not* talking about it today. Sorry."

There were a few groans as Mr. Costain erased the hair and the arrows, returning the two little stick figures to their original state. "These two little guys are *not* in love. They're friends. So how is friendship different?"

There was silence as the class digested this. Liz almost raised her hand; she wanted to hear Mr. C's explanation of why making it a boy and a girl automatically made it Eros instead of Philia (or could you

101

have both?), or if it *did* always make it Eros (which didn't seem quite right to her), or if Eros was as simple as adding sex to the equation (or whether it was even just that "butterflies in the stomach" feeling) or what. But she decided asking any of those questions would be too embarrassing.

Mr. Costain turned and drew some more on the board:

The class stared at the board in baffled silence.

"What's that rock doing there?" Miranda said in a sarcastic deadpan.

"That," Mr. Costain said, "isn't a rock. Or, I guess it *could* be a rock, but that wouldn't make for a very interesting friendship. But really, it could be anything. Anything that these two friends are interested in. A TV show, a band, a sports team, a book. The point is, they're doing it *together.* They're focused on *it,* not on each other, but they're *with* each other for the purpose of enjoying that thing together."

He drew another arrow, between the two stick people. Liz felt a kind of painful twinge in her chest. She thought of all the things she and Brian had done together. Played tennis. Walked in the woods. Prayed the rosary. Talking—lots of talking. Detective work. Getting Allie to come back to school at JP2HS. She realized, suddenly, that she had *liked* doing these things, even the more boring or unpleasant ones. Doing them with Brian had made all the difference.

"But me and my friends aren't *focused* on anything!" Miranda said.

"Yes, I've noticed," Mr. Costain said.

"Oh, ha ha, dad," Miranda retorted. "I mean, we just like hanging out. We don't *have* a rock thingy we're all looking at."

"Sure you do," Mr. Costain said. "You said it yourself. Hanging out."

"But—"

"Look," Mr. Costain raised his voice slightly. "You're always talking about *something*, and that *thing* can change all the time. And that's okay! That's what most friendships are like. They're casual. Free. Easy. That's what friendship is *supposed* to be like. Of all the loves, friendship brings the most innocent joy into life—yes, Mr. Kosalinski?"

James had raised his hand and was waving it. Liz couldn't see his face, but she thought his voice sounded even more irritated than usual. "Mr. Costain," he said. "This is all very *fine*, but I thought this was a *theology* class. What does this have to with God?"

"Excellent question, as usual," Mr. Costain said warmly. "You're forgetting, James, that Philia is one of the four loves. It *comes* from God. As I said in our first class, God *is* Love, and all love comes from Him. So when we learn about love, we learn about Him. Friendship, like God, is *good*. And friendship, like God, is *powerful*. So let's talk about why friendship is good. Besides being fun, friendship can draw us to God. How?"

He paused for a short moment, as if giving one of them a chance to answer the question—then he went on. "By example. We are all *influenced* by our friends. We become *like* our friends. We act like them.

103

We talk like them. So if you're really serious about getting holy, become friends with holy people."

Another awkward silence. Mr. Costain nodded slightly, as if he had expected this. "And if you have lots of friends, remember that you're influencing them. You have power. Friendship is a *very* powerful force in life. In fact, if you look at *any* powerful movement in history, you'll find, at its source, a close group of friends. How did the Church start? With Jesus and the twelve apostles. How did Communism start? With Marx and Engels. How did the Nazis start? With Hitler and Himmler and Goebbels—"

There were several shocked gasps, and a flurry of hands went up. "Mr. Costain!" burst out Josephine. "You don't mean ... Jesus and Hitler have *nothing* in common—"

"All right, all right," Mr. Costain said, and the class quieted down. "Of *course* Jesus and Hitler aren't the same. And it's possible for history-altering things to get done by groups of mere interested individuals, who don't care about each other but only about the goal. But the point is that groups of friends, which even otherwise bad people can be, are *extremely* powerful. They can change the world, for better or worse."

He paused, looking thoughtful. "You know," he said, "this school started because of a friendship."

Liz looked up. She knew a *little* bit about how this school had started, but mostly rumors. She had never heard the straight story. None of them had.

"Before starting this school," Mr. Costain said, "I lost my job teaching at St. Lucy's."

"What's St. Lucy's?" Kevin blurted out. At the same time, Joey said, "Why'd you lose your job?"

"St. Lucy's is our diocesan Catholic high school, Kevin," Mr. Costain said. "Some of your classmates used to go there. And Joey, the reason I lost my job isn't important. Let's just say that there was a disagreement between myself and the school administration."

Liz slumped back in her chair, disappointed. She had heard this already, but was never able to discover what the disagreement *was*. It was a nagging question, because Mr. Costain was such a good teacher, and also kind of a nice guy. Why would he get fired?

"Moving on," Mr. Costain said, "After I lost my position, I didn't know what to do next. And so I had coffee one day with my good friend, Dennis Burke. That would be *his* dad," he said, pointing to Brian.

"You and Mr. Burke were friends?" Kevin said.

"Oh, yes," Mr. Costain nodded. "We've been friends for years. And so he was concerned for me, and he helped me figure out what to do next."

"What?" Kevin said.

Next to him, Kristy Vogel snorted. "Oh, *I* don't know, Kevin," she said sarcastically. "Maybe, started this school, *duh?*"

"That's right," Mr. Costain said. "We did. Though there wasn't any *duh* involved." He shot Kristy a warning look. "It was Mr. Burke's idea, actually—to begin a new school that would truly reflect Catholic doctrine, and do the work of St. John Paul the Great in spreading the Gospel of Life, and… well, you know the rest," he said, smiling. "Or I hope you do. But I want you to all to see how *powerful* friendship is. Mr. Burke and I have had our disagreements over the years, but we've always stayed friends, and that's a powerful thing. For us, *this* –" he tapped the rock-thing on the board, "was the school you're in now. And this school wouldn't be here now if not for our friendship."

Mary Summers raised her hand. "Mr. Costain," she said, her breathy voice barely audible, "I have a question."

"Speak up a bit, Mary," Mr. Costain said.

Yeah, he can't hear her either, Liz thought irritably. She *hated* that stupid girly voice.

"Sorry. I was just wondering. Can Philia… can that ever turn *into* Eros? Can friendship ever turn to love?"

Liz gritted her teeth. *Of course.* Of course it would be that little twit Mary who wanted the same answers Liz did.

"Oh, yes," Mr. Costain nodded. "Absolutely. In fact, Eros often starts with Philia."

A hard little knot formed in Liz's stomach. She craned her neck, trying to get a glimpse of Mary's face, or of Brian's. She couldn't. But she could *guess* what Mary's face was doing. Oh yes, she could. She could just *see* Mary's smug, satisfied little smile…

"But that is a subject for another day," Mr. Costain said briskly, turning back to the board and writing. "For your homework, I need you to pick one the following Bible verses, and write a 200-word reflection on what it means: Psalm 133, John 15:12-15, Proverbs 22:24-25, Sirach 6:14-16…"

Stupid Mary. Of course you're going to ask about Eros. But Brian's never going to fall for you. He's not that shallow. Keep dreaming. He's not right for you, and you're definitely not right for him. Hm. Whatever. What do I care? I don't. I don't care. All I care about is you not hurting my friend.

W ow!" Isabel said as class broke up. "That was the coolest religion class I've ever had!"

Miranda just rolled her eyes, and said under her breath, "Looks like someone doesn't get out too often." Kristy and Vivian snickered.

"Actually, I thought it was really good, too," Jacinta said thoughtfully to Miranda.

Kristy and Vivian immediately stopped snickering. J.P. watched all of this while he put his books away and hoped that Miranda would hang back so they'd get a chance to be alone. Now that he was paying attention, though, it struck him how everyone liked Jacinta, and listened to her.

"This book is so hard to read, though!" Kristy complained.

"It's not that bad once you get into it!" Jacinta said. "Hey! I've got an idea! Since we're all in this class together, maybe we could read the theology chapters at lunch and discuss them so we all understand them!"

"That would help me," chirped Vivian. "I'm lost."

"So am I," Mary Rose admitted.

Wow. Vivian was part of Miranda's crew, all preppy and stuck up; Mary Rose was a frumpy homeschooler, a follower of Josephine. The

106

two couldn't be more different, but both listened to Jacinta. *I wonder what would happen if Jacinta wasn't here*, J.P. thought. *I bet there'd be a lot more fighting.*

They all exited, Isabel bringing up the rear. J.P. had hung out, waiting for Miranda, but she drifted off after the other girls.

Darn. Oh well. J.P. headed for his locker. He had brought some things from home—a few tools, and a cheap cell phone. He needed to work quickly though.

He had just ducked behind the wall of boxes when he heard approaching footsteps. *Hm. Wonder who that is.* J.P. decided to stay quiet, just in case he heard something interesting.

Two people were talking. "I don't think he was saying boys and girls can't be friends," Allie was saying. "He was just saying that, you know, sexual attraction, is something different. But if both a boy and a girl are looking at the same thing, then it's friendship." She laughed. "You know, like you and me talking about this class."

There was a murmur from someone male. J.P. figured it was George.

"But I think it's silly to say that a man and woman can't be friends. I mean, come on! It's like those people who think that everything's ALWAYS about sex, and that's dumb. I mean, I think friendships between men and women can be pretty powerful things, like Mr. Costain said…"

Her voice trailed off. J.P. put out his head just as Allie was walking around the corner. But he didn't see George. *Okay, time to move. Another special surprise for Mr. Costain.*

12

TRIVIAL PURSUITS

Liz couldn't find J.P. anywhere. Thinking she'd wait for him, she sat down at an empty table. Then Miranda Costain came and sat next to her. Liz eyed her and thought about asking her about J.P.

Before she could say something to her, Isabel Reyes came and plunked herself between them and said, "Hey, guys, I brought this Catholic trivia game to school and I thought it might be fun to play it. My family has such fun playing it, and it's really helped us learn more about our faith. My little brothers love it!"

Liz had already figured out that Isabel was a little out of it, and it was clear that she hadn't realized that she had picked the wrong people to ask. Liz expected Miranda to say something cutting, but instead, Miranda fake-smiled and said, "Oooh, sounds like fun, Isabel! Maybe later on."

"Great! Thanks! I bet you'll love it, Miranda!" gushed Isabel, and hurried off.

Miranda rolled her eyes at Liz. "Like I'm really going to play her dumb game. I cannot stand her," she said. "I mean, does she ever brush her hair? She always looks like she's been wandering in the woods!"

Liz felt divided. On the one hand, she was no fan of Isabel or silly games either, but on the other hand, if any of the freshmen needed to be taught a lesson, it was Miranda. Somehow she didn't feel like giving Miranda any ammunition. *Besides, she's a 9. She needs a good smackdown.*

But Liz couldn't think of anything to say except, "What's the beef with your sister? Why are you always out to get Celia?"

Miranda looked as though Liz was crazy. "Well, duh!" she said. "I mean, are you really all 'rah rah' school the way she is?" She lowered her voice. "You don't want to be here anymore than I do."

"Hey!" Jacinta came over. "Guys, we're going to be playing this really awesome game today, and we're picking teams now. Are you up for it?"

Liz was about to say no, and then realized that she should support Celia and say yes. But then a gorgeously wicked idea came to her. She said with a snake's smile, "Actually, Miranda was just telling me how much she's looking forward to playing it. Isabel already invited us. Right, Miranda?"

Trapped, Miranda fake-smiled again. "Right."

"Perfect!" Jacinta said, and grabbed Miranda's hand. "You're on my team. Hey, I got Kevin and Mitch on our side. Plus Josephine."

"Josephine?" Miranda's face twisted. "She's such a –"

"No, don't you get it? She knows ALL this Catholic trivia stuff. With her on our team, we'll win. Come over and help me persuade her."

Liz got up. "I actually have to do something for the school over lunch. But have fun!" Whistling cheerfully, she went out to find J.P. *I guess our little investigation* is *doing something for the school, right?*

J.P. was nowhere to be found. Liz passed Mr. Costain, Mrs. Simonelli, and Mrs. Flynn talking in one of the classrooms. Realizing that all the teachers were occupied gave her an idea. She walked casually down the hall and slipped into Mr. Costain's office.

W hatcha doin' down there?"

J.P. sat up in surprise and whacked his head on the underside of Mr. Costain's empty desk.

"Geez, Liz," he exclaimed, rubbing his head. "Don't sneak up on a guy like that."

"Yeah, well," Liz said, "You should learn to lock the door when you're doing nefarious deeds."

"I am *not* doing nefarious deeds," J.P. said, sounding hurt. "I'm trying to bring joy to the life of a sad, joyless man, who could use a good laugh."

Liz squatted down and peered at the cell phone in J.P.'s hands. "With that?"

"Yes!" J.P. said, as he checked to make sure the phone was on and then carefully inserted it in the little wooden hidey-hole he'd made. "Everyone loves a good joke. Look, see?" He pulled Liz sideways so

109

that she flopped onto the ground, then scooted over so she could get her head under and see and laid down next to her, shining his keychain flashlight up at the spot. "The drawer doesn't push all the way back even when it's all the way in, so there's this little space here." He pointed to the space. "So I made this little wooden box and borrowed some stain and wood screws from home and voila—" he pulled the phone out, then pushed it back in and shut off his light.

"It's invisible," Liz said. "Nice. But why?"

J.P. used his feet and hands to shove himself out. "The plan," he said, pulling out his own phone, "is to do this." He started a call on his cell, and the phone under the desk rang, slightly muted but also loudly, and in a ringtone nearly identical to Mr. Costain's desk phone. It even sounded like it was *coming* from his desk phone.

"Ahhh," Liz nodded knowingly. "And here I thought you were only going for the old 'hidden phone' gag."

"You can't beat the classics," J.P. said, getting up, "but you can improve on them. I've been sitting here at the beginning of every lunch period, for the last few days, calling this desk phone, trying to find a matching tone and figuring out where to put the secret shelf. It's right here, under Mr. Costain's *actual* phone. I figure the confusion should last at least a good five or six calls."

J.P. started to leave, then stopped and opened the office closet. "Almost forgot." He unzipped his school bag and took out two snack-sized packages of tapioca pudding, opened them, and buried the lids in the bottom of the office trash can. Then he stuffed the puddings carefully into the pockets of Mr. Costain's ragged old coat, one pudding on each side.

Liz giggled. "Gross. Well, come on; that junk food at SpeedEMart's not going to eat itself."

They slipped out the door, trying not to look like they were hurrying, and jogged to the path through the woods as best as Liz could manage on her ankle, slowing down when they reached the tree line.

"So," Liz said. "Who's this guy who thinks the shooter's still alive?"

110

"Oh, I forgot to tell you! It's Flynt. You know, the big goon who used to hang out with Tyler?"

Liz vaguely knew him. "Hm. Didn't he help beat you up once?"

"Yeah, well, water under the bridge," J.P. said lightly. "Anyway, he's on the football team now, and the day before school started, he told me some pretty weird stuff."

He related the conversation, and Liz listened with growing interest. "You know, he's not the only one who's scared. Some of the squad are convinced that cheerleaders are being targeted because two of the girls who were shot were cheerleaders."

"Wow, this is starting to look credible," J.P. scratched his head. "I mean, dumb Neil Flynt saying the shooter isn't dead is one thing, but *cheerleaders?* Whole different story."

Liz scowled. "Yeah, well, I met this police detective who also doesn't think Brock was the guy. He gave me his number and told me to keep in touch. Maybe your pal Flynt should talk to him."

J.P. shook his head. "He doesn't seem like the kind of guy who wants to talk to the police. Probably already should have a record and knows it."

"Hm. Well, listen to this." She told him about her phone call with Ginger Josslyn and Megan Brock and the mysterious phone call to Chinchilla's.

They had come to the slope that led to the parking lot at SpeedEMart, and J.P. gave Liz a hand down.

"Better stop talking now," Liz said. "We'll keep this under wraps. I'm glad you're keeping up the prank war, by the way. Guess I've just gotten too busy with cheerleading and finding a math tutor."

"Yeah, you're turning into a slacker, Simonelli. I'm trying to school all these freshmen by myself, and it's getting a little hard to wage a one-man-war against orderly procedures and school unity."

"Give me time," Liz said. "I'm more about improvising." She thought about Isabel Reyes and her impossible Kare-O ways. "I'm just looking for the right moment."

After buying their treats, they hurried back through the woods, sure that they were late for class. But when they snuck into the school, the classrooms were still empty.

"What's going on?" asked J.P. "Are they having another safety drill?"

"Hopefully nothing serious," Liz said. "Wait…"

She listened, and heard shouts and then laughter in the cafeteria. When they looked down the hall, they saw all three teachers were standing in the door to the cafeteria, watching something and laughing. Liz and J.P. edged down the hall and joined them. They saw all the students were piled around three tables facing Celia. Celia stood at another table in the front with a box of cards, calling out questions. The others shouted out answers. Joey was keeping score on a whiteboard and playing Vanna White to Celia's Pat Sajak. The competition was fast and furious. And to Liz's shock, *everyone* was playing.

George had Athan, Mary Summers, Vivian, and Paul on his team but it was clear his star player was Brian. *Of course, George was smart enough to get Brian on his team,* Liz thought. *And* of course *Mary was with Brian.*

The other team was Jacinta's, and she had Miranda, Isabel, Mitch, Kevin, and Josephine on her team. Between Isabel knowing the game and Josephine being smart, they were doing pretty well.

But the team that was smoking everyone else's, to Liz's astonishment, was Allie's. At first Liz couldn't figure out why they were so far ahead. Allie had Chris Manzini, Kristy, Agnes, Mary Rose—none of them intellectual heavyweights. But then when it was their turn, an authoritative voice intoned the answer. It was JAMES.

James was actually playing a trivia game, and everyone was cheering for him. He didn't look like he was enjoying it, but Allie looked like she was having the time of her life. Mr. Costain seemed to be relishing the game more than anyone else.

"And now it's time for the FINAL ROUND!" Celia bellowed, and read out the last question. "How many people saw Jesus after He rose from the dead?"

There was a breathless pause during which Brian counted aloud, Isabel and Josephine counted frantically on their hands, and James said loftily, "More than 500 people, according to the First Letter of St. Paul to the Corinthians, chapter 5, verse 6."

George and Brian moaned. Allie leapt onto her table with both fists in the air and belted out, "Woo hoo!" Everyone else roared. Mr. Costain clapped and said, "That was very enjoyable! All right, everyone to class!"

Liz watched agog as the students jumped down from the tables and surged down the hallway, everyone talking. Even Miranda was talking animatedly with Mitch and Josephine about the game. *Wow*, thought Liz, *for a moment, all the petty fighting is gone. Maybe there's something to this whole school unity thing.*

"Oh man!" J.P. said, stricken. "I can't believe we weren't here."

Part of Liz was disappointed, but she only shrugged and went up to Allie. James was ponderously getting his books. Allie waited for him. She put up her hand to give him a high-five. He returned it with mealy enthusiasm. "Miss Weaver," James said stiffly, and walked out of the cafeteria.

Celia came up to Allie, wide-eyed. "How in the world did you do that?" she whispered. "That was amazing."

She shrugged. "I told him I needed his help, that's all."

Celia seemed to be walking on air. She threw an arm around Liz and Allie and hugged them both. "Maybe this whole school thing is working out," she said.

"It's all Jacinta," Allie said. "She was working so hard to get everyone to play Isabel's game, and I thought, 'what the heck, maybe I can get James to play.' And he agreed!"

"Maybe more for the sake of showing up the rest of us, but I can live with that!" Celia said. "Though I admit I DID pick the questions I knew he couldn't start an argument over." She grinned rakishly.

Liz felt odd, being included as one of the top girls at JP2HS. No one seemed to notice that she hadn't even been there for the trivia game. *Zero again*, she thought.

Oh cripes! James is here already!

Liz took a running jump over the low hedge that separated the vacant lot from the public library parking lot, and landed on her bad ankle, resulting in a shockwave of pain. *Okay, that was a little much.* Cheer practice had been getting harder lately.

James's huge battered old black car was sitting in a parking space under a leafless maple tree. Over by the library entrance she saw James sitting glumly on a bench, his hands jammed in his lumpy jacket.

"Sorry! Sorry! Sorrysorrysorry!" Liz yelled when she was still twenty yards away as she limp-ran through the parking lot, clutching her algebra textbook to her side.

"You're late," James said curtly. He shouldered his backpack and stumped huffily through the library doors as Liz limped meekly after.

Past the checkout desk was a hall that led to a private study room where they could talk. It was a windowless room, brightly lit by overhead fluorescent lights. There were several long tables with plastic chairs. They took seats at one. Except for a college-aged boy and girl murmuring over a laptop computer that they were sharing, they had the study room to themselves. James drew a binder and a Saxon algebra textbook out of his back pack. Liz dropped her own textbook on the table with a slap, drawing sharp looks from the laptop couple. James looked at her book, then looked at her.

"Do you have a pencil, or are you going to do the problems in your head?" he said.

"I got one," she said, opening up the book. A chewed, eraser-less pencil was bookmarking the page of that day's assignment.

"And paper?" he said.

"I didn't want to have to carry a bunch of junk," she said. "I figured I'd just write the answers in the book and copy them to a piece of paper when I get home."

James muttered in disbelief, "You'll write in the book and copy..." He cut himself off with a sigh. "Look, the point of tutoring is I have

114

to see what you're doing so I can show you what you're doing wrong. You have to show your work. You have to write them out on paper."

"Okay, okay, no problem." said Liz. "See? In the back of the book there's a couple blank pages. I'll use those for today and remember to bring paper next time."

Sighing, James unclasped his binder, took out a couple of sheets of paper and slid them over to her. "Here, do your work on this. Now let's start with the review multiplication problems. You do know how to do long multiplication, right?

"Of course I know how," said Liz defensively. "It's just… it's just that even though I do exactly what you're supposed to be doing, I always come out with a different answer from what Mrs. Flynn writes on the board."

"Well, then, let's see you do the first one and see if we can find the error."

Liz took a determined breath, then looked at the first problem of her textbook.

$$\begin{array}{r} 116 \\ \times 25 \\ \hline \end{array}$$

She copied the numbers neatly on a sheet of notebook paper. Then, she laboriously worked it out, chewing her lip thoughtfully.

"There!" she said proudly, putting down her pencil. "Eight hundred and twelve!"

"That took you over a minute," said James in disbelief. "That should've taken only—Wait. You said eight hundred twelve?"

"Yes," she said, uncertainty now replaced the pride in her voice.

"Not even close. And you're multiplying by twenty-five. You know the answer can only possibly end in 25, 50, 75 or double-zero, right?"

"Uhh… Yes, of course I know that," Liz lied.

"If you know that, why'd you put 812 as the answer?"

"Cuz… Cuz…" Liz stammered at a loss. "Cuz I'm multiplying by… 116, not 25?"

James snatched Liz's work sheet and looked over her numbers. "This is wrong," he said after pondering her work for a few seconds. "Why didn't you move to the tens place?"

"Move to the…?" Liz said, baffled.

"Yes," said James, beginning to speak rapidly. "You're not supposed to multiply 116 times 2; you're supposed to multiply 116 times 20. So you need to move the second line to the tens place. That way when you add them up you're adding 580 plus 2320, but you added 580 plus 232 instead." He crossed out Liz's answer, drew a zero after Liz's 232, and then, ticking his pencil quickly over the digits, wrote the number 2900 below. "See? That's the answer you should have gotten."

"Oh, okay. So I guess that was my problem all along," said Liz. "Well, now I know what to do in the future. Thanks for clearing that up." She made as if to get up.

"Not so fast," said James. "You don't understand a single thing I just did there, do you?" He tapped his pencil on the corrected math problem.

Liz hung her head. "No," she admitted slowly.

"How can you be in an Algebra 2 course? How did you get through just the regular math course?"

Liz stared at James's pencil point, still pressed to Liz's corrected problem. At last she stuffed her hand into her jeans pocket and pulled out her cell phone.

"You call someone for the answers?" James asked, baffled.

"No," said Liz, feeling humiliated. Then very quietly, she added, "I use the calculator."

She couldn't face James, but she could feel his eyes boring right into the side of her head. Then after a long silence she heard laughter.

She turned to look at him. His eyes were screwed shut, and his wide, grinning lips were pressed together. His shoulders were shaking, and he was making soft chortling sounds in the back of his throat despite his apparent efforts to suppress them. All of a sudden, Liz felt the humor of the situation overtake her and she let out a loud snort. When she got

116

two more sharp glares from the laptop couple at the other end of the room, Liz put her hands to her mouth to contain herself.

Finally the laughter died away. And James sighed again, but this time in resignation rather than irritation. "Alright," he said taking up the textbook again. His manner was no longer stern and impatient but almost friendly. Friendly for James, anyway. "If we're going to do this, no more cheating, okay?"

"Okay." Liz smiled sheepishly.

James nodded, looking like he was trying not to smile. "Let's do the next one, and I'll walk you through it."

13

HOMECOMING

J.P. was pumped for his first official game as Sammy the Sparrow Hawk at homecoming this weekend. He'd had ample time to practice, but he still felt his nerves tingling as the crowd started filing in through the ticket gates.

J.P. ambled through the crowd (in a goofy, strutting kind of way; he'd decided Sammy would always have a "walk" when he made public appearances). He passed the gray-haired ladies from the Boosters Association selling Sparrow Hawk gear: red, white, and black T-shirts, sweatpants and hoodies, flags and pennants and bumper stickers, and even boxer shorts with the SHHS "lightning bolt and bird" logo on them. One woman was hawking full color programs to passers-by. J.P. had already checked one out when he'd arrived: he was quite smitten with the picture they'd gotten of him at practice in full bird costume surrounded by the cheerleaders. He'd had to tell George about his gig, but swore him to secrecy. He didn't want Joey loudmouth Simonelli to find out, and certainly not Athan.

"Good evening, ladies and gentlemen and supporters of Sparrow Hill's football team," an announcer said. "And welcome to homecoming!" Loud cheers erupted from the bleachers.

There was a short speech from the principal asking for a moment of silence for the victims of the past year's school shooting. Everyone bowed their heads and closed their eyes. J.P. did the same, then wondered, too late, if a giant bird bowing its head in sadness would convey the proper respect. He hoped no one else noticed.

"Thank you," the principal said after several heartbeats. "And now, I present to you our award-winning band who will lead us in the National Anthem." J.P. put his wing over his heart, feeling foolish again. *I've got to find out what the last mascot did at times like these.*

The second the final note was played, Sammy jumped in the air. *It's showtime.* He galloped around the football field, squawking, flapping his

118

wings, and shaking his tail-feathers. He ran up to where the cheerleaders were and stood right in front of Liz, who (still not knowing who he was) stared at him with annoyance. He mimicked the cheerleaders' dance moves, making as much of a comical nuisance of himself as he could. When the crowd started laughing, then cheering, then dancing as the fight song played and the drum line kicked in with the cadence, J.P. knew he'd found his calling.

Why does the mascot have to be so dang aggravating? Liz asked herself as the cheerleaders broke up to get ready for the next cheer. Sammy the Sparrow Hills Sparrow Hawk was making a pantomime of flirting with Madison. He made exaggerated gestures of embarrassment when Madison shooed him away. The crowd laughed.

Sammy covered his face in mock humility as he ran away past a row of cheerleaders. Liz pretended to ignore him, but then she was rudely shoved from behind.

She staggered back, regained her balance, and spun around, furious, to glare at Sammy the Sparrow Hawk. "Hey, freak, watch it!" she snapped.

Sammy put his "wings" to his face and trotted around in a circle, making a show of false concern over offending Liz.

"C'mon, dude. What is this?" Liz demanded, putting her hands on her hips.

Sammy put his dukes up, striking a pugilist's pose. He started bobbing and weaving around her, fists up like a bare-knuckle boxer.

"Hey, Liz! Fight me!" said a muffled voice from within the huge mascot head.

Liz, just an impulse away from decking Sammy, checked herself. "Fight you?" she said.

"Yeah! C'mon, Liz! It's me!" said the muffled voice as the mascot danced around her.

Liz regarded him skeptically. That voice sounded awfully familiar. "J... J.P.?" she said finally.

119

"Yeah, it's me!" said the fighting mascot. "I'm trying to do a bit here! Pretend you're angry at me!"

"What do you mean, 'pretend'?" said Liz, her voice rising. "Did you steal that—?"

Sammy gave her another shove with his "wings," and she lost her temper and punched the mascot square in his squishy foam beak.

"Thanks!" she heard J.P.'s voice say as Sammy the Sparrow Hawk bounced backwards and spun into a succession of sloppy rolls, as though Liz's punch had sent him head over heels.

The crowd in the stands roared with approval, and for the first time Liz was aware that her altercation with Sammy the Sparrow Hawk had been the subject of a lot of attention. Suddenly uncomfortable, Liz stepped back and tried to blend back into the group.

Whenever J.P. saw Liz in her cheering uniform, it reminded him of when she'd dressed up and acted like a ditz around Hank. Hank wasn't the only one flustered by her routine. Brian had definitely been distracted, too. *And truth be told… no. Truth will* not *be told. Even to myself. La la la self, I'm not listening.*

Brad threw a forward pass to Athan, who caught it. The crowd cheered, but Sammy the Sparrow Hawk was not impressed. *It's only Athan. Big whoop.* J.P. did his comedy routines, mocking the cheerleaders and taunting the other team, glad that the crowd couldn't see how annoyed he felt inside the suit. *As long as I do my Happy Dance, they'll think everything's fine.*

Halftime arrived with the score 17-3, Sparrow Hills. As the teams left the field, J.P. saw the thumbs up from the assistant coach, indicating it was the mascot's turn to get things moving. *Okay, Big Moment. Here I come!* Swallowing his nerves, he exploded off the sidelines and immediately started his routine, running back and forth, jumping up and down, and dancing along to the marching band music.

To his delight, the crowd loved every bit of it. He could see people in the stands dancing along with his moves, pumping their fists or clapping, and he could swear some of them were chanting "Sammy!

Sammy!" He put his wing to his ear in an exaggerated "I can't HEAR you!" motion, and the crowd cheered so loud that for a few seconds he couldn't even hear the music.

By the time it was the band's turn to perform he had everybody on their feet, spurred on by the announcers cheering him over the loudspeaker. "He's waaay better than the last guy!" he heard a girl say from the sidelines.

He jogged back to his seat at the edge of one of the team benches, every muscle heavy with exhaustion. He had only performed for a few minutes, but it felt like he'd been working out for an hour. J.P. grabbed his water bottle and drank through a convenient little flap under the beak. He wanted to remove the hawk head, but he'd been told by an assistant coach that he wasn't supposed to take it off in public; it "ruined the illusion", whatever that meant. *It's not like anyone actually thinks I'm a giant hawk.*

When he saw Brad hand the passing duties off to the backup QB and head toward the benches, J.P. walked over and sat down next to him. He couldn't help noticing how much older Brad looked, even though he had maybe only a year more on J.P.

"What's up?" Brad asked J.P. "How's your first gig going?"

"Just doing my thing," J.P. said, trying to sound as nonchalant as possible while practically shouting so he could be heard over the resurgent crowd.

"Yeah, you've got the jumping and flipping part down pat, and that's the hardest part. The other stuff basically takes care of itself." He gave J.P. a goofy smile. "Just don't go flirting with my girl Madison too much."

"Oh." J.P. hadn't known Madison and Brad were going out. He made a mental note not to do the flirting bit with her anymore, and laughed it off. "Hey, what can I say? Sammy's a chick magnet, and I'm an awesome Sammy. Way better than the last guy, at least."

Brad started and gave him a sharp look.

"What?" J.P. said, surprised.

121

"Er…nothing," Brad said after a moment. "I guess you don't know who the last guy was. Most people don't; it was kind of a secret." Brad lowered his voice. "It was Brock."

J.P.'s jaw dropped. "Are you serious?!"

Brad nodded slowly. His faced changed in some subtle way that J.P. couldn't put his finger on. Whatever it was seemed to darken his normally bright features, changing him from big-hearted, laid-back quarterback/buddy/prom king to… something that wasn't any of those things.

Suddenly J.P. didn't want to have this conversation, didn't even want to be sitting on the bench for fear that he'd end up stuffed under it soon. But he couldn't help himself. "You mean the same guy who shot people at the dance, then killed himself, was running around as Sammy the Sparrow Hawk most of last year?"

"That's right," Brad responded flatly.

"Were you and him…friends, or anything?"

Brad laughed harshly. "Him and his pals hazed me freshman year. That sort of put a damper on our relationship."

"Ah," J.P. said uncomfortably. "Yeah, you're not the only one. But he never seemed like the killer type. Makes you wonder, huh?"

The star quarterback scowled at him, and then got up to leave. The dark paint smeared underneath his eyes made him look even more intimidating. *What did I say?* J.P. wondered.

The next two quarters passed much the same way as the first two, with Sparrow Hills winning 31-16. By now, J.P. was exhausted, but all-in-all he knew it had been a great success, and possibly the best night of his life. Still, he knew he had some explaining to do with Liz, and he really didn't want to run into Brad right now. He was just planning how he was going to leave at the end of the game without anyone noticing when a hand grabbed his shoulder. "Yo, Sammy, we need to talk."

J.P. spun around. His eyes bulged when he saw a stocky guy with a blue mohawk and more piercings on his face than could be counted with a quick glance. "Meet me under the bleachers," he said, walking off towards the far end of the stands.

122

What does that guy want with Sammy? J.P.'s mind raced as he went back through the evening trying to think of what he might have done to upset the guy. Was he one of the people in the stands that Sammy was annoying? *Who knew being a mascot would be dangerous?*

One of these kids, Liz thought, scanning the crowd. *It could be any of them. The shooter.*

A few football players jogged passed her to take a water break, and Liz recognized one of them as J.P.'s new "friend," the reformed goon Flynt. He lifted a hand as he passed her, and she high-fived him. *Got to ask him about his story sometime*, she reminded herself.

The crowd roared suddenly. "All right, get ready!" she heard Simone yell. "Mighty Sparrow Hawk! One, two, three, four!"

"To BE! A! Sparrow Hawk you HAVE! TO! Move!
To be! A! Sparrow Hawk you GOT! TO! Groove!"

Liz went through the motions of the cheer with barely a thought—it was an easy one. They were *all* easy ones. She was finding cheering much less interesting than she had expected.

"You-can-never-be-a Sparrow Hawk-cause-you-can't-do-what WE do.
Saaaay what? Saaaay what?
CAN'T do—what WE do!"

The cheer over, Liz went back to checking out the crowd. *This guy is still out there.* She was more and more convinced of it. Even if nobody else believed her. Even if J.P. was too interested in playing Sammy the Sparrow Hawk. Even if—*oh.*

There was Brian.

He was sitting next to his little sister Melissa. She was talking animatedly, and Brian was nodding with a slight smile. He looked happy. Relaxed.

It was weird. Liz realized that she hadn't seen him look like that for a long time—not since the prom shooting. Brian used to look relaxed like that all the time back then, when they had first become friends. She had starting hanging out with him after school. They would play tennis together. Mostly they would just talk. He was incredibly easy to talk to.

123

She wasn't in Like with him then. She had been dating Rich Rogers, so the very idea of romance between them was off the table. They had just been friends. No anxiety, anger or sullen company. They were hanging out because they enjoyed each other's company. That was it. It had been… nice. So nice.

Suddenly all Liz wanted to do was walk up to Brian right then and there, ask his forgiveness for ignoring him, and beg him to hang out with her again. She had lost a friend, a really *good* friend, and she wasn't the type to make a lot of friends. And besides, Brian was smart. He could help her. Why *couldn't* she tell him about her investigation? What was the big deal?

And then she saw Brian turn to the girl on the other side of Melissa and say something—and Mary Summers, beaming happily, said something back and laughed.

Hanging out? Being friends? Forget that charade. They were on a *date*. Liz recoiled like she had been slapped in the face and looked away, grinding her teeth.

At least Melissa was there, too. Maybe it wasn't *really* a date. But Mary's happy face told a different story. Whatever they called it, it was a for-real date. Liz couldn't take it anymore. They couldn't be together— not Mary and *Burke!* They weren't *right* for each other! They didn't *fit!*

Or do you just wish *they didn't?*

"Ah, the heck with both of them," she mumbled. "I don't care."

Unfortunately, she knew a liar when she heard one.

Sparrow Hills ended up winning by a wide margin. As he stood by the entrance to the locker room near the bleachers high-fiving each player as they passed him by, J.P. suddenly remembered the Mohawk Dude who had approached him earlier. He remembered because Mohawk Dude was standing under the bleachers nearby, staring at him menacingly.

Hoping to appear nonchalant, J.P. followed the last player through the doors. He decided to wait inside for a few minutes, hoping that Mohawk Dude would just go away. He had a bad feeling about that guy.

He passed the time trying to imagine each student at JP2HS as a food, then as an animal (Athan was a cold plate of spaghetti, and a poodle). He listened to the coach give a little talk and heard all the guys cheer. Finally, after a few people began trickling out of the locker room, J.P. figured he couldn't hang around any longer. He hoped he'd given Mohawk enough time to get bored and take off.

No such luck. When he opened the door, J.P. saw that Mohawk was still there, in the same spot, and there was another punk-looking guy with him, this one with a shaved head of bright orange stubble and piercings running the length of his nose.

"Hey!" Mohawk shouted, and waved J.P. over. J.P. reluctantly trudged over.

Mohawk had a cigarette in his hand; he pointed it at Sammy the Sparrow Hawk's beak. "Hey, man, do you want to make this happen, or what?"

J.P. didn't know what else to do, so he shrugged.

"What?" said Mohawk. "What's that supposed to mean? Answer me. Are we doing this, or what?"

"Uh… um… are we…" J.P. stammered, muffled by the Hawk head but loud enough to be heard. "Um, no. I guess we're not?"

"What do you *mean* we're *not?*" Mohawk growled, leaning closer and grabbing J.P. by the chest feathers. "This is what you *do.*"

"Do what?" J.P. blurted out.

"Wait," Mohawk said, looking harder at J.P. and pulling him closer. "You're not him, are you? I mean you're not even the *guy.*"

J.P. was sweating profusely, and it wasn't from the heat. He was about to really panic when he heard a voice behind him.

"Oh, there you are, Sammy."

It was George. J.P. didn't know how his friend had found him, but he didn't care. He just wanted out. "I was just looking for you," George continued. "You need to go to the locker room. Like, now."

Mohawk let J.P. go roughly and stalked off, followed by his buddy. J.P. sighed in relief and turned to George. "Thanks," he said. "Um…do I really need to go to the locker room?"

"No," said George grimly. "You need to go anywhere but here. Who were those guys?"

J.P. rubbed his neck. "I have no idea."

14

THE BIG LIE

"Well?" James said after a long pause. "Do you *still* not see your mistake?"

Liz stared down at the worksheet James had given her. "I don't know," she grumbled. "Tell me, o wise one."

"You forgot to carry the 2," James said impatiently, and circled the 2 with his red pencil. (She *hated* that pencil). "See?"

"Argh!" Liz stood up, her chair scraping loudly on the floor. "I can't *do* this right now!"

"Shh!" James said, glancing around the library study room. "Of course you can. You just need to be thorough. Methodical. Math is an unforgiving discipline. Just like playing a church organ: you simply can't make any mistakes." He smiled smugly, as if silently congratulating himself for something. "You *can* get better at this, Liz, if you just *focus.*"

Liz sat down with a huff, and flopped her head and hands down on the table with a *bang*. A few tables over, a little old man gave them an annoyed look. "Focus, huh?" she muttered into the table. "Yeah, well, *you* try staying focused while freaking *Mary Summers* is messing with your head all the time."

"What was that?"

"Nothing." Liz sat up and rubbed her eyes. "C'mon," she said dully, "Woot woot, let's math it up."

James gave her one of his trademark long, piercing looks. Liz had nicknamed those looks "brain scans." She hated them. They made her think he was reading her mind. Hence the name.

"Actually," he said, putting his pencil down, "I'd like you to tell me what's bothering you."

"No." She shook her head. "Uh-uh. Don't wanna talk about it. None of your business."

"Liz, you're not unintelligent. You could be better than this. You can be quite careful and methodical if you want to. But we've had four sessions now, and you're not getting any better. Something is bothering you. I'd like to know what it is."

Liz blew a strand of hair out of her eyes with a *poof*. "Gee, I'm touched. Didn't know you cared."

James smiled thinly. "I *care* about not wasting my time. You need to deal with this distraction, so you can focus—" he tapped the worksheet, "—on more important things."

"What do you care?" Liz retorted. "You still get your twenty bucks no matter what."

"It's not a matter of money," James said huffily, "otherwise I'd be charging you much more." Liz was curious at that, but James continued. "It's a matter of pride. If I'm going to waste my time, I'd like to at least know *why*."

Liz groaned. "All right, fine. If you have to know, there's a girl at school…"

"Mary Summers?"

"Yeah. Mary. She's always getting up in my grill!"

"Your… what?"

"You know! Giving me the stink eye! Getting all up in my business! She's all like, waddup, and I'm all like, step off!"

"Er…she's…trying to start a fight? I don't understand."

"*She-is-a-NOY-ing-me.* Now do you get it? Geez, why ask if you don't even speak English?"

James shook his head like a bewildered bear. "I'm not the one using improper English. But anyway, why not ignore her?"

"I *can't* ignore her; you don't understand…it's complicated…" Liz flopped her head back down on the desk—*bang*. "I'm just so *sick* of her."

"I really thank God that I am male," she heard James mutter. "So, is she hurting you, somehow?"

"Well," she mumbled, "if you define *hurting* as 'making me feel like crap all the time,' then yeah, she's hurting me." She looked at James. "She just… ruins things for me. Yeah. She's hurting me."

"I see." James steepled his fingers and gave her another brain scan look. He kept it up until she was nearly squirming. "What?" she snapped.

"I'll give you some advice now," he said. "It's advice I gave myself a long time ago, and it's never steered me wrong, so listen."

"Yeah yeah." Liz sat up. "What?"

"If someone hurts you, you hurt them *back*."

Liz stared at him. She felt a little uncomfortable. Maybe it was the calm, placid voice James was using, or the odd, flat, disconnected look in his eyes. But something gave her the willies.

"James," she started. "Um… hurt her? How?"

"You'll figure it out," he said quietly, and picked up his pencil. "I think we should do some drills now," he said in a louder voice, pulling out another of his worksheets, this time covered with division problems. "Make sure to write your work out. I'll be watching."

J.P. was eating lunch with Liz when Brian walked up to them, alone. "Hey," he said in a guarded voice. "Can I join you?"

"Sure—" J.P. started.

"No!" Liz said at the same time. "Sorry, Burke. We're having a private conversation."

Looking disappointed, Brian walked away. J.P. turned to Liz, annoyed. "We weren't having a private conversation!"

"Yes, we were," Liz said. "I was about to talk to you about…binder stuff. The shooter investigation."

"So why can't you tell Brian, too?" J.P. said, exasperated. "He's smarter than both of us, put together!"

"What?" Liz snapped. "No."

"Come *on*, Liz, he's the missing ingredient! We never would have gotten Bickerstaff without him!"

"No," Liz said flatly. "Never."

J.P. stared at her. "They're just friends, you know," he muttered.

Liz spun around on him. "Who?"

"Brian and Mary. They're just friends. They're not really dating—"

"Hang on, hang on." Liz held up a hand with an incredulous look. "You think I care about that? You think I have a thing for Burke? Is that it?"

J.P. felt unsure of himself. "Um… yes."

"Wow. Um, wow." She snickered. "No, J.P. I don't. Never have, and never will. My problem with Brian isn't Mary. My problem is that he'd rat us out to Mr. Costain in a second. Got it?"

J.P. felt it was useless to argue the point further. "Fine," he said, slumping. "Whatever."

"Remember, we still have one lead. It could be some kid that Flynt and Brock and Tyler beat up. I'll keep my ears open at Sparrow Hills," she said. "You never know what people might say."

After science class, Liz shoved her books into her book bag one at a time, hard, and tried to zip it closed. It wouldn't close. She had packed them in wrong. Biting back a swear word, she dumped them all out on her desk and started again.

It took her a while to re-pack the books. When she finally slung her backpack on, her mom's classroom was totally empty. Grumbling to herself, Liz headed for the door. She had reached out her hand to open it when it opened on its own, and she found herself staring right into Mary Summer's face. "What do *you* want?" Liz said gruffly.

Mary looked taken aback. "I, um, forgot my purse," she said. "I need to—oh, what am I explaining to *you* for!" She scowled. "Get out of my way!"

She pushed past Liz into the room, stalked over to the desk where she had been sitting, and knelt down to retrieve the purse that was lying next to it.

"Mary!" Liz blurted out.

Mary looked up. "What?" she snapped.

"Just… hang on a sec," Liz bit her lip. A crazy idea had occurred to her. Maybe just crazy enough to work. It was a long shot, though.

"How's it going with you and Brian?" she said blandly.

"Yeah, like I'm going to tell *you*." Mary took a step towards the door.

Liz moved in front of the door, blocking her.

"Get out of my way, Liz."

"Hey, cool your jets. Look, I really need to know how you and Brian are doing."

"You think I'm stupid?" Mary said impatiently. "Why should I tell *you?*"

"Well, to be honest, I'm a bit worried. Because… let's just say I know something."

Mary's eyes narrowed. "You *know* something?" she repeated mockingly—but there was a bit of curiosity in her voice, too. At least, Liz hoped so.

"Yeah," she said, shrugging. "I've known Brian for a while. I was his friend before you—"

"Yeah, and you want to be *more* than his friend!" Mary cut in. "Which is why I can't trust you!"

Liz rolled her eyes. "I know you *think* that about me," she said. "But it's not true. I'm really *not* interested in Brian that way."

Mary gave her a long, suspicious look. "Are you saying," she said, eyes locked on Liz, "that you're *not* secretly in love with Brian and jealous of me?"

Liz gave a horrified gasp. "No!" she said fervently. "No. Absolutely not. That's *not* how I feel about him."

"Then why—"

"He's my *friend*," Liz said. "Brian is a great guy, and I really admire him, but we're friends. That's it."

It was easy to tell Mary this. It was all true. Of course she wasn't in love with Brian—the idea was crazy! Of course they were just friends! As for her Like, and the secret Something she couldn't remember… those were her private business. Mary didn't need to know. *Nobody* needed to know. Ever.

"Why don't you like *me*, then?" Mary said.

Liz snorted. "Believe it or not, lady, there are plenty of reasons not to like you without boys getting into it."

"Okay, then," Mary said coldly. "So why don't you just tell me what you want to tell me, and then leave me alone?"

Liz hesitated—but this was only for Mary's benefit. She knew exactly what she intended to say. "Look," she said. "I'm in a kind of awkward position here. I just want to do the right thing. Are *you* in love with Brian?"

"I don't know," Mary said, suddenly disarmed. "Maybe. I like him. I definitely like him a lot."

That tight, hot little knot formed in Liz's stomach. She ignored it. "I see," she said heavily. "I was afraid of this," she sighed. It was a pretty good sigh. Very convincing. "And how do you think he feels about you?"

"If you and him are such good friends, why don't you tell *me?*" Mary said hotly—but immediately she flushed red and looked at her shoes. "Sorry," she mumbled. "It's not your fault."

"What isn't?" Liz was genuinely curious.

"Brian has been acting funny lately," Mary said, her face getting redder with every word. "Sometimes I think he's avoiding me."

A light, fluttery, bouncy ball formed in Liz's stomach this time. She ignored *that*, too. "Darn it," she said in her best 'too bad' voice. "He hasn't *told* you, has he?"

"Told me what?" Mary said, looking a little scared. Even desperate.

A nagging voice started talking in Liz's head. *Don't do this*, it said. *This is crossing a line.*

Liz shook it off. *This won't hurt anything. It sounds like they're going towards Splitsville anyway. This will just help it along to its natural end.*

"Look," she said, making herself sound hesitant and even guilty. "A couple days ago, Brian called me up. He wanted to talk to me about…" She bit her lip.

"What? About what?"

"Nothing. Forget it." Liz started for the door. "Never never mind."

132

"Liz!" Mary stepped between her and the door. "Liz, what are you *talking* about?"

Liz gave her a long, anxious look, pretended to struggle for a bit, and then threw up her hands. "Okay, fine! But you better not tell him I told you! He swore me to secrecy!"

"Go on," Mary said in a steady voice, but she looked as though she was scared of what Liz would say. Which was exactly what Liz wanted her to think. *She already swallowed the worm. I just got to reel her in.*

"Okay, okay," she said, leaning in close and dropping her voice to a whisper. "Like I said, Brian called me a few days ago. He said he'd been praying a lot lately, and, well, he had mentioned becoming a priest *before*, but I never thought he was serious—"

"What?" Mary said. "A priest? He wants to be a priest?"

"He said he feels, you know, called," Liz said, nodding. "He told me so. He wants to go to the seminary right after high school. But he kind of feels trapped. Because…"

She trailed off delicately, and Mary jumped at the bait. "Because of me." She shook her head. "Oh. Wow. This explains everything. You know, just this morning I asked him how he was feeling, and he didn't answer. No wonder."

"Yes," Liz said, nodding again. "Yes. That's probably it." She had thought Mary would need more convincing, but she wasn't going to look a gift horse in the mouth. "Brian wants to be a priest, but he doesn't want to hurt your feelings. Brian's *very* sensitive about the feelings of girls." *Careful. Don't lay it on too thick.*

Mary collapsed in a chair, looking mortified. "Poor Brian. So, what was he planning to do?"

"He didn't know *what* to do," Liz said. "I'm real sorry. But you and Brian—that's never gonna happen."

She held her breath and waited. Mary was staring down at the floor, apparently pondering poor Brian's predicament. *Careful. All you need to do now is wait. Wait for it to sink in. You know what she'll decide.*

Mary stood up suddenly. "Well," she said heavily, "there's only one thing to do."

"You're not going to tell him you know!" Liz said in an alarmed voice. "I'm the only one he told! He'll know it was me!"

"No, I won't tell," Mary said heavily. "I'll just... I dunno, I'll just tell him I only want to be friends. That I don't like him that way. So he doesn't need to worry."

She sounded so sad that the nagging voice came back to Liz for a moment. *This is wrong. Stop it.* But Liz gritted her teeth and pushed it down. "Well," she said, "sorry to be the bearer of bad news. I'll, uh, see you later."

"Yeah," Mary mumbled. "See you." She walked out of the room and Liz pulled the door closed, still holding her breath.

I pulled it off! It worked! She broke into a wide smile. No nagging voice now—only joy. *She fell for it!* She skipped across the room, feeling light as a feather. *It's all gonna be okay! She'll break off their pretend-relationship, and she'll never tell him why! And then it'll all go back to normal! Brian will be* my *friend again! Just like before!* She felt like she was waking up from a long nightmare. *I wonder when she'll talk to him,* she thought. *Right away? I hope so.* She walked up to the door, pulled it open—

There was Mary, glaring at her, arms crossed.

15

HOSEY

"Hey," Mary said loudly. "Liz. When exactly *did* Brian call you about this priesthood thing?"

Liz almost took a step back, alarmed. "Um, Brian talked to me a few days ago. Wednesday, I think. Why?"

"Because *yesterday*," Mary said, "Brian specifically told me that he hadn't talked to you in weeks."

"Well, duh," Liz said, trying to remain nonchalant. "Of course he didn't *tell* you about talking to me; he wants to keep it secret."

"That's what I thought, too," Mary said through clenched teeth. "But then I remembered something. I didn't even *ask* Brian about you—he told me on his own. He was complaining about it. 'Liz never talks to me anymore, I miss her. Blah blah blah.' And you know what? I believed him. Just like I believed you."

Liz felt suddenly the need to vacate the premises, rapidly. "Look, Mary—"

"Which *means*," Mary said over her, "That either Brian is a really good liar, or you are. Gee, Liz, I wonder which one of you it is."

Liz opened her mouth. Nothing came out. Mary laughed harshly. "Brian told me about your *acting*. I should have remembered." She turned and walked away.

Liz stood gaping at her. Then, not knowing what else to do, she ran after her. "Mary! Wait!"

"Get away from me," Mary said as she kept walking.

"I'm sorry!"

Mary turned on her. "I *don't* forgive you," she snapped.

Liz blinked. That stung a lot more than she had expected. "Look, calm down. It was just a joke—"

"It was a *lie*," Mary said over her. "You *lied*, and now you're *lying* about a *lie*. You're pathetic."

"Oh, *I'm* pathetic?" Liz clenched her fists. "Like you're one to talk. You can't—"

"You are *pathetic*," Mary said again. "You act all cool, but guess what? You're not." She spun around, her brown hair flaring out and hitting Liz in the face, and stalked off.

Then she stopped again and turned around. Now she was smirking. "Oh, I almost forgot. You *are* in love with Brian, aren't you?"

"No!" Liz said fervently. "I wasn't lying about that."

"Aw, really? Are you sure?" Mary's voice was heavy with fake sympathy. "Because I hear from *everyone else* that you're head over heels for him."

Liz felt her face grow hot. It *couldn't* be true. Mary was lying now. Wasn't she? Normally Liz could tell. But not now, not with this pounding in her head and the walls closing in.

"So sorry, Liz," Mary said, mocking. "You and Brian—that's never gonna happen. Not after I tell him what you just tried to do." With a little smirk, she turned and walked away.

Liz couldn't move. She felt like her limbs had been turned to stone. Like a sandbag had been placed on her back, rooting her in place. Every part of her body felt cold and heavy, except for her head. Her head was burning.

Mary was going to tell Brian. She was going to tell him Liz was in *love* with him, and that she had tried to trick them into breaking up. And what would Brian think? He would be outraged. Outraged and worse, disappointed.

She couldn't stop seeing sneering faces, hearing the whispered conversations. The snickering that started as soon as she was out of earshot. Pathetic? *Pathetic?*

If someone hurts you, hurt them back.

Her limbs didn't feel heavy anymore. She imagined punching Mary's pretty face. She imagined punching *all* their faces. She couldn't do that, but she could do something else. Quick, before it was too late.

She ran down the hallway, through the cafeteria and out the back door. Once she was outside, she ran around the school to the parking lot. It was the end of the school day, and cars were pulling into the parking lot, parents coming to pick up kids.

Liz dashed to the familiar clump of bushes situated just by the corner of the school building, and found what she was looking for: the coiled hose, one end attached to the spigot, the other end with the gun-like spray nozzle. She grabbed the spray nozzle and turned the spigot.

"Come on, Hosey. Come on come on come on," she mumbled to herself as she waited for the hose to fill with water. Finally it was ready and she crouched behind the bush, watching, heart pounding like a drum. She spotted Mrs. Summer's black boxy car, parked in the front row. That meant Mary was still here. All she had to do was wait. She knew they would all come out in a rush.

The door banged open and a crowd of kids spilled out. Liz waited, gripping the nozzle. *Where is she?... Where is she...?*

There. She saw Jacinta emerge, laughing at some unheard joke, and then a flash of golden brown hair as Mary emerged, her back to Liz.

Liz jumped out and pulled the trigger, and with a loud hiss the water arced out and struck Mary right in the back.

Mary made a funny squawking sound and turned around, her mouth open in a stupid expression of surprise. Which was perfect.

Liz kept the spray steady, moving up and down, soaking Mary from head to foot until her hair was lank and dark and her white blouse and black skirt was soaked and sticking to her. Liz made sure to fill her stupid open mouth with a powerful jet of hose water.

Liz turned off the spigot with a flourish, and stepped out triumphantly. "Hey!" she said, waving it at Mary. "*Now* who looks pathetic?"

For half a second she felt amazing. But then she noticed several things at once that made it all come crashing down on her like a rock slide. Everyone—including about a dozen boys—stood staring at Mary. Her blouse was soaked, and it was doing what cloth did when it was soaked—sticking to skin, becoming form-fitting. And Mary's blouse was particularly thin.

Mary made a whimpering sound and ran back into the school. Jacinta shot Liz a disbelieving look and then followed her sister. Teachers, parents, and students were yelling, talking, asking each other what had just happened. A few of the boys like Kevin and Mitch were laughing, but everyone else was staring at Liz, looking just as outraged as Jacinta.

"Um…" Liz said, smiling uneasily, holding up the sprayer, "Prank?"

"You!" She saw Mrs. Summers push out of the crowd, swelling with rage. "Put that down! Come here!"

Liz dropped the hose and ran.

I…I can't *believe* you, Liz!" Liz's mom said for what seemed like the hundredth time. She paced up and down the dining room, wringing her hands. "You soaked that girl…in front of everyone…Mrs. Summers is *so* angry…that was entirely inappropriate and wrong!"

"I'm sorry," Liz muttered.

"Don't you have *any* control over your emotions?" her mom went on. "Don't you realize the damage you've caused? Well, you're going to pay for this, missy. You'll stay after school with me the rest of this year, sweeping floors…you'll eat with me, too, in my office, and help me grade papers…"

"Hey, Tammy, come on," her dad said. He was home for the weekend, and was watching both his daughter and his wife with an alarmed look. "Is it really that bad? It was just a prank."

"You don't understand!" her mom said. "That woman…she's trouble! This could get out of control *really* quickly. And all because our daughter thought it would funny to—"

"I didn't do it be because it was funny!" Liz stood up, fists clenched. "I did it because she deserved it!"

"Liz…"

"Just…leave me alone!" Liz stomped out of the dining room, up the stairs and into her room. She slammed the door extra hard, sat on the bed and stared at her shoes, breathing hard.

138

A few minutes later, when she was calmer, she heard a knock on the door. "Liz?" It was her dad's voice. "Can I come in?"

"Yeah," she said mournfully, and her dad opened the door.

"What's going on?" he said.

"Nothing," she muttered. "Look, Dad, I'm sorry that I—"

"Let's go get some ice cream."

"What?"

"You. Me. Ice cream. Come on." He beckoned to the door. "Now. That's an order."

They went to Buffalo Blues, a little restaurant just down the road from their house. Going out for ice cream was something they hadn't done since Liz was a kid. It was a special time where they could just hang out. And maybe, talk.

They ended up talking for a long time, about many different things: New York, cheerleading, cars, sports, school, construction… but it was never anything more than fun. It never got deep, until, on his fourth cup of coffee, her dad said something that Liz hadn't expected.

"Hey, Liz," he said. "I'm sorry I fired you."

Liz looked down at her melted half-eaten sundae and stirred it. "That's okay," she mumbled.

"No, it's not," her dad said. "It wasn't fair to you. On that day of the school fire—I kind of knew, deep down, that it wasn't you—that you wouldn't be that careless. But I just didn't see who else it could have been."

"Yeah, it was Bickerstaff," she muttered. Bickerstaff had triggered a fire in the school by plugging her tools in and turning the power back on. "But you had no way of knowing—"

"I should have, though," her dad said firmly. "You did. I should have respected you enough to listen to you. You're my daughter, for crying out loud!" He shook his head. "So that's why I'm not going to ask you why you did…what you did to Mary. Not unless you want to tell me."

Liz stared at her dad for a long moment. "Dad," she started. "Dad, I—"

"Can I clear those up for you?" Their waitress came by and started gathering their plates and silverware. Liz, distracted, stared at her. She was tired, harried-looking, with a weak chin and straight brown hair. As she leaned over their table, Liz caught the whiff of tobacco. She straightened, and there was something in her face that looked familiar. But Liz couldn't figure out what.

"Liz?" her dad said. "What, Liz?"

"Um…never mind." Liz said, her eyes on the waitress as she walked away.

That night, after her parents had gone to bed, Liz got her coat on and slipped out the front door.

She walked to the end of her street, then took a right, walking quickly. It was dark. If her parents discovered she was missing, they would probably freak…but Liz didn't care. *I know I've seen that waitress before.* She stopped at a red light, pushed the button and waited for the *walk* sign. *If only I could remember where. I just need to see her again. Maybe take a picture.*

When she arrived at Buffalo Blues, she snuck up to one of the windows and peered in. She couldn't see the waitress. *Darn. Maybe she's done for the night.*

Then she remembered the smell of tobacco. *Maybe… there's a chance…*

She crept down the side of the building, staying in the shadows, until she got to the kitchen exit in the rear. There were a couple of dumpsters, the back door with a light above it, and a few parked cars. And sitting on the hood of one of them, taking a drag of a cigarette, was the waitress.

"Hello?" Liz walked up to her. "Hey, sorry…can I talk to you?"

The waitress peered at her. "I know you," she said. "You were here before, with a big guy. He was a good tipper." Her accent was

140

a thick local one, the kind people imitated when they made fun of Pennsylvanians.

"Um…yeah. He's my dad," Liz said. "Look, are you Megan Brock?"

The waitress hung her head. "Aww, crap," she muttered.

"I'm just asking because you look a lot like—"

"Stop!" The waitress jumped off the car and waved her hands angrily. "Just… just stop! My name is Megan *Hemmingway* now, okay?" She glanced at the door that led back to the restaurant. "Don't call me that *other* name."

"But…why?"

"Because I want to keep my job, okay?" the waitress hissed. "So shut up and go away!" She tossed the cigarette away and started for the door.

"I don't think he did it!" Liz called after her.

The waitress stopped, and slowly turned around. "What?" she said.

"I don't think Brandon did it," Liz repeated. She had figured out what had happened to this woman. It wasn't that hard to understand. "And I want to figure out who did. That's why I want to talk to you."

The waitress stared at her for a full ten seconds—then she walked slowly back to the car, pulled out a pack of cigarettes from her apron pocket, and lit a fresh one. She offered one to Liz, who declined with a wave.

"What's your name?" Megan Not-Brock finally said.

"Liz Simonelli." Liz extended a hand. "Nice to meet you, Megan."

The waitress hesitated, and then shook her hand. "*Hemmingway*," she said under her breath. "Remember, okay? I have to keep this job."

"Is Hemmingway a made-up name?"

"It's my mom's maiden name," Megan mumbled. "So who are you, exactly?"

"I'm a student at John Paul 2 High," Liz said. "You know…that school down the road from Sparrow Hills."

"Yeah yeah, Tyler's ex goes there, I remember." Megan took a drag of her cigarette. "So, you don't think Brandon did it, huh?"

"No," Liz hesitated. "Do you?"

141

"Of *course* he didn't," Megan said scornfully. "I've been saying that ever since he got killed. Not that anyone believes me."

"Well, I believe you," Liz said. "But...if you don't mind my asking, how do you know?"

"Cause he's my little brother!" Megan said vehemently. "My brother! Don't you understand? I *know* my brother! He wasn't a freaking criminal mastermind! He couldn't even keep a secret! He was kind of dumb, and kind of a bully, and yeah, he got in trouble a lot. But it doesn't mean he did it, and it doesn't mean we deserve to be treated like *this!* No one talks to us anymore. People throw stuff at our house. They throw rocks at my dad's car. And why? Because the—"

"Yo, Megan." A man appeared in the open doorway, his shadow falling across both of them. "I need you back in here in ten minutes."

"Yeah, sure," Megan muttered. "Be right in, Mike."

Liz watched as the man disappeared again. "Does your boss know your real name?" she said.

"Yeah," she said. "But I'm not allowed to tell anyone else here, just in case. He makes me wear my hair down, too. He thinks I look too much like Brandon when I pull it back." She let out a shaky laugh.

"That's... awful," Liz said after a moment. "How could he *do* that?"

"I don't blame him," Megan said brutally. "He's got to keep this place open. I'm just happy he gave me a job at all. He didn't need to. No one else would. Small town, and all that."

She lapsed into silence, staring blankly into space. Liz glanced up at the sky. It was a clear night, but she could barely see the stars because of all the glaring yellow street lamps around here. She could hear the bang of dishes inside the restaurant and an occasional car down the road. How many people lived in their town—ten thousand? Twenty thousand? She had no idea. She tried to imagine how it must feel to have twenty thousand people know and hate you.

"Why don't you move?" she said. "Go someplace where nobody knows you?"

"That's what I'm trying to do," Megan said quietly. "That's why I need to keep this job. I'm twenty-four years old, I got a high school diploma and a baby daughter. I live in my parents' basement. I'm *trying* to get out of here. I just need to save up some money, then I'm gone." She closed her eyes. "How'd you even find me anyway?"

"Just dumb luck," Liz said. "I heard you worked at *La Chinchilla's*, but when I called them, they acted all weird and pretended that you never worked there."

"Pfft. Yeah, that sounds about right." Megan's face tightened. "You know my uncle owns that place? I've been working there since I was fourteen. But after the shooting, people heard who I was, and he fired me. Won't even talk to me now, or my parents. None of them will. None of my friends."

"Wow. Just… wow." Liz faltered and fell silent. *I never thought about the Brocks—I mean, thought of them as real people. I've been treating this like a game or something.*

"Hey," she said. "Have you talked to this detective, Thomas Irving?"

"Oh, Tom?" Megan shook her head. "Yeah, I know Tom Irving. He's a good guy. He's come by a couple times. He's the only cop who listened to me. I appreciate it, but he's all alone there. Nobody else listens. They all think it's over."

"But it's not," Liz said. "Is it?"

Slowly, the tightness drained out of Megan's face. She went back to staring at the pavement, but her gaze didn't look blank this time. Her eyes were wide, very wide, as if she was looking at something and she couldn't look away.

"No," she whispered. "No, I don't think it is."

16

LOST DOG

"Why not?" Liz asked quickly. Maybe there was new information to be found.

Megan lit another cigarette. "Boone's gone."

"Boone?"

"Our dog. Boone. He's gone. Disappeared last month and never came back."

"Oh," Liz said. "Um… okay. So, your dog ran away—"

"No, he *didn't*," Megan said. "Boone was thirteen years old and he had arthritis. He didn't run away; he could barely hop up on the couch. Somebody took him. We woke up one morning and he was gone. We put up signs everywhere—my dad loved that dog. But we never got a call. We never heard anything."

"Oh," Liz said. "But maybe he just wandered off and, you know, died? If he was really old."

Megan shook her head. "We got a fence around our yard. The gate was closed and Boone was gone. And…" Megan shuddered, and hunched her shoulders, as if trying to make herself smaller. "I think somebody's watching me."

Liz frowned. "Like a stalker?"

"I don't know, I don't know!" Megan swore and threw the cigarette away. "Every now and then, when I'm coming from my car to my house after work, I feel *eyes* on me."

"What do you mean?"

"Haven't you ever gotten the feeling that someone's watching you? Like, that tingly feeling?"

Liz had. She wished she hadn't. "Okay," she said, trying to keep her mind trained on the facts. "So you feel like someone's watching you."

"Not just watching. I feel like he's laughing at me." Megan kneaded her forehead with her fingers. "No, I never actually saw anybody. But I knew he was there."

"Huh," Liz grunted. *Great. Another 'I got creepy feelings' story just like Flynt's.* "What do you mean, he's *laughing* at you?"

"I've heard a laugh, once or twice." Megan shuddered again. "Maybe I just imagined it."

Liz looked up. "What kind of laugh?" She suddenly remembered.

Megan's eyes, if possible, looked even wider. "It was like a nasty, gravelly laugh. Like," Megan lowered the pitch of her voice and let out a chortle of three even, scratchy breaths, "*heh-heh-heh.* Kind of like that."

Liz didn't answer. She remembered the night of the shooting. Running through the woods with Celia. Hearing someone laughing at them as he raised what looked like a rifle... *heh-heh-heh.*

"Have you ever talked to anyone else from my school?" she asked. Only Celia had heard the laugh. And Allie, from what Liz had read in Allie's notes.

"No," Megan said, surprised. "Why?"

"Nothing. Never mind...Are you sure about that laugh?"

"No, I'm not. Like I said, I could have just imagined it."

Somehow Liz didn't think so. But this was worse than ever. It was a clue, but *not* a clue. It seemed that whenever she got close to this guy, he was just out of reach. An odd laugh. A shadow in the woods. A pair of eyes watching—but never a trace. He was like something seen out of the corner of your eye, only real for a moment, and then vanishing again—only he *was* real. As real as two dead bodies—no, three. *Four, if you count the dog...*

"You know what I think?" Megan said after a moment. "I think he's gloating. He ruined our lives, he killed my brother, and he just likes gloating over it." She scowled. "You want to know who I think the real killer is? He's some kid living in my neighborhood, Shady Acres. That's where you should be looking."

"What do you mean? Why?"

"Brandon, Neil, and Tyler used to go around—ever since they were little kids—and beat up people. Kids. All the time. And now two of them are dead. Someone's getting revenge."

145

"Really?" Liz's interest was piqued again. "All right! We got to look at all the kids your brother and Tyler and Flynt beat up, and—"

Megan was shaking her head. "Liz, I told Tom everything I'm telling you, and he thought the same thing. He spent weeks tracking down every kid that my brother beat up in school. He just about went door-to-door in the neighborhood before he was called off because people were complaining. He never got any results."

"But—" Liz spluttered. "But—*argh*, it makes *sense!*"

"Of course it does," Megan said. She sounded much older now, old and worn out. "I just think he's too good, this guy. He's too smart. He hasn't left any trace."

"So, what are we supposed to do?" Liz said impatiently. "Just give up?"

"I already have." Megan stood up. She opened the door. "My break's over. I got to go."

"Wait!" Liz said. "How do you think he planted the evidence on your brother—?"

"Just give up, Liz." Megan shook her head. "I'm glad you care and all. But seriously—leave it alone."

Leave it alone, huh? Liz thought grimly as she walked home. *He may be smart. But I'm smarter. Believe it or not, it's not the first time I've had someone aiming to kill me.*

...I didn't get out of that one by myself, though.

She stopped and looked around. It seemed a long walk back to her street, and off the main drag there were no street lamps. There was a little light from the moon, and that was it.

She glanced at the woods just to her right. An uncomfortable thought popped into her head: *if someone was looking at me right now, I wouldn't be able to see him at all.*

She imagined eyes looking at her, and shivered. *Why the heck did I do this?*

Suddenly, to her annoyance, she found herself thinking of Brian. Specifically, of how nice it would be to have Brian here right now. Not for his brains or anything—not even because he was a boy, and stood a better chance of beating the crap out of some creep sitting in the bushes.

She needed him, just for him.

And that thought drove her crazy. *I don't need him!* she thought. She had never felt this way before. *I don't need anybody, and especially not a boy! I'm a strong independent woman, and—*

Somewhere nearby, an owl hooted, startling her.

Um…yeah. Sorry, ankle, I'm gonna run the rest of the way home.

It was lunchtime, and J.P. was headed to his locker to get his lunch. As he got close he smelled something. Strawberries. *Hoo boy.*

It was Miranda. Miranda Costain was once again standing beside the locker next to his. "Just moved in!" she chirped, closing the door. "Looks like we'll be locker mates!"

"Oh!" J.P. said, nonplussed. "Um…are you sure you're allowed to do—"

"Hey," she said over him. "Want to go to SpeedEMart? You and me?"

"Um…uh, I don't think freshman are allowed to leave the school," he said. It was too risky; she was the principal's daughter—

"Aw, come on," she said. "I thought you didn't believe in limits." She leaned a bit closer. *It isn't that risky, is it? No, actually, not risky at all…*

A few minutes later they were walking into the woods, and he had given Miranda five dollars (the last of his monthly allowance) for lunch.

He was just about to walk in the door when he caught a glimpse of a girl with dyed red hair at the counter. Ergh. Courtney's working there today. Courtney was his ex-girlfriend, and J.P. got embarrassed every time he remembered that they had dated. He managed to sidle in the door and duck behind a counter when Courtney was checking out a customer. She looked like so much trailer-trash compared to Miranda.

"What are you doing?" Miranda asked, when he didn't follow her down the candy aisle.

"Ah—" He focused on what was in front of him and found it was a display of ratchet sets. "I, uh, need to replace something on my mom's car. You go ahead and pick something out for me."

So Miranda browsed with his five dollar bill while he squatted down and familiarized himself with travel sewing kits and hood ornaments. While he was waiting, he couldn't help overhearing someone talking on a cell phone in the next aisle over. The voice was familiar, and he caught a glimpse of her when she paced down the end of the aisle. It was the head cheerleader, Madison, and she was ticked off.

"What's with the interrogation?" she was whispering into the phone. "I don't need to tell you everything I'm doing. What? No, I never told anyone how you ditched me the night of the dance. Look, Brad, you owe me big. You owe me tons. So stop being a whiner."

Huh. Wonder what that's all about. J.P. didn't have time to wonder much, though, because at that moment Miranda came back with her hands full of candy bars, and a moment later they were hurrying back to the school.

"We better get in there," Miranda said, "I have class in like, less than a minute. Thanks for the candy!"

"Yeah. Sorry we didn't actually get to *eat* any of it."

"That's alright," she said, pulling him to a halt. She wrapped her arms around his neck and hugged him. "It was worth the trip."

J.P. just stood there. His brain was doing that not-working thing again.

"Well, are you coming?" Miranda asked, releasing him and trying to lead him inside by the hand. "We're gonna get in trouble."

"I... uh..."

"Well, it's probably better if we go in separately anyway. Don't want my dad getting any ideas."

"Ideas?"

"Yeah, you know. About us."

"Is there... an 'us'?" *Please let there be an 'us' please let there be an 'us' please let there be an 'us'—*

Miranda smiled demurely. "Maybe. Yeah, maybe. I know you've been really sweet to me. And I don't care about that stupid dating rule, and neither do you. *Do* you?"

"No. No, I do not."

"I didn't think so," Miranda said with a half-grin, and then stood on tiptoe and kissed him on the cheek. "No limits for J.P."

Her lips seemed to linger ever so close (but not quite close enough) to his own for an eternity, before she stepped back and patted J.P. on the cheek. "Well, bye, *boyfriend!*" She gave a little squeal of delight, then turned and ran into the school.

J.P. wandered away in a stupor, letting his feet take him on autopilot while he tried to process what had just happened. One thing was for sure: he had achieved his goal. He was dating Miranda. Officially, really and truly dating Miranda. His first reaction was outright panic. Dating the principal's daughter! What if Celia found out?

But never let it be said that a Flynn isn't up for a challenge. This was… kind of exciting.

Liz poked her plastic fork at her lunch. She had brought a disposable plastic snap-top container of tortellini, leftover from Sunday dinner, which she had just nuked in the school kitchen's microwave. Liz hated microwaves. If she was at home, she would have gently reheated the tortellini, and it would have been just as delicious as it had been last night. The microwave made the noodles dry and rubbery, scalding on one side and stone cold on the other. She mixed both sides with her fork, trying to even the heat out and get some sauce over the hardened, dried-out bits.

"Ugh." Allie sat down next to her. "That's gross."

"Well, it was fine on Sunday," she mumbled, replacing the lid on the container and shoving it to the side.

"So, Liz," Allie said, sitting down next to Liz at the cafeteria table, "I hear James has been helping you."

"Yeah," Liz admitted. And to be honest, he was. Some of the stuff he'd shown her the first day had actually been a revelation, although occasionally she still got confused. It was frustrating; why did people have to put such a high value on math, anyway? She wanted to be good at other things: reading, history, sports, pranks, firing a .40 caliber handgun, psychoanalyzing people, cooking Italian food, using nunchucks and butterfly knives. All the things that really mattered in life.

But since James was a math genius and Liz wasn't, it made her feel like *she* had to get good at it, too. Even though she couldn't imagine ever having to use it for anything outside of school.

"There's James now," said Allie. "Hey, James!" she waved him over.

James walked over and sat down. "Hello, Liz. Hello, Allie." He opened his lunch bag and took out a ham sandwich.

There was something about James that struck Liz as odd, but she couldn't tell what. Then it hit her: *nothing* was odd. James was acting… normal. He wasn't haughty or grumpy or even withdrawn. He looked like a normal, boring person, eating a normal, boring ham sandwich, relaxed and even happy. Weird.

"So, Liz," he said after a moment, "I see you're prepared for this evening's *tête-à-tête*." He indicated her open algebra book and loose pages filled with her messy ciphers.

"Our Teddy Ted? Um, sure. I'm totally going to rock the Teddy Ted."

"*Tête-à-tête*," James corrected. "It means 'a meeting of the minds.'"

"Right, I knew that," Liz said cheerily, wondering if *tête-à-tête* was somehow related to the word *tutor*. They both had a lot of t's. "In fact," she continued, "I was just going to suggest giving you the nickname Tutor Ted."

"Don't call me Tutor Ted—" James started.

"Hey, guys!" Celia walked up to join them at the table, followed by George.

The cafeteria was filling up. Liz suddenly noticed something else weird: Mary wasn't around. Neither was Jacinta. She was relieved, but also confused. Maybe they were both sick? Had she given Mary pneumonia? Liz didn't want that. Maybe only a mild flu, not pneumonia.

Isabel walked in, carrying her bag lunch in one hand, and her swinging guitar case in the other. *Oh no*, thought Liz, *what's she bringing that in for?*

"Whacha guys talking about?" asked Celia and she tucked into her own brown bag lunch.

"We're making up nicknames," said Liz. "I think we should start calling James 'Tutor Ted.'" Allie laughed. James looked exasperated.

"Why Tutor Ted?" asked Celia. So Liz explained it, despite attempted interruptions and corrections from James. Celia giggled and George was clearly amused, but James, to Liz's surprise, seemed to take it well—at least better than his usual humorless, prickly way.

The cafeteria filled up with conversation, and soon Liz had put her homework away and tried her rubber tortellini again (it had finally cooled down enough to eat). The whole table was chatting away; even James seemed to come out of his shell again, once the topic turned away from nicknames. Liz was feeling good.

Except every now and then, she wondered again why Mary and Jacinta weren't there. She noticed Brian sitting by himself, looking sad, and suddenly her rubber tortellini tasted like just rubber. *Ugh. What does he look so sad about? So I shot his not-girlfriend with a hose. Big whoop. Does he miss her that much? Eh, what do I care?* She clenched her fists. *I don't care. I don't—what's that sound?*

She looked around and saw Isabel. She had a guitar strapped over her shoulders and she was plucking its strings.

Oh, no. What is she doing?

Liz could hear Isabel saying something like, "Are you guys sure you want to hear this?" and the girls at her table going, "Yeah! Play it!"

You have got to be kidding me. She is not going to—

"Okay, you guys," Isabel raised her voice, and while no one quite stopped talking, the cafeteria noise dimmed to a volume where Isabel could be heard clearly. "I've gotten a couple song requests, and I think it might be fun to…"

She trailed off as she started fingering her guitar more adroitly now. She strummed a couple times, then twisted the tuning knobs. "I'm not used to playing for an audience, but here goes."

Isabel began delicately plucking out a treacly tune, and after a few bars she began singing:

> *Your grace fills me up,*
> *With the words of eternal life...*

Oh. No. Liz *knew* this song. It was one of the ones her mother would play in the car, and sometimes sing along to. Over the years, Liz had come to *hate* it. She looked around. Many of the students seemed puzzled or irritated at this impromptu show. *Dang right*, she thought. Others, though, brightened up as they recognized the melody and began singing along with Isabel.

> *And I will fall before your throne,*
> *Fall before your throne...*

Liz noticed Celia and Allie smiling in appreciation. Celia was even mouthing the words along with Isabel. *Ugh.*

Isabel ended her song to a scattered, polite applause. "Anyone mind if I sing another?" she said.

Most of the students said nothing, but a few shouted for more. A couple of the freshmen guys covered their mouths with their hands and moaned, "Nooooooo." But Celia shushed them and they stopped, and Isabel launched into another song.

It was another one of her mom's favorites: one of those up-tempo barn-burning songs that started out quiet and ended with a huge swelling chorus:

> *From the foundations of the earth,*
> *To the firmament above,*
> *There raises from all corners*
> *A song of praise... to Him in love*

Now more and more of the students (mostly girls) were singing along. Quietly at first, but then louder as Isabel's song began to rise in volume and intensity. By the end, you could barely hear Isabel's guitar for all the kids shouting/singing:

> *Hallelujah! Hallelujah!*
> *He reigns from above!*
> *He reigns from above!*

Now Celia had her arms raised, her hands up with palms to the sky. Liz could see several other students doing the same. Liz looked over toward James and made the "crazy" circling motion with her finger. James, as she expected, had reverted back to his usual grumpy self. In fact, he was positively seething. He probably considered this blasphemous or something. Liz just found it annoying.

Isabel finished the song to wild applause. Even students who weren't into it were clapping just out of peer pressure.

Liz started to worry. Was Isabel going to do this every lunch period? How big an embarrassment would that be? Liz could not imagine bringing a *normal* person to this lunchroom to have to suffer through that outburst. This whole school would gain a reputation as a haven for nuts!

Looking for an ally, she leaned across the table and whispered to James, "Some freak show, huh?"

"Indeed," James muttered darkly. "Ridiculous. Totally unbecoming. I have half a mind to tell them all off right now."

"Well, why don't you?"

James hesitated, and then glanced at Allie, who was smiling and clapping with the same enthusiasm as the others. "Because I don't think it's the right time. That's why. Besides, I'm not at your beck and call. Don't make the mistake of thinking I am."

Isabel removed the guitar and was leaning it against her chair so she could throw her lunch trash away when Liz heard Celia dreamily say, "That was nice."

"That was *not* nice," said James grumpily. "In fact it reinforced my long-held belief that every Protestant-inspired, carnival calliope pop-music church book and song sheet in this country ought to be thrown onto a bonfire and burned, followed by all the guitars used to play them."

Celia looked hurt, but Allie only laughed. "Aw, come on, James! Lighten up!"

Rats. James won't do anything about this. Guess it's up to me. She already had a plan. Not a very well-formed plan, but a plan nonetheless. Now J.P. wouldn't be able to accuse her of slacking off in the war on the noobs. "Not to worry, Tutor Ted," she said, "I've got it covered."

"Don't call me—"

But Liz was already rising from her chair. "I'm either gonna nip this in the bud, or else make you love guitar music forever!" Liz strode from her table just as Isabel crossed to the trash can. Before Isabel could respond, Liz picked up the guitar and settled down in Isabel's spot on the table.

Now, she thought grimly, *the schooling begins.*

17

PANDA BEAR ROCK

Liz threw the guitar strap around her shoulders. She cleared her throat and said, "Well, hey! Since we're all having such a rocking good time, let's keep the party going."

She started strumming a tuneless, twangy tune, using the two chords she knew: D and G. Liz barely knew how to play guitar, and it showed.

Laughter and groans filled the room. Liz smiled wickedly. Playing guitar was a stupid skill anyway. Guitar players deserved to be mocked. And Liz had excellent mocking skills.

She started singing in the most wavering, wussy voice she could muster:

> *Hippy-happy! Everyone's happy!*
> *Rainbows and flowers and everything's there!*
> *Skip stomp! Clap your hands like a lunatic!*
> *We're feelin' happy like panda bears!*

Lots of people were laughing now. Liz strummed even more vigorously and started gyrating around to the cacophony she was creating. She threw out a few more nonsense lyrics:

> *Ninjas and pandas! What a wonderful world!*
> *Everyone's happy! Put your hands in the air!*

She leaned back, eyes closed, and jammed on the strings as hard as she could in imitation of a big finale.

"Stop! Stop!" Isabel was saying. "You're wrecking it! Stop doing that!"

Liz stopped playing and opened her eyes. Isabel was standing in front of her, trembling with fury, looking on the verge of tears.

"Sorry," Liz said with a smirk. "I was just trying to fill in while you took a break."

Surrounded by laughter, Isabel took the guitar, packed it back in its case and stormed out of the lunch room. "Thank you! Thank you! I take cash and Paypal!" Liz bowed to the laughter and sarcastic applause.

Lunch was over now, and the students were dispersing, many still chuckling over Liz's performance. Liz knew they were talking about her song because a few guys high-fived her, and she could overhear several students laughingly talking about panda bears.

She was met back at the table by a livid Celia. "Why on *earth* did you do that?" she demanded.

Liz met her gaze evenly. "Do what? Oh, you mean interrupt lunch break to sing some goofy song? I didn't know we weren't supposed to do that, 'cause it wasn't a problem when Isabel did the same thing."

"That was not the same thing," said Celia, "and you know it. You mocked her. She's having a hard time fitting in here, and you just made it ten times worse for her."

Liz reached out to Allie and George. "Aw c'mon guys. You know it was funny."

"Funny or not, that was pretty mean," said George.

"It wasn't funny at all," said Allie, glaring.

"Gimme a break," said Liz defensively. "Look, I just made a little fun at Isabel's songs. If I hadn't, then we'd have these dopey little praise and worship songs going on at every lunch break."

"I would have *liked* it if we did praise and worship for every lunch!" cried Celia. "I thought it was beautiful!"

"Really?" Liz stammered. "*Every* lunch break? Are you serious?"

"Of course I'm serious," Celia said passionately, and threw up her hands. "What do you think I'm doing all this for?" She got up and ran out of the cafeteria. Allie followed her.

Out of the corner of Liz's eye, she caught Brian slinking away.

"Brian!" Liz called. "You don't think what I did was all that inappropriate, do you?" Liz knew Brian was one of those Latin Mass types. He was as allergic to charismatics with their Glory & Praise music as he was to poison ivy.

"Well," Brian started off weakly, "I didn't really care for Isabel's music. But I did feel that your response was, you know, maybe in poor taste."

Liz stared at Brian, gape-jawed. Brian merely shrugged and said, "Sorry, Liz. I just don't think you should have done that." Then he walked out the door.

Whether it was Brian's rejection, or Celia's anger, Liz found herself regretting her actions. The next day, she decided to try and make it up to Celia.

So before school started, she searched and found Celia huddled together with George and Allie in homeroom. They were talking in whispers, and Celia looked upset.

"Hey," Liz said, sitting down next to them. "Look, Seal, I'm sorry about—you know. Are you guys still talking about it?"

George looked up. "No, Liz," he said. "We're talking about something else." He glanced at Celia, who nodded. "It's Miranda," said George. "Seal found out that she's dating one of the guys in the school."

"Really? Who?"

"I don't know!" Celia said with some exasperation. "She just told me this morning, 'I have a boyfriend now and you can't do anything to stop me!'"

"Wow," Liz said. "That's not—too surprising, I guess. I guess I'm just surprised that it took so long."

"Up until now, I don't think she thought she could get away with it, but now that she knows…" And Celia trailed away, looking embarrassed. "She's thinking that the atmosphere in the school is about to change. And so she's going to change it."

"What?" Liz was confused. "Okay, well… wish I could help."

"Do you know who she's dating?" George asked.

Liz shrugged. "Miranda and I aren't exactly pals. But I haven't heard anything. You said she's going to get herself a boyfriend today?"

Celia spread her hands. "That's what she said."

"Well, I know it's not you, George, and it's not Brian, and—I'm going out on a limb here, but I'm guessing it's probably not James—so that means it's got to be one of the freshmen," Liz finished.

George put his head to one side. "I guess that makes sense. But it wouldn't be Athan, or Joey. I mean, they promised not to date, and I think they'd take it seriously."

Liz couldn't imagine Joey being serious, but she also couldn't imagine Miranda hitting on her chubby little brother. "Yeah, it does narrow the field. Come on, Celia, let's find out what's going on."

The first boy they saw was Kevin Snyder. He was pulling some books out of his locker, and he was pretty much all alone in the hall, so it was a good opportunity to confront him. Celia walked up to him and Liz followed.

"Hey, Kevin, I was wondering if maybe you could help me out with something," Celia began.

BAM! From the opposite side, Liz slammed the palm of her hand on the locker next to Kevin's head.

"Okay, Snyder, this is your last and only chance!" Liz snarled. "We know it's you so don't even bother to deny it!" She couldn't help but feel a little thrill when she saw the look of fear in his eyes. *Maybe I do intimidate them,* she thought.

"Look, Kevin, you're not in any trouble," said Celia gently. "We just want to know if maybe any of the boys have been talking? Maybe something about getting a new girlfriend?"

Ah, Celia's playing the Good Cop/Bad Cop thing. Okay, I can do this. "No, not in any trouble at all." Liz said putting as much menace in her voice as she could. "Just dating the principal's daughter. That's all." *BAM!* "Not smart, Snyder, not smart at all."

"Liz, you don't have to slam the lockers," said Celia. "And Kevin, I'm not accusing you of anything. I just want to know if you've heard any rumors."

"Uhhh… uhhh…" Kevin stammered.

BAM! "What do you know?" Liz barked. "Spill it!"

"I have no idea what you two are talking about," Kevin said meekly.

Liz was about to draw back her arm to slam the locker again, but Celia put her hand out and stopped her. "Okay, Kevin," said Celia. "We believe you." She pulled Liz away with the hand she had on her arm.

"Yeah, sure, Kevin. We believe you." Liz started walking away backward, glaring. "But we'll be watching you." She held two fingers to her eyes and then pointed those two fingers at Kevin in the universal I've-got-my-eyes-on-you gesture before Celia hurried her away.

"Hee! That was kinda fun," said Liz, once they were far enough from Kevin.

"Keep your focus, Liz," said Celia. "We're trying to get information, not become the school bullies."

"We gotta rattle their cages, Seal," said Liz. "You know how guys are. They always protect their own. They've got their good ol' boy club, and the only way to get them to betray their inner circle is to show 'em you aren't taking any guff."

"Let's just try it my way next time," said Celia. "You know the old saying, 'Catch more flies with honey than with vinegar?'"

"Not with this guy, you won't," said Liz, spotting their next target. "HEY, YOU!" she yelled as Mitch Wilson came out of the freshman homeroom. Mitch jumped six inches backwards, his tie flying. "WHAT'S UP WITH YOU TRYING TO DATE MIRANDA? You caving in? You breaking your dating promise??"

Mitch's eyes bulged out of his freckled face as Liz leaned into him. "I didn't!" he gasped. "I swear I didn't!"

"But you sure WANTED TO, didn't ya, Wilson?" Liz growled at him.

Mitch shook his head frantically and backed away from Liz. She looked around the room. The other freshmen boys in the classroom were staring at her with looks ranging from terrified (Chris Manzzini) to incredulous (Paul Wolczak) to hysterically amused (Joey: he knew she was putting this on).

"Look, I'm sorry," Celia said quickly. "I don't want to be giving anyone a hard time, but…"

159

Athan stepped into the classroom. "Um, Celia? George said you guys should come out here…" For some reason, Athan didn't appear to be either scared or snickering. He just shrugged his shoulder towards the door, and quickly vanished.

Liz and Celia, followed by the other freshmen boys, hurried out into the hallway, and beheld… Miranda. She was standing by her locker with a gleam of triumph in her blue eyes. One hand was locked possessively through a bemused J.P.'s arm. And, if any more evidence was needed, on his freckled cheek was a lipstick mark from Miranda's smirking red lips.

"There's your cave-in," Kevin Snyder muttered, and he walked away, after giving J.P. a dark look. The other freshmen boys trickled out of the hallway, leaving Celia, Liz, and George looking at Miranda and J.P.

"How could you?" Celia whispered.

"We've been over this before," sniffed Miranda with a toss of her ponytail. "You don't make the rules."

"It isn't a rule," said Celia.

"Seriously, J.P.?" said Liz. "She's like, three years younger than you! You're old enough to be…" She was about to say, *old enough to be her older brother*, but somehow that didn't really convey the sense of a dramatic age gap, and so she just trailed off.

J.P. just grinned sheepishly and looked away.

"You made the promise, too, J.P.!" said Celia, turning on him.

"I made the promise last year, with you guys," said J.P. defensively. "Miranda wasn't *going* here when I promised not to date anyone from this school."

"J.P., I can't believe you did this without even telling me!" said Liz. "Not to mention the fact that you're robbing the cradle! I mean, you were probably potty trained before she was even born!" *Nope, still not dramatic enough…*

"That's not true!" J.P. protested. "I wasn't… I mean…"

"C'mon," said Miranda, taking J.P.'s hand. "I gotta take care of some stuff before class." With a careless wave, she led J.P. away, and he seemed just as eager to go.

Celia was staring daggers after them. Finally she spoke. "If she wants to hate me, fine," she said with a trembling voice. "But why does she have to take it out on the school community? And right on top of…" She stopped talking and walked away.

Liz was still putting it all together in her head. "Um… Did J.P. just tell us that he wasn't potty trained until he was three?"

A few days later, J.P. stared at the muscular St. Francis figure painted on the wall and wondered how long it might take him to learn to paint like that. He'd finished up his business in the bathroom a while ago, and now he was checking out the picture, a habit he'd fallen into recently when no one was in there with him. He hated to admit it, but it was really good. Inspiringly good, even—if he forgot who painted it, and that it was on a men's room wall.

"Stupid Athan," he mumbled to himself. He turned around, and almost had a heart attack. Celia stood in front of the bathroom door.

"Aren't you even going to wash your hands?" she asked sternly, arms crossed.

"Celia! You can't be in here!" He tried to scoot past her, but she wouldn't budge.

"You've been avoiding me all week, so this is the only way I'm going to get to talk to you alone."

"Girls can't come into the boys' bathroom!"

"Oh grow up," she scoffed, rolling her eyes. "I've got brothers, you've got sisters. And no one else is coming in. I have George standing guard outside."

"Fine, fine. You got me, okay? We'll talk after school. I promise." He tried to move past her, but once again she blocked his path.

"No deal."

"C'mon! I said I promised!"

161

"Well, that's the problem, now, isn't it? You making promises and then not keeping them?"

J.P. sank against the wall, defeated. He'd been trying to avoid facing Celia for days now: he felt he had to get it over with. "Go ahead. Just make it quick; I already got a talking-to from my mother after you blabbed on me, so I don't really need another one."

"What did your mom say?"

"She said your dad didn't want me dating Miranda because your family doesn't allow dating." J.P. didn't mention that his mom clearly was resigned to the idea; she'd long ago realized that trying to get Flynn boys to not date in high school was like herding cats. "She told me I wasn't allowed to see her alone outside of school. But," he added, "She also said I could hang out with any of the kids here in groups, and that she can't stop me from liking someone. So, is your dad going to keep Miranda from going out with her friends?"

Celia looked a little uncomfortable, but pressed on. "Probably not. And I don't want to stop you from liking anyone either. Even if you made a stupid decision," she said under her breath, then continued, "but that's not the point. You made a promise, J.P., and you broke it."

J.P. didn't care—even if he knew, deep down, that Celia just wanted everyone to be happy. J.P. didn't care about being happy. He cared about kissing Miranda. "Yeah, well, I wasn't serious. None of us were." He nodded toward the door, where George was standing on the other side. "I know you have a thing for George…"

"*I* was serious!" Celia said. Her face had turned red, from anger or some other emotion, J.P. couldn't tell. "I'm not dating George! Have you seen us kiss? Or even hold hands? Have you seen us do anything other than act like good friends?"

The door opened a crack. "Hey, uh, lunch is gonna be over soon," George murmured, "and this is the only men's room in the school. I can't turn away everybody, so hurry it up in there, okay?"

"Sure, just a sec," Celia whispered, then pushed the door shut and turned back to J.P. "J.P., please! George and I have known each other forever and we're mature enough to handle what we're doing. But I know my sister, and she's not! She's only fourteen."

"She's...old enough to make her own decisions," J.P. said lamely. But he already knew that Miranda was kind of immature. Though he wasn't going to give in to Celia. "Just because you don't get along with Miranda doesn't mean you're right about her. You don't get to make decisions for other people."

"Arrrgh!" Celia slapped the wall in frustration. "Let's just drop the whole promise thing, J.P. Can't you see what you dating Miranda is doing to the school? This isn't some big public school where there's a huge population and everyone expects stuff like this. We're small, we're struggling, and individual decisions matter here! And it's going to get worse and worse! Because..." She bit her lip, hesitated, and then said again, "Please, J.P. Please! Between the pranking, and you dating Miranda, the school is suffering."

Even though he felt terrible now, J.P. didn't back down. He pulled open the door and shoved past George, then turned back. "Look, I'll... I'll talk to Liz, okay? We'll stop the pranks. But the rest isn't going to happen. It's not up to you. It's up to me and Miranda. You don't run our lives."

"Hey!" George called after him as he fled down the hall, but J.P. didn't turn back. *I faced down High Priestess Celia*, he thought, and felt a little smile growing. He couldn't wait to tell Miranda.

Liz decided to eat lunch outside. She wanted to review Allie's notes anyway, which she had recently scanned and uploaded to her phone. Now she could review them whenever she wanted. And she could add some notes of her own. *Someone from Shady Acres. That's what Megan said.*

It was a cold, dry day. Liz was just settling down on one of the picnic tables when she realized that she wasn't alone. Mrs. Summers' car was in the parking lot. She could just see the shapes of Mary and Jacinta's heads inside. More importantly, she saw Brian, talking to them through a passenger side window.

Bang. The double doors flew open, and Mrs. Summers stalked out, looking positively livid. Thankfully, she didn't notice Liz but went straight for her car.

Brian backed away from the car as she approached. Mrs. Summers said something to him — Liz couldn't hear what exactly, but it didn't sound nice — and then waved him away. Brian just stood there a few paces away, watching as Mrs. Summers got in the car, started it, and drove away.

What the heck was that all about? The Summers hadn't come to school at all this week, and now they come for just a few minutes?

Brian kept standing where he was, watching the trail of dust the Summers' car had kicked up. After a few moments, Liz started to worry about him. *Maybe I should say something...*

But at that moment Brian turned around, and saw her.

"Liz!" He walked quickly towards her.

She sat there, frozen. *Oh crap.* She had gotten so caught up worrying about him that she had forgotten to avoid being alone with him. Now it was too late.

"Um, hey, Burke," she mumbled. "Long time, no—"

"Can we talk?" he said tersely. "Please?"

18

SMASHING PUMPKINS

They walked around the school and towards the woods. "Where are we going?" Liz said.

"Somewhere private," he answered without looking back.

They took one of the many paths that crisscrossed the woods behind John Paul 2 High. This one happened to lead to a small clearing and a patch of rough grass and a log, only a hundred yards from the school. Liz glanced around, feeling a weird sense of déjà vu. She had been here before—when? And with who?

"Can you sit down please?" Brian gestured to the log.

Liz obeyed, feeling both nervous and depressed. She hadn't talked to Brian for a very, very long time. *Well, go on then*, she thought sadly. *Get it over with.*

Brian leaned back against a tree trunk, facing her. "Look," he said, clasping his hands together and glaring at the spot of grass between them, "I'm sorry. Okay?"

"Sorry?" Liz looked up, surprised. "For what?"

"Well, I must have done *something* to tick you off," Brian snapped. "Why else would you avoid me? Why else would you not talk to me for months?"

"I haven't been avoiding you," Liz stammered. "I mean, you're always with Mary—"

"Yeah, and whenever I want to talk to you, you always leave. You always run away before I can say a word."

"That's because I was mad at you," Liz mumbled. She didn't even think about lying to him. What was the point?

"Why?"

Liz stared at the ground. "Because you were dating Mary. Or hanging out with her. Whatever."

"I was *never* dating her! And you said it was okay to hang out with her!" Brian said indignantly. "You looked me right in the face, and you *told* me it was fine!"

"Um, yeah. I was lying."

"Lying?" Brian looked shocked. "*Lying?* Liz, why do you think I *asked* you?"

"I dunno," Liz muttered. "Look, Brian, I know I did some stupid stuff and you're mad at me so just yell at me and get it over with, and then we can go back to normal."

"Normal? You mean like, I'm with Mary and you ignore me?" Brian snorted. "Well, we can't go back to *that*, Liz. Mary's gone, and so is Jacinta."

"Yeah, I saw them leave."

"I mean they're *gone*, Liz, for good. Forever."

She looked up. "What?"

"Mary just came up to me, crying her eyes out," he said darkly. "She told me her mom was pulling them both out of school. And then her mom walked over and took her away. I tried to talk to her mom, but she didn't listen. She drove away. We'll probably never see them again."

"Oh," Liz said blankly. *She's gone. She's finally gone.*

She blinked several times. She felt like…a balloon. Full of air. Like she had just *stopped* choking. She felt *untightened*. Every muscle in her body seemed to unflex at once. "Huh," she whispered. "Wow. Didn't expect that."

And then she realized Brian was staring at her, his face showing outrage. "Liz?" he said sharply. "You…you're *happy* about this?"

She looked up at him, her mouth open, wondering desperately what to say.

"Liz, you…*gah!*" Brian threw his arms up in the air. "I am such an idiot! You planned this, didn't you?"

"No!" Liz shook her head. "No, I didn't!"

"Of course you did! You probably, I don't know, found ways to annoy Mrs. Summers, or spread rumors, or did *something* to make her hate the school, and then you started persecuting Mary, being *so mean* to

166

her day after day after day, insulting her and her family and her mother and you finished it off by squirting Mary in front of everyone—"

"I didn't squirt her because of that, I did it because—"

"And that was the last straw! Was it all calculated? Did you plan it all out? Huh?" Brian pointed at her, accusing. "How much work did you put into this? Why would you *do* this? What were you *thinking?*"

"*Shut up!*" Liz sprang to her feet. She had finally found her anger. She clenched her fists and stalked up to him. "Just shut up, Burke, and leave me alone!"

She got up to go, determined… and then looked around the clearing. She *had* been here before. She and Brian. They had fought… and then they had made up. Hadn't they?

Or was it all a dream? She was starting to think it was. She was starting to think that they would *never* make up. That this whole thing— their friendship, or whatever—was over. Forever.

"Liz," Brian took a deep breath. "Listen—"

"I didn't make the Summers leave," she snapped. "I didn't plan for them to leave. So just shut up about that."

"Then why did you lie to me?"

"*Because I had to!* Because you're not my slave! Geez, Brian, why did you even *ask* me? Why didn't you just do whatever the hell you wanted? That's what a normal guy would do!" She laughed bitterly. "But if you were a normal guy, I wouldn't have—"

"Do you like me? Is that what this is about?"

"No! You freaking idiot! I don't like you, I lo—"

She caught herself just in time. She turned away from him, heart pounding. *No. Don't say that. Don't even think that…oh, God, please don't let him think that I was going to say that. I can't let him see through me…*

"Fine," Brian said after a long moment. He sounded angry and resigned. "So you just wanted to be mean to Mary. Well, you know what, Liz? I don't want to hang out with someone like that. I don't want to be with somebody who's just mean to people for kicks." He took another breath. "So, I'll leave you alone now. And you leave me alone. I need space. Maybe we both do. Maybe…maybe that's for the best."

167

She could feel his eyes on her for a long moment. Then she heard him walk away.

She listened to his footsteps growing fainter and fainter, thinking desperately of how she could get out of this situation she'd created… how she could convince him that she wasn't that bad, that Mary totally deserved it, that she, Liz, was good enough for Brian, that she *needed* to be good enough, that she couldn't stand this, that she *wouldn't* stand it, that he belonged to her, *her*, and why couldn't he see that…?

But before she could say any of those things, his footsteps had faded away entirely, and she was left in the woods, in this clearing where something had happened once—and would never happen again.

Whatever it was.

She was alone.

Hey, Flynn!" Brad called J.P. over. It was Friday night, Sparrow Hills had won another football game, and J.P. was hanging out in the locker room with the team, feeling pumped up.

Brad gave J.P. a manly slap on the back while Flynt helped him take off the mascot costume. "Nice job out there tonight. You put on a pretty good show. I was looking to see if you're up for hanging out for a while with the team."

"Sure!" J.P. said happily. "Sounds good! What are we doing?"

"Just a little winning home game tradition of ours. Lots of us players will be there. You in?"

"Yeah!" J.P. glanced around, and realized he was the only JP2HS kid left in the locker room. George and the freshmen boys had apparently left. *Well, I guess they weren't invited…* He realized that for the first time, he had been picked out of the group to do something cool. *Him*, not George, not Athan. It was a good feeling.

Brad grinned. "Then let's go. J.P., you can drive. We need someone with a clear head behind the wheel, there and back. You don't mind, right?" He held out some car keys.

"Nope," J.P. said, taking the keys, "I just got my license. I'm good."

Flynt snickered. "Good. We need a DD. Gonna do some celebrating tonight."

Dyl, Fatty and X were all waiting for them near a huge black pick-up truck with a bunch of crates in the back, parked near a couple other cars full of football players.

Brad and Flynt climbed into the cab and a couple other guys jumped in the back with the crates. J.P. opened the driver's side door and stepped up onto the running board. This was a nice truck. And a *big* truck. He also noticed a few cases of beer on the floor at Brad's feet, unhidden.

"Whose truck is this?" he asked Brad curiously as he got behind the wheel.

"My mom's boyfriend's. It's all good though. He knows we're gonna be out late."

J.P. felt a little apprehension driving such an expensive truck, but that vanished when he hit the gas. This truck was awesome. He was soon on Sojourner Road, the other cars following along behind him. Flynt pointed. "Take a left. We're headed up to the old railroad bridge. You know where that is, right?"

J.P. did know, although he had never pulled in there. But he played it cool. "Who doesn't? We go there sometimes."

Flynt laughed and sparked a lighter in the cab, then lit up. "I didn't realize you Catholic school kids hung out at our bridge."

"Um, yeah, sure," J.P. said when he made the final turn toward the bridge down a dark, deserted stretch of road. A few moments later, the truck was parked on a gravel shoulder, and Brad and Flynt were piling out with the beer. The whole group went into the darkness.

"Do you always come up here after games?" J.P. asked the group as they started walking on the skeletal railway bridge that loomed out into the darkness, nearly a hundred feet over the road. You had to walk from one tie to another with an abyss yawning below you.

"Usually, if it's a home game we win," answered Dyl.

"So, pretty much all of 'em," said X with a grin and a grunt. He and a few other guys were lugging some of the heavy-looking crates from the back of the truck. Fatty was dragging two by himself, one with each hand.

The guys broke out the beer and started passing it around; when Dyl offered one to J.P., he reached for it eagerly, but Flynt barked, "Hey, morons, he's the designated driver!" And that was how J.P. found out what DD stood for. *Darn*, he thought. J.P. had drunk beer before—a little, at family dinners. Never out in the woods, and never more than a few swallows.

After a few minutes of watching the others have More Fun Than Him, it occurred to J.P. that drinking underage and sitting on a dangerous railroad bridge was probably illegal. When he mentioned it to Brad, the quarterback just snorted in derision. "The cops aren't coming out here, dude."

"How can you be sure?"

"Because they don't want to arrest the whole starting lineup of the football team. We're pretty popular around here, you know."

"Wait… really?" J.P. couldn't believe it. Was that really true? But then again, this football team was the only claim to fame this town had… and it explained why Brad and the others acted like royalty. *Imagine a life with no rules. What would you do?* He glanced at the crates, and was suddenly curious. "So what's in the crates?" he said.

"Go get the crowbar out of the truck bed, and we'll show you," said Brad. J.P. was kind of glad for an excuse to get off the bridge— with nothing to drink, his mind kept focusing on the hundred feet of air below them.

By the time he got back with the crowbar, some of the guys had lit up cigarettes. He could see the cherries glowing in the dark as he walked back.

"There's the man!" Brad said, holding up a beer as J.P. returned with the crowbar. He motioned to one of the crates. "Do the honors! Open it up!"

J.P. felt excited. He was finally being accepted as one of the guys. And not just any guys. Football players!

"Okay then!" He inserted the end of the crowbar into the crate and pulled back. It gave with a crack, revealing a whole lot of… *pumpkins?* Kind of rotten pumpkins, too.

"Heh," he said, a tad disappointed. "You guys must really like pumpkins."

"We chuck 'em," Dyl said. "My uncle grows them and he lets us take as many of the rejects as we want. Brad picked these up before the game."

Brad grabbed a large pumpkin from the crate and hefted it onto his shoulder like a shot-put. "Watch." He spun in a small circle and hurled it over the bridge's side. It landed quite a distance away with a satisfying splat. Flynt and the others followed his lead, raining pumpkins down on the road below.

"Twenty points if you hit a car," X called out.

J.P. blinked. "Has anyone actually done that?" He couldn't help imagining a pumpkin landing on his mom's car or something.

"Nah," Dyl said with a grunt as he pried open the other crates, "this road's pretty deserted—it's a dead end. I suppose it could happen though. You never know."

"Do you ever wonder who cleans up the mess down there?" J.P. asked. They all looked at him like he had two heads. *Right. No rules.* "I mean, who cares about the mess? Let them eat pumpkins, I say."

They threw pumpkins for a while, competing on who could throw the farthest. Fatty was the clear winner; he had the spinning throw down to a science. J.P. was dead last. Not only were his throws shorter than anyone else's, but one time he tripped and accidentally smashed his pumpkin into X's shoulder, splattering him. Luckily X had downed five beers by then and didn't seem to care.

"You're a strange dude," Brad laughed. "But you're growin' on me. So," he said as he picked up another pumpkin and chucked it, "what's up with that girl at your school?"

"What girls do you mean?" J.P. asked, suddenly feeling wary.

"That girl you were talking to the other day when I came to your school." Brad turned to him, a kind of sly smile on his face. "Are you guys going out, or what?"

"Heh. Yeah," J.P. said, "I think we are."

"You 'think' you are?" Brad said, thoughtful. "Huh. So you guys just hook up?"

"No!" J.P. said blankly. He knew what 'hook up' meant. "I mean... yeah, we're dating. It was kind of a big deal at the school."

"What, is it against the rules or something?"

"No, it's just..." J.P. sighed. How could he explain the whole messed up dating situation at John Paul 2 High? "Last year when there were only seven of us, this girl Celia and a few others came up with this stupid idea that we wouldn't date anyone at the school."

"Celia made that rule?"

"You know Celia?" J.P. said, surprised "Oh right, you met her at the school. Yeah, she came up with the rule, but a lot of people agree with her."

"Why?" They had walked off the bridge, and now Brad sat down near the lip of the ridge that led down to the road, leaving space for J.P. to sit next to him.

"Well," J.P. said, sitting down. "I guess... Celia's dad is the principal, so she kind of sees the school as..."

"She sees the school as her family, huh?"

J.P. was stunned into silence for a moment. "Yeah. I guess that *is* how she sees it. I never really thought of it that way before." *But it sure explains a lot*, he thought.

"So," Brad said, "then the girls figured it would be bad to date in such a small group, because a bad breakup would just make a bunch of cliques and enemies?"

"Well, yeah."

Brad shrugged. "Doesn't sound like a stupid idea to me."

"Re— really?" J.P. asked.

"Sure. I've seen bad breakups ruin all kinds of friendships. Devon over there," Brad pointed to one of the players on the bridge, "he was going out with Jacob's sister. Then when that blew up those two didn't speak to each other. That was two years ago, and they're still not right."

"Oh," J.P. had to think this over. He was surprised to find Brad on the "prudes" side of the question. "You know," he mused. "This all started after George and Allie broke up. After the dance. The same night as..." He trailed off uncomfortably.

"The shooting." Brad looked grim.

"Yeah." J.P. remembered it like it was yesterday. He had gone there with Courtney, who had dumped him that night. He vaguely recollected Brad and Madison going into the dance together, but he'd never heard Brad talk about it. J.P. suddenly remembered something he had overheard Madison saying, "How you ditched me at the dance." Did she mean THE dance? The dance where the shooting...?

"Hey," Brad said suddenly, turning to look at J.P. "Aren't you breaking the dating rule?"

"Well, sort of, I guess," J.P. said, even more uncomfortable.

"No sort of. You promised your friends you wouldn't date, and now you are. You quit once it got tough, and broke the rule."

"It's not a rule!" J.P. snapped, suddenly angry. "Geez. You were the *last* person I thought would lecture me on this."

They sat silently for a moment, listening to the other guys whoop and holler. J.P. brooded. He felt like Brad was messing with him. Brad wasn't supposed to care about this stuff. Brad wasn't supposed to make J.P. feel guilty. *That's* why he was mad.

Than an even more uncomfortable thought came: *That's what makes you mad? Feeling guilty?*

"Look," Brad said quietly, "I don't know what you've heard about me and girls, but I can guess."

"Listen, I didn't mean—"

"No, just... I want to tell you something. Whatever bad things you heard about me, it's probably right. I mean, I'm not even sure they're bad things. I'm not big on the whole 'good and bad' thing. But I mean *you* probably think they're bad things."

173

"Well, I don't know… There's such a thing as right and wrong, but… uh…" J.P. wasn't very good at this sort of thing. He kind of wished Brian were here. Or George. Or even Allie.

"I'm not dating Madison. We just hook up, that's all."

J.P. gulped. "You mean… for sex, right?" *Why is he telling me this? I don't want to talk about this.*

"Yeah," Brad went on, but now he sounded kind of defensive. "When we started hooking up, it was cool. We were safe about it, and everything. I mean she was the real safe one, you know? Always condoms. *And* her pills. She was real good at that part. So no worries, right? We're just together for fun, right? It's not like we're getting married or anything. I don't care."

"Uh huh," was all J.P. could think to say. To him, it sounded like Brad really *did* care, but didn't want to admit it. He felt, somehow, that the darkness around them was even darker than before. Almost pitch-black. He thought, suddenly, of how easy it would be for one of the guys on that bridge to slip and fall off, the others wouldn't even notice. It was that dark.

It wasn't safe. None of this was. J.P. felt like he should say, or do, something. But he didn't want to. That wasn't his job. There was always someone else who did the worrying and the thinking and the forbidding. But what if there wasn't? What if his life was like Brad's? He had always assumed that Brad's life was awesome. No rules. Fame. Sex. Lots and lots of sex. That must be awesome, right?

But Brad didn't sound like he even *liked* sex.

Brad seemed to sense his discomfort. "Hey, this isn't a problem, is it? I mean, I know you guys over there aren't into that… sex and all. And I know George is a pretty stand-up guy. So if you're, you know, inexperienced or whatever, I won't hold it against you."

"Oh. Thanks," J.P. grumbled. Then, before he could stop himself, he added, "If you think George is such a stand-up guy *because* he doesn't do that kind of thing, then why do you do it? I mean, if it's good not to, then why *do* you?"

174

Brad looked at him as if the answer was obvious. "Well, because it's fun, duh. And because I'm normal. You know, not religious or anything. I don't have all those rules. But George does, and I guess you do, so you should live by them."

J.P. knew what Brad was saying was bogus. But he also knew he didn't have any idea where to begin disproving him. So he didn't even try. Instead he tried to focus on Brad's problem with Madison.

"Look, if Madison's not acting like being… with you… is special, then maybe to her, it isn't. Maybe she thought it was going to be but then it wasn't, and then she had all this expectation built up and she's just disappointed with the whole process. So to her, that's all it is. A process. It's just a thing you do."

"Yeah! Yeah, that's how it seems to me, too. She's all messed up."

"Well, yeah, maybe, except you yourself said it *was* just supposed to be a thing you do for fun, right? But what if it's supposed to be more than that?" *Good, J.P.! He walked right into that one. We'll have this guy reading* Humanae Vitae *before the night is over! Then maybe he can tell me what it says, and do my homework.*

Brad looked at him seriously for a moment, opened his mouth like he was going to say something, then seemed to think better of it and settled back into his spot on the grass. "I don't know, man. On the one hand, it's just sex. On the other hand… I don't know. Maybe it's not. Sometimes I feel like it's not. I'm not saying it's wrong," he looked at J.P. very pointedly, "but maybe there's something else to it." He shook his head as if to clear it. "But for sure I think you're right about Maddie— it's definitely nothing but a time waster for her."

He had that dark look in his eyes again. "Sometimes I think everything is a time waster," he said. "Like there's no point to anything, you know? I mean, what does it all mean? What does anything mean?"

J.P. was trying to figure out what to say next, and had opened his mouth to say something when he looked at Brad's face, and felt that creepy feeling again. Like there was just something wrong inside Brad, something that was making him sick from the inside out. And that was giving J.P. a very bad feeling. So much that he couldn't think of what to do next.

Brad dug in his pocket. "Light up?" He held out an unlit cigarette in one hand. J.P. hadn't smoked since back when he was hanging out with Courtney. He still kind of craved it sometimes, even though he knew it was bad for him. *But hey, here's something cool and bad I can finally do.*

"Thanks," he replied, accepting the cigarette. "I need a break now, you know?"

"Yeah I do," Brad said as they walked off toward the truck and sat in the gravel near the front wheel well, leaning against the tire. The other guys had come off the bridge. Brad pulled another cigarette and lighter out of his jacket pocket, and lit up. J.P. flicked his lighter, and took a huge drag. This cigarette tasted different.

J.P. held his breath for a moment, then exhaled. "Huh. Different bouquet. Not bitter. More… plant-ey. I say, sir," he said in his best Stuffy Brit voice, "Good show. Very good show indeed!"

The other guys had come off the bridge. A few of them were starting a bonfire, using the broken-up crates as fuel.

Brad and J.P. watched in silence as the fire grew to a pretty good size and the embers floated up into the night air.

"You know," Brad said, "I got into football because it was fun, and I was good at it. Now I'm just in it because I'm good at it." He took another drag. "I'm starting to think that football is bull, too. Just like everything else."

J.P. tried to think of something to say, but for some reason, he couldn't quite find the words. Instead they sat by the truck in silence, both of them taking periodic drags and continuing to not say anything. J.P. bummed a second cig off Brad. Then a third.

"I want to tell you something else," Brad said suddenly. "Something weird."

"Uh huh," J.P. said. "What?"

"It's about this dream," Brad started, but then stopped himself. "Nah. You know what? Never mind. Forget it. Like I said, everything

176

is bull. Girls, football, everything. I used to have all these ideals, you know? But not anymore. That's all over."

"Nah," J.P. shook his head. "No way, dude. It ain't over." His head felt heavy, for some reason. Eventually the fire started to die down, but both boys just sat and listened to the sounds of the night, and of the other guys talking in the distance.

Eventually Brad broke the silence between them. "I wonder if it's finally done now?" he said laconically.

"Yeah," J.P. said. "Done." He wasn't sure what Brad was talking about. He was feeling... funny.

Dizzy. Sleepy. Happy? One of those dwarves, anyway. It was like he was there, but not. Like he'd fallen asleep for an hour and just half woke up, but it really wasn't more than a minute later. Or was it? He couldn't tell. He felt like he was looking out from inside his own head, but it wasn't his head. Or something. Whatever it was, it was funny.

"Hey, guys." It was Flynt. What was Flynt doing here? Oh, wait. He'd been here the whole time. He'd also just come up from in front of them, but somehow J.P. had missed it. He craned his neck to look up. Flynt was funny. And he looked like George a little bit. And James. Tall like George, bulky like James. Not fat though. Not fat like Fat James.

"Hi there, Mr. Muscle George," J.P. said, smiling. "Mr.... Mr. Skinny James." He chuckled.

Flynt stared at him. "Oh. Oh no. Brad!"

"What?" Brad said, turning toward him irritably. "Don't shout, dude. Don't shout."

Flynt pulled J.P. to his feet and looked him in the eye. "Aw, man, he's *totally* stoned!"

Stoned? J.P. knew what "stoned" meant. He'd never *been* it before, but he knew what it meant.

"Aw, man! He was supposed to be our DD tonight!" Flynt said angrily.

Brad looked up at him. "Nah, he's fine. J.P., you're fine, aren't you? Mostly?"

J.P. looked at Brad dumbly. Was he fine? Was he stoned? He sure felt like, if stoned was a thing, he might be it. "Yeah," he intoned. "Stoned." He was going to be in trouble. That was confusing. He sat down again, trying to figure out what he was supposed to do.

He only half heard Flynt arguing with Brad about… whatever. Brad was saying something about how he 'only had three.' Three whats?

Three joints. You smoked three joints tonight, dumbell. Not cigs. You're high. You're high on drugs. You're a drug user now.

"I'm a drug user now?" he asked out loud.

No one heard. Brad was standing up, looking for something. "Where are my keys? Oh yeah, you have them. You need to give them to Flynt."

J.P. fumbled in his pocket for the keys. Found them. Accidentally dropped them. Bent over to grab them and fell over. *I bet that looked funny.* He chuckled.

Flynt grabbed the keys off the ground. "You lucked out. I haven't had anything but half a beer. I'll drive you home." Then he turned to Brad. "Come on," he said, grumbling. "Guess I'm the DD tonight. We'll come back for the others later."

They climbed in the truck, with J.P. in the middle. Brad shouted something out the window to one of the other guys, and then they were off.

The ride back was a whirl of sound. Music and the truck engine and conversation all mixed together into a weirdly numbing cacophony that brought back that feeling of being there-but-not-there. The next thing J.P. knew, he was being led out of the truck (he tripped trying to step down out of the cab, scraping his hands on the gravel in the parking lot) and into Flynt's car.

The movement or the fall must have cleared his head a little, because he was lucid enough to hear Flynt saying to him, "Guess you stay clean, huh? Don't smoke your weed? That's smart."

"I've *never* smoked weed before. Nope. No weed. Never weed. Because it's bad." He looked Flynt in the eye. "It's bad for you, Flynt," he said as seriously as he could manage. "Don't smoke weed."

Flynt stared at him, and then snickered. "Um, yeah, sure. Like you really want people to not buy weed from you."

J.P. scoffed. "I'm not selling *weed*, Flynt. I don't even know what weed looks like! I mean I know what *weeds* look like; everybody knows what *weeds* look like. But not *weed* weed. Weed weed. Weeeeeeeed. That sounds funny. Ever noticed that?"

"But Brad said he gave you *all* the stuff," Flynt said, confused. "With the game suit!"

J.P. tried to focus on what Flynt was saying. "He didn't give my anything but the suit," he said drowsily. Man, was he tired! "He just put it in the trunk of my mom's Beemer."

"He put all the mascot stuff in your mom's trunk? Like, all of it?"

"Yup."

"Including four pounds of weed?"

J.P. smirked. "Nooo. No he didn't. Did he? Oh no." His smirk faded, then instantly reappeared. "Now *that's* funny."

"You know what?" Flynt said, "Let's go back to your place. Give me your address."

19

MAKE UP, MADE OVER

"Uuunnnnnhhhh."

"J.P., is that you? What are you doing down here?"

"Mmffph." J.P. rolled over on the couch and pulled the throw pillow over his head. He was in the basement. Apparently he had been lying on the floor. He felt like it, too.

"And you slept in your clothes? What time did you get home from the game?"

J.P. peeped one eye out from under the pillow and tried to focus. When that didn't work he tried to go back to sleep.

"Come on, lazybones. Get up!" His mom smacked him on the bottom. "It's almost 10 AM!"

"UUUNNNNNHHH," J.P. moaned loudly. But after another minute he did sit up.

Or attempted to. He only got about halfway when he immediately felt nauseous and vomited on the cement floor, then flopped back onto the couch.

"Oh dear!" his mother cried. "Oh, my baby! You're sick! Oh!" She ran to the bathroom and came back with a plastic bucket and a bunch of towels. "Here," she said, handing him the bucket, "if you have to do it again, do it in this." She started cleaning up the floor.

When she was done, she felt his forehead, then sat down next to him. "J.P., you were drinking alcohol last night, weren't you? *Weren't you?*"

"No," he said weakly.

"You promise?"

"Yes. I promise. No alcohol." *Well, that's true,* he told himself. *I didn't do any drinking.* "I swear on your grave, Mom. I swear. And Eddie's. And Patrick's. And Colleen's…"

180

"Good," she said, looking slightly more relieved, "because if you turn out like Eddie, I swear I don't know what your father and I would do. Are you hungry?"

He nodded. Despite feeling sick, he felt like he could eat a horse.

Five minutes later J.P. was alone in the basement under a blanket, a glass of water in his hand, wondering how exactly last night had ended. He remembered Flynt driving him home, but that was about it.

Eventually his mom brought down a bowl of chicken soup and crackers. "We can't trust your sick tummy with anything else," she said.

"Thanks," J.P. croaked, taking the bowl and gulping the hot soup down eagerly. It wasn't a horse, but it was something.

"All right. I love you. Just lie low and watch some movies." She kissed him on the head. "I'm picking up your dad in the city and we'll drive up to his conference. It's only two nights: we'll be back on Monday by the time you get home from school." She retreated up the stairs.

It wasn't until he heard her car pulling out that J.P. remembered that her trunk was full of marijuana.

Liz walked through the front doors behind a bunch of other students, avoiding eye contact with any of them. It was Monday morning, and she didn't want to be there. She wished she could skip. She *would* have, if she could summon the effort to do anything. But she couldn't—there was no point. There was no point to doing anything. All the crap she had been excited about—pranking, stupid secret investigations—it was all pointless. What did it matter if the shooter came back? Liz only hoped that he would shoot her first and put her out of her misery.

She had thought she would feel better after a few days. She didn't. She felt worse. She had spent the weekend in bed, or lying on the couch. She'd been positively savage to her brother and mother, only doing her chores grudgingly, and not bothering to do any of her homework. She had expected—no, hoped—that her mom would get mad and punish her or something—but oddly enough, her mom had just looked sad and concerned. Liz didn't know why. *I'm certainly not worth being concerned over.*

181

She walked over to her locker, opened it, and took off her black leather jacket. As she did so, she happened to catch a glimpse of her face in the mirror she hung on the inside door. She had bags under her eyes. Her skin was greasy and dull and pockmarked. Her perm had grown out, and her hair was lank and lifeless. *Ugly fat pig. Zero.* She felt her eyes get wet. Oh no, not again. Liz had been crying so much this weekend that she was thoroughly disgusted with herself. *Get over it, pig. You're ugly. No wonder he went for Mary…* That did it. She let out a sob, then slammed the locker shut, furious with herself. *Get over it.*

"Liz?"

Liz looked around. The hallway was empty except for Allie, looking her usual glamorous, gorgeous, grown-up self with long blonde hair and flawless skin. "What's wrong?" she said, looking concerned. "You need some help or something?"

"No," Liz mumbled. The last thing she needed was pity from Perfect Allie right now. "You can't help. It's not something you'd understand."

"Oh come on," Allie said gently. "Try me."

Liz laughed bitterly. "I just feel ugly, okay? Like I said, you wouldn't understand."

Allie gave her a sad kind of smile. "I do, actually." She thought for a moment. "Tell you what. About 11:45, meet me in the girls' bathroom, okay?"

"Okay," Liz mumbled. "Whatever."

"Come on. We're late for rosary."

W hat about you, Mr. Flynn?"

"Huh?" J.P. stared dumbly at Mr. Costain standing at the front of the classroom, chalk in hand. He had no idea what Mr. C. was asking him, or what the class had been talking about. All day his head had been filled up with worries. What if his mother opened the trunk? What if his dad recognized the drugs? His dad was giving a talk on the deterioration of Christian culture in America—J.P. could imagine him haranguing his audience from the lectern, brandishing the bag of drugs from the trunk…

"Well, Mr. Flynn?"

"Well… huh?"

"Can you name a reason the British were defeated in the American Revolution?"

"Um. Because… George Washington?"

George Washington was about the only thing J.P. could remember about the Revolution. Washington and fifes. And he was pretty sure the British didn't lose because of fifes.

Mr. Costain smiled a knowing smile, but wasn't ready to let J.P. off the hook just yet. "I see. Because George Washington. Can you perhaps be more specific?"

"Well, Washington was the… um… American general, and he was very… inspiring. He led his men in a bunch of battles and, and…" Something was coming to him. What was it Washington did with a river? And which river was it? "He crossed the Delmonico and attacked some Russians. Um… his men had fifes."

A snicker from Brian. Groans from everyone else.

"Not the answer I was looking for," Mr. Costain said, putting the chalk down and crossing his arms. "Anyone else?"

James raised his hand and provided what was probably a correct answer, but J.P. didn't care. He had already stopped paying attention again. As he had been doing since getting out of bed that morning, he'd spent the day freaking out, but trying not to *look* like he was freaking out.

He'd woken up to a text message from Brad asking him to turn in his "first profit." Unless this was an increasingly elaborate practical joke, Flynt hadn't been kidding about the marijuana in the trunk, and J.P. was in real trouble.

There was always the police, but that was another problem altogether. What if they didn't believe his story? What if they arrested him? Brad had said at the tracks that the police pretty much let the team get away with whatever they wanted. What if they just blamed it all on J.P., to keep the team image clean? What if he went to jail? Even his rascally brother Eddie had never been sent to juvey; J.P. couldn't imagine what *that* would do to his mother.

The end of class came and J.P. stumbled along to his next one, then the one after. He couldn't concentrate on anything; even Miranda talking to him in the hall didn't make him feel better.

"What is wrong with you? Are you even listening to me?" Miranda demanded. He suddenly realized she was right in his face, staring at him with her big blue beautiful eyes.

"No," he said, without thinking.

"Yah! Thought so!" she said, stamping her foot. With a toss of her ponytail, she went to walk with Kristy and Vivian. He didn't even try to stop her. *She's immature*, he realized. Just like Celia said.

But the realization didn't solve his problem. Soon he was so frazzled that he felt like he was about to explode. He had to do something. *Anything*. By the time the bell rang for lunch, he'd figured out what.

"Hey, Mr. Costain," he said. "Uh—I left something important at home. Can I borrow your car to go home and get it?"

Liz gritted her teeth, bent over her paper and thought as hard as she could. *Almost done... yes!* She wrote the answer down, stood up and walked over to the teacher's desk.

"I'm done," she said, slapping down the test paper.

"Already?" Mrs. Courchraine asked. She was a pretty, young mother who was subbing while Mrs. Flynn was away on a trip. "It's only 11:47; you have 12 minutes left. Are you sure you don't want to double-check your answers?"

"Nah, I'm sure they're fine," Liz said hurriedly. "Could I go to the bathroom?" She lowered her voice and leaned a bit, giving the impression that she didn't want Brian and J.P. to hear. "I kinda don't feel good, so I might be a while."

Mrs. Courchraine seemed to take the hint immediately. "Oh, okay," she said sympathetically. "Go ahead."

Liz walked out the door, inwardly thanking James that she was able to do algebra faster now. The hallways were quiet; everyone was in class. Whatever Allie had planned, she picked a good time.

Allie was waiting for her. She had set up a wooden chair facing the mirror, and she had some makeup spread on the bathroom counter. "Hey," she said as Liz walked in. "You're late."

"Sorry," Liz said. "I had a pop quiz. Um…is this what I think it is?"

"Yep," Allie grinned. "You said you felt ugly. I can help with that." She handed Liz a small squirt bottle of soap. "Go wash your face and then we'll get started."

Liz washed, dried with a paper towel and then sat down in the wooden chair. "So, um," She laughed awkwardly. "Are you sure you know what you're doing?"

"Trust me." Allie unscrewed a bottle. "It'll be fine."

Another worry struck Liz. "Wait! Don't make it too obvious! I don't *want* to look all made up, I'll look stupid—"

"Shh. Don't worry." Allie started daubing her cheeks. "We're just going to do some foundation, and concealer for under your eyes, and a bit of eyeliner. You're gonna look *fine*. Nice and natural."

Liz sat quietly and just let Allie work, hoping she knew what she was doing. Liz had only had a makeover once, at the same place where she had her perm and dye job. But she had paid for that one. She had never gotten a makeover like this—she never knew any girls well enough to ask for one.

"Have you done this before?" she asked.

"Oh, yeah." Allie was dabbing under her eyes now with stuff from a different bottle. "Me and Nikki used to give each other makeovers all the time. This concealer won't get rid of the eye bags forever, but it'll cover them up for the rest of the day." She picked up an eyeliner pencil. "Close your eyes."

Liz obeyed. *Why don't I have any girlfriends? I mean, real close girlfriends.* It had never seemed that important to her. Now she wondered what it was like.

She felt Allie working deftly with the eyeliner. *Maybe I should ask Allie what it was like, being friends with Nikki. Nah, she might run away crying or something. Why is she being so nice to me, anyway?*

"Okay, I think I'm done." Allie said. "What do you think?"

Liz opened her eyes and looked at her reflection. She looked pretty. Not made up at all. Just pretty. No pockmarks, eye bags or dullness. Her eyes looked brighter and bigger. She had jumped from a 4 to a 5. Get rid of the unkempt hair and she would jump to a 6.

She resisted the urge to touch her face. "Wow," she breathed. "Um…thank you. Thanks a lot."

Allie smiled. "You're welcome. Now put this on—" she handed Liz a tube of lipstick, "—and lose the ponytail. I'm going to peek outside to make sure we're still clear, and then brush out your hair." She walked out the door.

Liz puckered up and started applying the lipstick. It was the perfect shade for her—just a bit pinker than what her lips were already. *Allie's really thought this through.*

Feeling grateful, she decided to help clean up. She grabbed Allie's purse from the counter, and started shoving in lipsticks, sponges and bottles.

Allie came back in. "We're all clear. What are you doing?" She frowned at Liz, who happened to have her hand in Allie's purse.

"Just helping clean up," Liz said, "to thank you." She felt something in the purse—something smooth and metal, but too small to be lipstick. "What's this?" She pulled out the last thing she expected: a little brass tube.

"Allie," she said, confused. "Where did you get this from?"

"Oh that?" said Allie with some surprise. "I forgot all about it. It's nothing—just a memento. I think it's part of a church organ."

Liz stared at her in disbelief. Why would she think this is part of an organ?

"Why are you looking at me like that?" Allie laughed nervously. "I think it's just a metal thingy from a church organ. Maybe a knob or a button."

"How on earth did you mistake this for a metal thingy from a church organ?"

"Do you know what it is?" asked Allie

"How did you not know? Here, look," Liz turned the flat bottom of the casing toward Allie. "What does it have stamped on the bottom?"

Allie looked close at the tiny markings. "Umm...Nine. Em. Em."

"What does that tell you?"

"Uh... nothing? Is it a parts number or something?"

"9. M. M. Which means..."

Allie looked at her in incomprehension.

"Nine millimeter!" Liz said again, "As in 'nine millimeter handgun!'"

"That's a part to a handgun?" asked Allie.

"This is a bullet casing!"

"Why would a bullet need a casing?"

"It comes off when the bullet is fired." Liz was in amazement that Allie could have no idea what this brass casing was. "Have you never seen a gun fight in an action movie?"

"Right. My favorite genre of movie," said Allie sarcastically. "Just last night I curled up to watch..." She faltered for a few moments. "Uh...to watch *Shooty...Dead-Kill...MacSplosions.*"

Liz made a mental note to find out if J.P. had a movie camera so they could script and film *Shooty Dead-Kill MacSplosions* before saying, "You were researching guns all summer. You printed out pages and pages of guns from the internet. You had all these notes on them. And you still don't understand how a bullet works?"

"I was researching guns, not bullets! I was trying to find out what kind of gun he used! What did I care about his bullets?" Allie glanced down at the casing again. "Okay, I see it now. That's like the bottom half of a bullet without the little nose. I didn't know they were supposed to come apart like that."

"Yes! Of course they come apart! What did you think, the whole cartridge just goes flying out the barrel of the gun?"

"Well, duh. Of course that's what I thought. That seems way more common sense than assuming the bullet splits in two in the gun and only the nose half goes flying."

"And why on earth did you think this was part of a church organ?"

"Because I found it in a church!"

"What church? How did it get there?"

"Liz, do you want me to brush your hair out of not? It's still messed up. It doesn't match your face, and we are *running out of time.*"

Liz glanced at herself in the mirror. Allie was right. "Okay," she said grudgingly, and sat back down.

Allie pulled off Liz's hairband (a little harder than Liz thought necessary) and started brushing vigorously. She still looked annoyed—and a bit anxious. *There's a story behind this,* Liz thought. *But I have no idea what it is.*

A few minutes later, Allie put the hairbrush down and combed through Liz's hair one more time with her fingertips, tossing it lightly and bringing it down so it framed Liz's face. "I'd wear it like this. If I had some hairspray, I could have done it better. Is that good enough?"

Liz looked at herself in the mirror again. "Yeah," she said. "Allie, this is really good. I really owe you one."

"Good." Allie frowned. "Then maybe you can stop looking through my stuff."

"Your stuff?" Liz blinked. "You mean your purse? Sorry. I was just trying to help—"

"I mean my notes from my binder. The notes I threw away. You grabbed them out of the trash, didn't you?"

"Uhhh…" *Oops. Me and my big mouth.* "I may have taken a tiny peek in the trashcan after you left."

Allie's eyes narrowed. "A peek, huh? I think you actually stole them, and you've been looking over them."

"Now wait a minute! How could I have stolen it if it was in the trash?" Liz protested meekly. She could tell from Allie's clenched jaw that she was really angry, but restraining herself. And when she looked at her reflection, she felt kind of bad about it.

"Sorry," she mumbled.

Allie heaved a sigh. "Whatever. I don't care. Just don't do it again, okay?"

"Okay," Liz said. "Allie, um… thanks. Really. I mean, you didn't need to do this. So thanks."

Allie shook her head. "Don't worry about it. And let me know if you need anything else, okay? I mean it."

Okay, here goes nothing. J.P. parked the Costains' Volvo near the front doors, grabbed the uniform out of the box, and went through the entrance toward the gym.

When he rounded the corner of the Athletics wing hallway, J.P. bit back a curse. The assistant coach, Mr. Abernathy, was still in his office. He had been hoping he could leave the mascot uniform with a note that said, "Sorry, I quit," but that wouldn't happen now. Before he could retreat out of sight, the coach saw him and waved him in.

Nervous, J.P. waved back and furiously racked his brain for ideas as he walked in. After all, he couldn't exactly tell Abernathy that he was quitting because drug dealers were after him, but he didn't have any other good reason. Except that the priest he had gone to confession to on Sunday (right after Mass) had told him he should quit. But he couldn't exactly say that to the coach either.

"Hey, Mr. A," J.P. said, traipsing into the room and dropping the uniform on a chair. "Here's the suit like you wanted."

"Thanks. Wait, what?"

"The suit. The mascot suit. You wanted the mascot suit."

"What? I never said that."

"I heard you wanted the mascot suit."

"Who told you that?"

J.P. shrugged. "Someone. One of the guys on the team, maybe. Maybe not. Probably not. I don't know. Anyway, it works out fine because I was thinking of quitting anyway."

"What? You're quitting? *Why?*"

"Oh, a bunch of reasons," J.P. said. "They don't matter though. I wasn't sure, but when I heard from whoever that you wanted the suit, I figured it was important. So this works out for both of us." *Don't look him in the eye. Keep moving around the room.*

"But I never said I wanted it back!"

"Well, then, why would anyone have said you did?" J.P. replied, moving near the wall and running his finger absently along the school plaques and pictures hanging there.

"I don't know!"

"I don't know either," he said, stopping near the door. "Because I know it wasn't a prank because I'm really good at them, so it can't be that."

"You're good, that's true, but..." Abernathy sputtered.

"I know it's true, but thanks for saying so."

"You're... you're welcome, I guess."

"Great! And I know you don't not want me to not leave the suit here, but that's OK, because here it is, like someone wanted."

"Now wait a minute—"

"It's OK," J.P. said, backing out of the room. "I don't mind. It's kind of dorky being the mascot anyway."

"Well, sure, a little," Abernathy said, looking confused.

"Great!" J.P. exclaimed. "We agree!" He turned to go, then turned back. "And thanks again for being so understanding, Mr. A. You're a great coach!"

"Thanks Flynn, but—"

"No problem!" J.P. shouted over his shoulder as he ran down the hall. *One part of the problem solved...*

But now he had to go back to school. And he honestly wasn't sure what he was going to be doing next.

20

DANGEROUS

This time when the school bell rang, J.P. didn't jump up. He just sat there, wondering if this was going to be his last day at John Paul 2 High. Or worse, his last day on earth. *If it is, I've spent my life in a really stupid way,* he couldn't help thinking. For a long time, he just sat there, watching the other kids get up from their desks, mill around, talking.

Mr. Costain got up, stacking together his papers. Behind him on the board, there was another one of those Greek words written: EROS. J.P. vaguely recalled that today's lecture had something to do with that. Romantic love. J.P. turned his head slowly to look at Miranda, but she was already leaving, slinging her bag over her shoulder and chattering to Kristy, flipping back her dark curly hair. She had really beautiful hair. She really *was* beautiful, even if she didn't really care much about him after all. And J.P. reminded himself that the entire reason he'd done most of the stupid stuff he'd done—the stuff that was probably going to get him killed by drug dealers, was because he wanted to kiss Miranda.

His eyes traveled back to the blackboard. Again, Mr. Costain had written the word POWERFUL on the board. And next to it, DANGEROUS. J.P. was getting the idea that love was a really dangerous thing. It got you in trouble. It messed up your plans.

He looked up at the crucifix over the board. Yep, even Jesus got in trouble because of love. That's where it all ended.

He felt sick. He got up, but no one said to him, "Are you ok, J.P.?" Someone should have, but no one did. He felt like he was at another one of his family's massive reunions—seventy-five loud people in one house, everyone talking at the top of their voice, no one paying attention to him. That was pretty much his whole life.

As he walked out through the door into the hall, most of the other students had left, except for one girl who was standing at her locker. One of the freshmen. As he passed her, he noticed something about

191

the way she was standing. Her shoulders were slumped in such a way that J.P. guessed that she was crying, or had been.

He stopped, but wasn't sure what to do next. He never knew what to do when girls were crying. And this was Isabel, the Mexican girl with the messy hair and the guitar.

She turned to go and saw that he was looking at her.

"You okay?" he asked, and his voice sounded far away to him.

She nodded, and then shook her head, and her face kind of crumpled. "I miss Jacinta," she said. "She was really my only friend here. No one else here likes me."

"That's not true!" J.P. said. "Man, that's not right... I mean, what about Liz?"

Isabel's face hardened. "Liz? She hates me! That's why everyone else has been so mean to me! She made fun of..." she trailed off and shook her head. "No, I was just dumb. I'm never going to do that again."

"Do what?" J.P. asked, wondering if he were still a little stoned.

"Not play my songs for people, ever again." Her shoulders slumped. "I thought this school would be different, but it's just like everywhere else after all."

Sadly, she closed her locker. "I gotta go," she said. "See ya." And she walked off.

J.P. stood watching her go, and suddenly he felt sadder about Isabel than he did about anything else. It actually made him feel better, for a few minutes.

He walked outside. Isabel's mom had picked her up. All the other kids had gone. He vaguely remembered that Celia had taken Miranda out grocery shopping or something. Only Liz was in the parking lot. Her shoulders were hunched against the cold wind, but he realized that she looked... well, cool, somehow, in her black leather jacket, with her dirty blond hair blowing in the wind. Like a female spy or something.

He didn't think she was the kind of person who would want to see a girl like Isabel crying into her locker and vowing to never play guitar again. But he didn't quite know how to bring that up.

"Hey, Japes," she said as he came up. "What's going on?"

He didn't know what to say. Mrs. Simonelli banged out of the school then, and Liz strolled over to the car, lifting up her hand for the car keys. "Hey, Mom! I got this!"

"Hey, Liz—" he started to say. "Do you need to go somewhere?"

She swung around to him, her hair swishing around her face. He couldn't figure out why she looked so good. Was it her hair? "Yeah, I do. Library. Tutoring with James."

"Oh."

"Why? Do you need something?"

"Nothing," J.P. swallowed. "Well…" He glanced at the cell phone, wondering if he should tell her about Brad's text.

Just then another car pulled into the lot: his mom's BMW. His mom waved cheerfully at him as she pulled into a space.

"Hi Mom!" He practically bounded over to meet her.

She got out of the car, ruffled his hair, felt his forehead, and then looked at him suspiciously. "You look happy to see me!"

"I—I am! Did… did you and Dad have a good time?" *If she saw the drugs, she'll say something right away.*

But she just smiled. "Oh, we had a wonderful time. Your father's talks went very well. They usually do. Oh, and your dad said…" She got her purse out of the car. "He said he hopes you're feeling better. I'm just going to get my teacher's manual so I can go over next week's lessons. Are you coming home with me or going home with one of your friends?"

"I—"

"Well, let me know by the time I come out," she said, kissing him and bustling inside. He saw Liz wave as she got into the driver's seat and slammed the door. The Simonellis drove away.

J.P. was alone in the parking lot, looking at the BMW. Took a deep breath. Walked to the back of the car.

With exaggerated casualness, he popped the trunk, but didn't see anything obviously out of place. He stacked the books, but they weren't hiding anything. He dumped out the plastic bags, but they were only full of odds and ends meant for the charity donation center. He rummaged through the no less than three different gym bags in there, all full of nothing but his parents' gym clothes.

Wha... There's nothing here.

Moving as much to the side as he could, he lifted the flap and pressed wood board that covered the spare tire. Under the board he found the spare tire, a jack, and nothing else.

J.P. slumped to the ground. Surely, if his mom had found it, she would have asked him about it. Even if—well, *especially* if she didn't know what it was.

It's not here. There's nothing here. Where in the world did it go?

He felt dizzy with one kind of relief and sick with another kind of realization. But before he could sort out exactly what to do next, a big black pickup swung into the parking lot.

Brad stuck out his head and waved jauntily, but his eyes were dark. "Hey! Get in! We need to talk." He was grinning his goofy surfer-dude grin, but he didn't seem inclined to take no for an answer.

After Liz's mom had dropped her off at the library and driven away, Liz made for the doors. She grabbed the handle of the closest one and tried to pull it open, but to her surprise, it was locked firm.

"What's going on here?" she asked herself and went around to the other door. A couple quick jerks confirmed it was locked as well. She went around again, this time to cup her face with her hands and press up against one of the windows, trying to see if she could spot anyone inside.

"You should try reading signs," said a voice immediately behind her. This startled Liz. She jumped and turned to see who was speaking.

"Oh, hi, James," Liz sighed in relief. "They locked us out."

"Yes, I know," said James. "They left a note telling us so." He gestured toward the main door, the first door Liz had tried to open.

Liz went back to the door, and this time she noticed a flier taped to the inside of it. She pulled out her keychain flashlight J.P. had given her for her birthday a couple weeks ago, and read:

Due to budget cuts passed by the Sparrow Hills Municipal Council this past June, the William Pitt Memorial Library will no longer be open on Mondays. We apologize for the inconvenience.

"What?" cried Liz. Then she cupped her face to the glass door, trying to see through the reflection into the darkened building. "Hey! Is someone in there?" She yelled and started banging on the glass with her fist. "You can't close! Mondays are our study day!"

"Looks as though they just moved our study day," said James. "I guess we meet on Tuesdays from now on."

"That's fine for next week," said Liz, still looking through the glass in the vain hope that someone might be inside. "But this week I need help with work I'm supposed to turn in tomorrow."

"Okay, so this week we can meet at your house," said James.

Horrified, Liz pictured in her mind the scene of doing algebra with James as her mom hovered over them, making her comments every time she messed up and James had to correct her.

"I've got a better idea," said Liz. "Look around for a big rock, and we can break this glass…"

"Miss Simonelli," said James. "I am not going to help you break windows. If we can't use your house, then—"

"Then… we can use *your* house!" said Liz with sudden inspiration.

"I don't know if that's such a good idea," said James.

"Why not?" said Liz. "I've never even *seen* your house. C'mon!"

"I'd really rather not," said James sullenly.

"Why, James?" said Liz silkily. "You're not hiding anything from us, are you?"

"No," said James defensively.

"What am I going to find there?" taunted Liz. "Now you've got me all suspicious."

"Leave it alone," grumbled James.

"What's the big secret at your house? Are you running a meth kitchen?"

"I said—"

"I've got it! You're secretly a brony!" said Liz triumphantly. "You don't want me to see your bedroom's full of lil' pretty pony toys!"

"Okay! Okay! I'll do it! I'll let you study at my house!" cried James in defeat.

Liz and James walked to James's car, and Liz opened the passenger side. The seat and floor were stacked with books and papers. From the driver's side, James began clearing the seat for her, tossing the junk in his back seat. Liz helped by grabbing a stack of books off the floor. She was about to drop them in the back when one of them caught her eye. It wasn't a school book, and it wasn't one of James's horror novels. The cover showed a police mug shot of a man, and the title printed above the mug shot was *Justifiable Murder*.

Before she could look more closely at it, James rudely snatched it and the other books out of her hands and thrust them in the back seat.

"Your seat is clear," he said gruffly. "You can get in now."

Liz got in and rode in silence to James's house. *Maybe this wasn't such a good idea…*

Brad had parked in an empty lot behind a dilapidated old factory, the abandoned one on the edge of town with the smokestacks that made a creepy silhouette against the dim sky. The whole factory complex was far back from any main roads J.P. was aware of, surrounded by forest. It could only be reached by a long industrial road with no turn-offs or other buildings, just a straight shot from the intrastate highway to the lot. Until Brad had brought him out here tonight, he'd had no idea how to reach it.

"Well, he'll be here in about fifteen minutes," Brad said, "So let's get everything figured out before then."

"Wait, what? Who'll be here?" J.P. asked.

Brad scowled at him. "My supplier. Come on, J.P., you know how this stuff works. Who did you *think* we were meeting out here?"

J.P. felt the blood drain from his face. "Your supplier? *That's* why we're out here?"

Brad looked confused. "Why would I drive us all the way out here just to talk? We could have done that in your driveway." Brad's eyes narrowed. "Wait, you didn't forget the money, did you?" He leaned in slightly closer to J.P. "Please tell me you didn't forget the money."

Sweat broke out on J.P.'s brow. He had no words. He was caught up between the idea of lying and saying he *had* forgotten the money, and just telling the truth. But he knew the lie would only buy him a little time, and might make things worse. Although, how things could be worse than meeting with two drug dealers after dark in the middle of nowhere when they expected either money or drugs and he didn't have either one, he couldn't imagine.

"Look Brad—" he started.

Brad shook his head. "No. No no no. Oh no. You are not going to tell me you don't have the money." Suddenly the demeanor J.P. was so used to seeing on Brad's face, the cocky, friendly, kind of unfocused goofball look, was gone.

In its place was something else. Someone else. "You better not be trying to rip me off," Brad said with menacing slowness, a quiet threat dripping from every word. "Because I don't have the time or the patience to put up with any crap from you." He lurched forward suddenly, grabbed J.P. by the collar, and shoved him hard up against the passenger door. "*Where. Is. My. Money?*"

"I don't have it! I never did! That's what I wanted to talk to you about!" J.P. had turned his head away and closed his eyes reflexively when Brad had gotten in his face; now he cracked one eye to see if a punch was coming.

It was.

J.P. had been punched before, and as punches went, this one wasn't so bad. It was what he called a "soften you up" punch, one that caused just enough pain to promise even more pain in the very near future. The kind he'd received many times from his brothers when they were trying to intimidate him. It always worked for them, and it worked even more for Brad now because J.P. knew, in his heart of hearts, that his

197

brothers wouldn't actually kill him and stuff his body in the cold, dusty black furnace of an old factory smokestack.

Brad seized J.P. by the lapels of his winter jacket and got right into his face. "I don't want to *hear* that, J.P. I want to hear that you have either my money or my supply, and if I don't hear one of those things, then—"

Brad didn't get to finish. When it came to "fight or flight," J.P. was firmly in the "flight" camp, and in his panic he'd managed to reach behind himself and pull the door latch. The passenger door swung wide and spilled the two boys onto the pavement.

It was a relatively high drop, and a lucky one for J.P. He managed to twist on the way down, more of a scramble than an actual attempt to escape, but his reflexes kicked in so that he tried to breakfall on his front, turning Brad so that the larger boy hit the pavement first.

Brad cursed as he fell, the breathe whooshing out of his body as he landed. J.P. rolled off and got to his feet. But Brad wasn't a star quarterback for nothing. He grabbed J.P. by the ankle and sent him sprawling to the ground. By the time J.P.'s eyes had stopped spinning, Brad was standing over him, fist brandished. J.P.'s self-control snapped, and he went into full-scale panic mode as Brad grabbed his shirt collar.

"Start talking," Brad said.

"You think I'm a drug dealer?" J.P. yelled. "You think I was trying to get into selling drugs? I had no idea that's what this was all about!"

"Oh come on!" Brad hissed. "No one's that dumb!"

"I am!" yelled J.P. He frantically searched for something, anything, to say that might buy him some time to think, or to change Brad's focus. He quickly settled on something. Not a good something, given the circumstances, but something. "Well, if we're asking questions, I have just one to ask you."

Brad drew back his fist. "It had better be a good question and not a dumb one," he said.

J.P. braced himself for the coming punch. This one was NOT going to be a soft one. He squeezed his eyes shut and yelled, "Where were you the night of the Sparrow Hills shooting?"

Nothing.

Except that Brad let go of him.

He cracked open his eye. Brad had staggered back, and was staring at him.

J.P. saw his chance. *Run now!* His brain was screaming. *Shut up brain! I need to know the answer to this!*

"Why?" Brad asked. "Why do you want to know?"

J.P. felt his palms sweating. "Well, you know… it's kind of like, everyone knows just where they were when the Twin Towers fell down, or when JFK was shot… so… where were you when the shooting started?"

Brad turned his dark eyes towards J.P. and J.P. felt sick. Where *was* Brad on the night of the shooting?

"What kind of game are you playing here?" Brad almost whispered. "Has this whole thing been a set up?"

J.P.'s heart was beating fast; he wondered if he was close enough to the highway to make a break for it and frantically hitch a ride before Brad could run him down. Not likely.

"No games, Brad! Really!" he said, holding up his hands. "Just a question. My friends and I, we've been poking around. The case against Brock has some holes in it. And Madison said you ditched her the night of the dance. I guess it was a dumb way to spend my time. You know, considering my apparent life expectancy… at this moment…"

Something seemed to snap inside Brad. "You're right about that," he said, jerking his head around. "Ok, explain, and explain fast. So what are you trying to tell me? You guys were investigating and that's why you wanted to be the mascot? You didn't know that the mascot's the one who sells drugs?"

J.P. shuddered. "No! I had no idea."

"But that still doesn't explain why you don't have the stuff, when I know I put it in your mom's trunk."

"Heh," J.P. stammered, "Yeah, that's… that's funny. I didn't even know they were in there. My mom's been driving around with a couple hundred dollars' worth of pot in her car."

"Try a couple thousand." Brad checked his phone's clock. "And talk faster."

"OK, OK. So the night I went out with you guys to the tracks, that was my first time ever smoking weed. When Flynt drove me home he figured it out, and then started grilling me about the drug selling stuff, and when he figured I didn't know what he was talking about, he told me the truth. But, uh… when I checked the next morning, all the stuff was gone! My mom had cleaned out the trunk, I guess."

Please, Lord. Please please please please please. I can't die out here. That's not what you made me for, is it? To die in an abandoned coal factory parking lot? No, it's not! Please don't let me screw this up any more. J.P. got ready to take off for the tree line though, just in case God wanted him to run for his life.

"All right. I believe you, but now we've got a bigger problem," Brad grabbed J.P.'s arm, hurried to the truck and threw open the door. "Get in here. Now." He shoved him into the truck. J.P. let himself be shoved.

"Are we leaving?" J.P. asked.

"No chance. My guy will be here any minute and even if I drive with the lights out, he'll know it's me if he passes us on the road."

He started the truck again without lights on, and drove slowly toward the factory itself. "You'd better pray one of these things is still unlocked."

There were a row of garages behind the factory, and Brad pulled up to the third one, got out, and motioned J.P. toward the driver's seat. "When the door's up enough, just pull in."

J.P. slid over and grabbed the wheel. Brad lifted the door about two feet off the ground and propped it open with an old tire lying beside it. Then he crawled under. A few seconds later the tire fell over as the door slid the rest of the way up. J.P. cringed at the sound it made, but soon enough he was able to drive the pickup into the dark rear of the factory floor.

Brad shut the garage door. "Kill the lights and get out of there."

J.P. did as he was told, but they were in total, complete darkness. He had always been afraid of the dark. "Um. Now what?"

"Now we wait," Brad whispered. "But we need to make our way toward the front windows over there, so we can see when he pulls up and when he leaves."

"Oh, I have a flashlight on my keychain," J.P. said proudly, producing the keys.

Brad swiped the keys from his hand and turned on the flashlight. "Follow me." He led the way to the windows, keeping the beam of light toward the floor so they could see all the old bits of machinery and other detritus that littered their path. When J.P. realized some of it was pieces of the ceiling, he looked up and realized he could see the darkening sky through the holes.

"This place isn't going to collapse on us or anything, is it?"

"No."

"How do you know?"

"Because it hasn't yet."

"How about asbestos poisoning?"

"Don't know. Don't care. Shut up."

"Well, I tried to warn you 'asbestos' I could."

Brad just held up a fist. J.P was quiet again until they reached the large windows near the front of the factory. They were at least ten feet high, with many broken panes. "So...who is this guy we're waiting for anyway?" he whispered.

Brad looked at him strangely, then said, "Someone you wouldn't expect. Now stop asking questions. If he hears us, we're screwed."

J.P. gulped, then nodded. They turned off the flashlight and settled themselves in for a wait; the windows came down so low the boys could sit on the floor and still see out without craning their necks. Soon enough the hum of an engine could be heard, and then J.P. saw headlights, followed by a four-door car of some kind. Someone stepped out, and leaned against the car with his arms folded.

Whoever it was, was almost a hundred feet from the factory. J.P. couldn't make out any features, except that it was someone about George's height, wearing a cap and a trench coat. *The perfect image of a shady drug dealer. The movies were right!* They watched as the guy started pacing, then pulled out his phone.

Suddenly J.P. could hear rap music coming from somewhere. It sounded muffled, but not muffled enough. Brad yanked his phone from his pocket.

"Shhhh! Shhhhhhhh!" J.P. hissed at Brad as the older boy frantically fumbled at the volume slider, trying to turn it off. That wasn't fast enough for J.P.—in a near-panic, he snatched the phone from Brad's hands, dashed it on the ground, and smashed it with a large piece of concrete.

Brad stared murder at him in the darkness, but J.P. pointed at the phone, which was now silent, and held out his hands as if to say, "Hey, at least it worked." Then he held a finger up to his lips, and nodded his head toward the car.

The supplier glanced around, then tried his phone again. Thankfully Brad's phone didn't ring; J.P. must have smashed it pretty good. He could very vaguely hear the angry tones of a male voice floating on the air from the direction of the car.

After what seemed like forever (and two more phone call attempts), the supplier got back in his car, slammed the door, and sped off down the road. He didn't even bother turning off his headlights.

"That was a $500 phone," Brad growled when the dealer was gone.

"Sorry," J.P. said, taking the flashlight back from Brad and standing up. "I'll try to find the money to buy you another one." He was still pumped with adrenalin from the close call. "So… where *were* you on the night of the shooting?"

21

SHADY ACRES

Liz hummed a little tune to herself. She was in a good mood; she had often wondered what James' house looked like and now she was going to find out. Would it be a castle? A big gothic mansion? An underground bunker? Probably not—but what if it *was?* She started banging out a beat on her legs to go with the tune she was humming.

"Will you stop that racket, please?" James said sharply.

"Oh! Sorry."

"Would you like me to put on some music?"

"Sure! Pump up the jam!"

James switched on the car radio. Some classical music started playing. Liz groaned. "Really? James, that is the exact *opposite* of pumping up the ja—Hey, wait." She had noticed something. "We just passed Buffalo Bill's!"

"What?" James said sourly.

"You know, that restaurant back there. I went there with my dad awhile back, and we met Megan Br—" Liz stopped herself.

"Who was that you said?" James gave her a sharp look.

"Megan…Brock," she said awkwardly.

"Oh…" James said in a cold sneering voice. "Oh, I know about *her*. Unwed mother, sister to the late unlamented Brandon Brock." James snorted as he made a left onto Pottstown Lane.

"Oh, well, um…" Liz trailed off awkwardly. Time to change the subject. "Hey, are we heading for West End?"

"Yes."

"Why?"

"Because that's where I live."

"Oh," Liz said blankly. "That's… nice." *James lives at West End… and he knows about Megan Brock. Does he live near them?*

"Miss Simonelli," James said. "Is something bothering you?"

"No!" Liz said. "Nothing!"

Actually, she was excited. If James knew the Brocks personally, that may mean that he *lived* near them, and that meant he would know all about the neighborhood where the real shooter lived. Liz couldn't believe her luck—James could be the source that helped her get the final piece of the puzzle!

It could still be nothing, of course. After all, the Brock family was infamous now, so it made sense that James had heard of them. Nothing unusual there. And thousands of people probably lived in that part of town. It didn't mean that James lived anywhere near the actual neighborhood, Shady Acres.

But Megan had said something about the real killer being a Shady Acres kid, so if James was familiar with the neighborhood, she might have her lead, after weeks of nothing! No matter how reclusive James might be, he must have interacted with the other kids in that neighborhood. Heck, he might have even known the real shooter and not known it.

For the next ten minutes she plotted about how to interview James without it actually *looking* like an interview. Just in case.

They eventually turned onto an unfamiliar road and drove awhile longer, until finally the car slowed down and James put on the turn signal, across from an old dirt road that the road sign identified as "Dunhallow Crossing." Liz glanced at another sign ahead, off the side of the road where they were turning. It was the kind of sign they put in front of suburban developments to give them fancy names. The sign was in pretty rough shape though, all weather-beaten with letters missing. It said:

Welcome to

SH- -Y AC- ES

"a n-ce place t- settle do-n"

"So this is where you live, huh?" she said. *This must be the back entrance to the neighborhood.*

"No. I'm just stopping by to visit."

Liz almost said "Really?" before she caught the heavy sarcasm in his voice. *He does live here. I can't believe it.* "Okay," she said, deciding to play dumb for now. *I need to figure out how to start the conversation.*

James drove for a little while longer, past houses new and old. The new ones looked unoccupied, and the old ones were generally in disrepair. It made Liz feel sad and lonely, even though she was with someone. Finally, James stopped the car close to a silver Toyota Camry that was parked outside a single-story brick ranch house. There was a space between the Camry and another car parked in front of the next house down. James tried parallel parking in the space, but gave up after two or three tries. "I don't have room," he said finally.

"Park on the other side," said Liz helpfully.

"I'll block the driveway if I do that," said James. Instead, he wheeled the car around to the opposite side of the street and parked there. "The neighbors hate it when I park on their side, but they'll just have to get over it."

Liz and James got out of the car and crossed the street to the brick house. The yard was overgrown, full of weeds, and encircled by a rusty chain-link fence. The Camry was parked right in front of the gate and walkway to the door.

"This is a terrible place to park. Why'd your parents block the gate and leave you no room?" said Liz.

"It's not my parents' car," said James quickly.

"It's not? Then who's parking right in front of your walkway?"

James was already walking toward the door with his back to Liz. "It's Tyler's," he said over his shoulder without looking at her.

"Tyler Getz?"

"Yes. That's Tyler Getz's car parked in front of my house." James sounded irritated. "The Getzs' live in Shady Acres, too."

"Yeah," Liz said to herself. "I know." She followed James to the front stoop where he was fumbling with a big ring of keys, trying to find the house key. "So, do the Getzs' live on this street?"

"Yes, right up there." He pointed to the next house down.

"Well, who dropped the car off? They didn't do a very good job."

"I have no idea. Whoever drops off cars after someone gets shot." James was struggling to find the right key on his massive key ring. His apparent agitation was making it harder.

Now that Liz thought of it, he had seemed to get agitated as soon as he had seen the Camry. Tyler's Camry. And that brought up something she hadn't thought of until now.

Brandon and his friends must have beaten up every kid within a ten-mile radius of our house, Megan had said.

Did that include James? *How can I bring up the subject?*

"You sure gotta lotta keys," she said after a few more seconds of watching him fumble.

"I work a lot of odd jobs after school," said James. "Most of these keys are for jobs." He started to examine his keys again, when he stopped and put his hand experimentally on the doorknob. He twisted it, and the door opened. "Of course," he said. "Unlocked the whole time." He entered and Liz followed.

Once inside, Liz felt almost overwhelmed by the oppressive gloom of the place. It was a normal living room to a typical ranch-style house, no stone gargoyles or skeletons propped up in standing coffins as she had half-expected. But the place was so depressing. Surely the ceiling was the normal height, and yet Liz almost felt like she had to stoop because it seemed so low. *I wonder what it was like to grow up in this place.*

"Let's get some light in here so we can see," she said. She went to the living room curtains and flung them open. She turned to look about the room. The late afternoon daylight helped dispel the airless oppression of the room, but it also highlighted the dust that covered every surface. All the furniture was at least a couple decades old. The TV in the corner was one of those kinds with the tubes. Liz hadn't seen a tube-style TV since she was ten or younger.

"James? James, is that you?" An irritated woman's voice said from down the hallway.

"Yes, Mother," said James. "I'm here with the student I told you I'm tutoring."

A woman with frazzled gray hair emerged from the hallway. She was heavyset and wore a long denim dress that reached all the way to her stocking-and-sandaled feet, a pale, long sleeved t-shirt, and a very large crucifix that hung around her neck by a thick brown string.

"What, you've brought a friend home?" She looked sourly at Liz. "Well, I hope you didn't tell her she was invited to dinner, because I've only got the two-pound chicken, and there won't be enough for sandwiches tomorrow if we—Oh, now who did this?" Mrs. Kosalinski crossed the small living room to the front window. "We'll have all the neighbors gaping in here, watching us like we're fish in a fishbowl." She yanked shut the curtains that Liz had just opened moments ago. "There, that's better," she said looking with satisfaction at the living room, now gloomy and dark once again. "Have a decent bit of privacy."

Liz was amazed; apparently Mrs. Kosalinski *liked* living in depressing gloom. That, or else she honestly believed she was surrounded by neighbors with nothing better to do than look through windows hoping to catch a glimpse of a sofa purchased during the Clinton administration and a TV with a real cathode-ray tube.

"She's not my friend; I'm tutoring her," said James, and Liz couldn't help but feel a little hurt at that. "We are going down to the basement where we will go over tomorrow's algebra homework. She will be gone within an hour."

Liz found it rather shocking the way James spoke to his mother. Not that Liz never back-talked her own mom. "I talked back to my mom several times since my last confession," was a line she was so used to saying to the priest that it was automatic by now. But the way James talked to his mother, it seemed as though he was almost disdainful of her.

"And I didn't invite her to dinner," James continued. "So don't worry. I'll be sure to call ahead if I ever do think to bring one of the John Paul II students home to dine with us."

"Well, be quiet, then," said Mrs. Kosalinski. "Your father finally just got to sleep. If you and your friend here wake him up with your ruckus, the pain's just going to keep him awake."

At first, Liz found it amusing that Mrs. Kosalinski was expecting James and her to be causing "a ruckus" in the basement loud enough to wake her snoozing husband. But the mention of "pain" made Liz figure it might actually be something serious. She was immediately curious.

James said nothing, but walked from the living room to the adjoining kitchen. Liz followed, feeling depressed in this strange place, with these strange people. As she passed from the living room to the kitchen, she had a chance to shoot a glance down the hall that Mrs. Kosalinski had emerged from a minute ago.

The master bedroom at the end of the hall was halfway open, and although Liz could not see a bed or Mr. Kosalinski, she did note that there was what appeared to be medical monitoring equipment set up in the room. The equipment was attached to tubes and cords that stretched away to connections that Liz couldn't see.

At the far end of the kitchen, James rounded a corner and disappeared. Liz followed him around the corner and found a narrow, low-ceilinged staircase leading down into the basement. She descended after James into the darkness.

"Is there a light switch?" Liz asked, feeling the banister and wall as she went.

The lights came on, and Liz found herself looking at a wood paneled basement, her feet deep in shag carpeting. It was a little like her living room at home, but not as roomy, and not at all as cheerful. There was barely any furniture in here, just a sofa and a coffee table. At one end of the basement there was a doorway to an unfinished section. Through the door, Liz could see an old bike propped up against a water heater, and some taped boxes in the darkness behind that. At the opposite wall was a home bar setup, with barstools and a place to put in beer taps.

No beer taps were present though, and the bar wasn't stocked, which made sense to Liz since the Kosalinskis didn't seem much like a family to have use for a home bar. It had probably been installed by the previous owners of the house. What Liz did find odd was that in all their years of living there, the Kosalinskis had never done anything to their basement.

"Well," said James gruffly, "we can work on the coffee table," he gestured toward the sofa, "or we can sit on the bar stools and work on the bar. Do you have a preference?"

"The bar, I guess."

"Fine," James grumbled, "let's get to work."

I must have a death wish, J.P. thought. *If Brad's the Sparrow Hills Shooter, we're in a perfect position for him to kill me. He's bigger, stronger, and we're someplace far from help.*

But if he doesn't kill me, I might just get to go to jail for drug dealing. J.P. inhaled deeply, and kept a steady hold on the flashlight, shining it on Brad's chest instead of his face. He didn't want to annoy the guy more than necessary.

Finally Brad spoke up. "So… you want to know where I was on the night of the shooting?"

"Yeah," J.P. said. *Not that I'll live very long after you tell me.*

Brad sighed. "I guess you know pretty much everything. I mean, you know that I'm a drug dealer. Not a cool quarterback guy. So you can guess where I was and what I was doing."

J.P. waited.

Brad swallowed. "I was right here at a drug pickup."

"Oh. Okay." J.P.'s mind was racing. "Can you prove that?"

Brad barked out a harsh laugh. "Do you think I *want* to?"

"No one else was here?"

"Oh, no, there was someone else here. And not just the supplier either. Someone else came down before me to intercept my supply. He wasn't supposed to be here, but he thought he'd come down early and try to get away with my stuff." Brad took a deep breath. "I was driving down the road with my lights off, and I saw two guys right out there. Their phones were lit up so I saw their faces." Brad paused. "And I recognized the guy who was here, who'd come to steal my stuff before I could get to it. It was Brandon Brock."

J.P.'s mind reeled. "Wait. Are you trying to tell me that at the time of the shooting, Brandon Brock was here, trying to take your drug supply?"

Brad nodded. "I took a picture of him with that phone you just smashed."

"Uh, oops."

Brad shook his head. "I have a copy on my hard drive at home."

"Oh. And you didn't tell this to anyone?"

Brad smiled, but there was no humor behind it. "I didn't know it was friggin' important until Brandon shot himself and everyone started saying he was the shooter. And who could I tell? The cops? Right. 'Hey officer, I can clear the suicide kid from murder charges because I saw him at a drug deal. But don't ask why I was there, thanks.' And who else am I going to tell?"

"You knew it wasn't him," J.P. repeated, as he slowly put all this together. "You knew all this time that Brandon Brock couldn't be the shooter and you didn't tell anyone." Fury sparked inside of him. "Damn it, Brad! Don't you care? All those people believing a lie, thinking they're safe—and Brandon's family, thinking he's a killer? You selfish, stupid…"

"Calm down!" Brad said, from somewhere between cool and concerned. "Look, I'm a mess, all right? And who are you yelling at? You haven't been doing so great either. And now we're both in a steaming pile of crap, with no idea how to get out of it."

That shut J.P. up for a moment. He realized that he and Brad were, for better or worse, in this together. Brad was… not a friend. *Maybe* a friend. J.P. didn't know. He and Brad might have *Philia*, but in this case the rock on the chalkboard was a missing packet of drugs, and they definitely didn't care about it for the same reasons.

And Brad really did seem like a decent guy to J.P., despite the fact that he'd punched him. He could tell Brad wasn't mean, just kind of messed up. Brad sold drugs; he also had sex with his girlfriend, both things firmly in the "mortal sin" category. But J.P. found he didn't stop liking Brad or trusting him. In fact, the talk he and Brad had on that topic had convinced J.P. that his maybe-friend was genuinely confused, and really didn't know any better. Maybe it was the same way with the drugs? "So how did you get involved with drugs in the first place?" J.P. asked.

Brad sighed. "I don't know. We've always been kind of poor. My dad's a deadbeat. I don't think my mom even knows where he is." He made a wry face in the darkness. "When we moved here from California, my mom started hooking up with a new guy every other month. So I guess I had to grow up pretty quick. I got into the drug thing a couple years ago. The whole team was into it at the time and when I was playing football so well, everyone offered me pretty much everything. Whatever I wanted. Then someone asked me if I'd start selling. Said I was so popular at the school it could make a ton of money. So I did."

"You've been selling for that long?" J.P. asked, awed and horrified at the same time.

Brad ignored the question. "I guess I kept the old, laid back attitude around because people liked it. It fit with the popular QB thing, you know? But I didn't *feel* very laid back. I never do anymore. I couldn't just let everyone do everything for me, not after sales picked up. It was mostly just pot, but not always, and I did so well I got responsibility for bigger stuff. I don't like that too much though."

"Why not?"

"Because... just because. It's too much trouble. I mean look at the mess we're in now." Brad suddenly looked dejected, and worried. And that made J.P. worried. "I have no idea how we're going to get out of it," Brad said. "I can buy us maybe a few days, but after that, we *need* to have that money, or the drugs."

"Forget about that for a minute. You're the key to this whole shooter thing now. You can prove everything!"

"I already told you I'm not going to the police," Brad said harshly. Then his expression softened; he must have seen the look of total disdain on J.P.'s face. "Look, the shooter guy got away with it; he'd be crazy to come back. He's probably skipped town and went off to party in Mexico or something."

211

Brad said it like he believed it, but J.P. could tell by the look on his face that he wasn't so sure. He remembered a trick Liz taught him, about being quiet and staring at people. So he was quiet, and stared.

Brad turned away in frustration, then back toward J.P. "OK, fine. Probably not. It's not like I'm not worried. I am. About Sparrow Hills, about everybody. I can't say for sure there's no danger. I know that."

It's working, J.P. thought. *Thanks, Liz!* More silence, more staring. He slightly arched an eyebrow, just for effect.

"*Damn it, J.P.!*" Brad slammed his fist into his palm. "Where do you get off judging me? This has been on me for months now. *For months!* Do you know what it's like to carry around something like that? Do you? Well, it sucks! I mean, what would *you* do?"

Brad really looked like he wanted to know what J.P. thought. His face was contorted into a mask of anguish, like one of those sad tragedy masks from the theater, and his eyes were half-wild and searching. J.P. had never been around anyone so desperate for an answer. His fear disappeared and was replaced by awkwardness. He hadn't expected Brad to give in so easily, and now he was kind of weirded out that this big tough guy was threatening to get all whiny. It really *must* have been eating him up.

What would *I do?* he thought. *I'd talk to Brian. Talk to George. Talk to Liz. Talk to my brother.* But Brad didn't have any of those people. In fact, now that J.P. thought about it, Brad didn't appear to have any good friends at all. "Look," J.P. said, "I'm not the first person people usually go to for good advice," he said, "but if it was such a burden, maybe you shouldn't have been carrying it alone."

"I didn't have anyone I could trust! I wouldn't have trusted you either, except that now I don't have a choice." Brad groaned and sunk back into the seat, eyes closed. "For God's sake, I'm only seventeen! Why do bad things always happen to me? How am I supposed to come clean without getting in trouble?"

"Huh," J.P. chuckled.

"What? *What?* This isn't funny."

"Oh, I'm not laughing at you," J.P. said, "it's just that I was saying the same thing a little while ago, when I had to come clean about something but didn't want to get in trouble."

"Yeah?" Brad sullenly sneered, "Well, what did you do?"

"I came clean to you about it. Like, an hour ago."

Now it was Brad's turn to stare, blankly at first but then as realization dawned, slightly confused and, if J.P. was going to be completely honest and not at all prideful, a little awed. Brad sank back into the seat again, and shook his head. "I guess you're a braver man than I am. I don't know what to say."

"Well, you could say, 'Hey J.P., do you have any helpful ideas?' Because it just so happens that I do." J.P. had suddenly realized what the answer was. And it was a kind of humiliating answer, but if it worked it might resolve everything more or less for the best. *OK, Lord. I hear you. Thanks, I guess?*

Brad's eyes had narrowed, but he still looked hopeful to J.P. "You have an idea? About the shooting, or the drugs?"

"Both."

"Really? What is it?"

"It seems to me like you need a really good lawyer. One you can trust, that can keep you out of jail. And I happen to know where to find one who'll talk to us. Like, right now."

Brad sat up. "Where? What are we waiting for?"

"First you have to promise something serious though."

"Sure, anything. I'm so sick of this, I just want it all off my chest."

"OK, then. You've got to quit doing all the stuff with drugs. This guy, he's not going to help if you don't try to clean up."

"J.P.," Brad said earnestly, "there's nothing I'd like more. I promise, no more drug stuff. I'll come clean, just help me. Please."

J.P. didn't know whether he believed Brad or not, but he figured giving him the benefit of the doubt was the right thing to do. "Fine. No promises, but I'll see what I can come up with." He pulled out his phone. "I have to call a... a friend."

22

HOUSE OF FEAR

Instead of paying attention to James' droning lecture on proper equation form, Liz was wondering how long James's dad had been sick. A lengthy illness would explain why they had lived in this house so long and done nothing to the place since the '80s. She wanted to ask him what was wrong with his dad, but thought that might be a touchy subject for James. Besides, there was another touchy subject she'd much rather talk about.

Liz decided to take the plunge. "Hey, James?" she interrupted.

"What? Do I need to repeat something?"

"No, it's something else. Why didn't you tell me you lived in the same neighborhood as the shooter?"

James froze. "What?" he said after too long a pause. He sounded surprised, almost shocked.

Liz cringed on the inside, but went on. "You know, Brock. The Sparrow Hills shooter. Everyone knows it's Brandon Brock, right?"

James stared at her. For an instant, she saw something unmistakable on his face... furtiveness. A secret. *He* does *know something!*

Then James let out a little snort and just looked grumpy and ill-tempered as usual. "I'm sorry," he said. "Was I supposed to reveal every facet of my personal living situation to everyone?" He picked up his books and crossed the room to the coffee table. "I notice you've never confided to me the names of your next-door neighbors. Do you not have next-door neighbors, or are you keeping secrets from me as well?"

He said 'secrets' in a scornful way. But Liz hadn't imagined that look. There *was* a secret behind it. And she meant to find it out. She *had* to find it out.

"Are the Brocks your actual neighbors?" She asked as she turned the page of her notebook casually. "Do they live on this street, too?"

"No," James muttered. "Next street over."

"So you lived in the same neighborhood as Brock *and* Tyler? And you haven't told any of us this whole time?"

"Honestly, it never crossed my mind."

"Heck, even before the shooting, Tyler was always coming over to pick up Allie from school and acting like a jerk to the rest of us. All that time he was coming over, and you never thought once to even mention that you grew up with the guy?"

James' face tightened a bit. "It's none of my concern who Allie used to date," he said gruffly.

Liz scoffed. "Yeah, well, what about when he was beating up our boys? He beat up J.P. *and* Brian, he tied up George… Heck, you're the only upperclassman at our school he didn't pound."

"If only," said James moodily, flipping pages in his textbook.

"What's that supposed to mean?"

"Nothing. Bring your homework over here. There's better lighting."

"You said, 'if only.' What's that mean? If only what?" She brought over her books and plopped them onto the coffee table.

James was staring down at his textbook. "Liz," he said again, "we have to be quieter. We can't wake my father. Now focus on your math homework."

"Not until you tell me—"

"Tell you *what?*" he hissed, slamming the book closed and glaring at her. "What do you want to know, Liz?"

"Hey, hey," Liz said, alarmed. "Take it easy."

"Just focus on your math homework," he snapped, still glaring at her sidelong.

Liz started to look down at her books… but she just couldn't let it go. "So Tyler *did* beat you up?" she said casually.

James' eyes bulged a bit, and, abruptly, he let out a harsh laugh and shook his head. "You're not going to let up, are you? Okay, fine. The answer is yes. And no. Yes, Tyler was responsible for beating me. Many times, in fact. And no, Tyler didn't ever beat me up—by himself."

Liz blinked. "What—?"

215

"I was too big," James said coldly. "He couldn't risk properly humiliating me alone. No, it was always Tyler and his two friends Brock and Flynt who did it together—they would hold me down, and he would do the rest. And they did it for years, since we were all young. So you see, Tyler and I go *way* back."

Liz immediately felt guilty for pressing, and yet now that they were getting down to it, now that James was finally talkative, she wanted more. It wasn't pleasant, but this is what she had wanted all along. "I'm sorry," she said, and thought about putting her hand on his shoulder, but didn't. "When did all this start? Why didn't you tell anyone?"

James let out another harsh laugh. "I didn't always go to Catholic schools. I went to Woodhaven Elementary when I was a kid—the same public school as Tyler. He was a bully even back then. He made me miserable. Every single day he made me miserable. Do you have any idea what that's like for a child? To dread the dawn of every new day?"

"No," she said. "I suppose I don't."

"I was about nine when he formed his little posse with Flynt and Brock, and that just made him worse."

"Yeah, I heard that," Liz said. "I heard they beat up a lot of the kids around here. Do you know any of those other kids? I'd like to know—"

"What? You want to hear stories of childhood beatings?" James said contemptuously. "You find that sort of thing interesting? Fine, how about this—when I was twelve Flynt and Brock held my mouth open and Tyler threatened to urinate in it. Interesting, huh?" he sneered. "Or how about that one time when I was nine and Tyler hit me repeatedly in the stomach and the head with a sack of potatoes and mocked my father's illness the whole time? Oh, the mocking happened quite often. Still want me to go on?"

Liz's mouth dropped open. There was a look on James' face that she'd never seen before, more than simple emotional turmoil over reliving old memories—it was like the memories were fresh for him, like he was telling her about something that happened only yesterday. "Um…" She licked her lips nervously. "What?"

"Do. You. Want me. To go on?" James said again, clearly struggling to keep at least the veneer of calm.

Something was wrong, and she suddenly felt uncomfortable, like she was reading James' diary while he sat there simultaneously allowing it, and condemning her for it. But she was rooted to her spot anyway, like a gawker who can't stop staring at a train derailment. Even if she was in the path of the train.

"Yeah, go on," she said quietly.

He stared at her for a moment, his eyes full of pain, but with a small, vicious smile on his lips. "Alright. When I was thirteen, they hogtied me and left me in my back yard. You know what that is? That's when they tie your legs and arms together behind your back. I was out there for a couple hours, until my mom came home from work. They had pulled my limbs well past the point where I could stretch them comfortably on my own, so when she untied me I could barely move my shoulders or knees, and they hurt for weeks. I got to learn a lot that day—I even learned why Tyler did it. Want to know?"

Liz nodded her head. She was starting to feel a chill in the pit of her stomach.

"He did it simply because he *could.*" James hissed. "And he wasn't shy about telling me so. He leaned down to me and said it right to me. 'This is so you know you'll never be safe.' He actually said that. Right to my face. I was lying on the ground crying and he said that to me."

"Why... didn't your par— your mom do something?"

James shook his head in disgust. "Oh, she said something the first few times, but it availed nothing so I stopped telling her when it happened. Besides, do you really think monsters like that come from happy homes? Healthy homes? Do you really think their parents would have cared? If they could have or would have done something, they would have already. So, no, I never really felt like telling people how I knew Tyler. He was a terrible person back then, and he was a terrible person when he died. But no one wants to talk about that. No, we want to put up a big picture of Tyler smiling for his school photo and put a wreath around it and say," here James began speaking in a mocking simper, "'Aww, Tyler, you left us too soon. Heaven's getting another angel.'" James resumed his cold, contemptuous tone. "Well, it's a lie. No one misses Tyler, and no amount of prayers are going to help him now. Not where he's gone."

"You...you think he's in hell?"

"I *hope* he is," James snapped. "Now... are there any other questions?"

"Um, no," Liz said in a small voice.

"Fine. Now hand me your homework, and I'll correct it."

Liz got out her homework—a few wrinkled pieces of loose leaf—and handed it over. She felt scared now—scared of James. She had sensed the anger underneath his cold exterior in the past, but just now she'd seen it seething close to the surface. And it was a *lot* of anger. He was like a volcano. And she was alone in this room with him.

What if he got angry at *her?* What could she do? She looked around the room; she had a sudden impulse to find an exit. Just in case.

At the same time, though, she was horrified at what he had said, and angry, and feeling sorry for him. She had forgotten about interviewing James about other Shady Acres kids like him, any one of which could be another victim who finally snapped and started fighting back. Heck, she almost felt *sorry* for whoever he was. If his story was like James' story, maybe he had the right idea—

"So what did Megan Brock tell you?" James muttered, marking up her homework.

"Oh...um...nothing," Liz said, caught off guard.

"Too busy taking care of her illegitimate child, is she?" James said with a nasty laugh. "Oh, I know all about her. I've been watching her, you see."

Liz felt an icy coldness in her stomach. "What?" she said involuntarily. "What do you mean, watching her?"

"You can't trust people like that," James said. He seemed to be speaking almost to himself now. "Scum like that. The whole family. The Flynts, the Brocks, the Getzs—all scum. Getting what they deserve." He snorted, and shifted a little in his chair.

218

He continued marking her homework. Liz stared at him.

I've been watching her...

Something collapsed inside of her.

"James, I... I feel a little...sick," she said in a calm voice. "I kind of need to go to the bathroom. Where is it?"

James looked up, shot her a look of annoyance... and suspicion? "Upstairs and to the right," he said after a moment. "I'll show you—"

"No thanks, I got it," she said, calmly. And then she took her purse and walked upstairs, calmly. Fortunately it had been so cold in the basement that she'd left her black leather coat on.

She found the bathroom—a closet sized room with a toilet, a smudged mirror, a sink and no windows—shut the door quietly, and then bent over the toilet, her stomach churning.

"No," she muttered shaking her head. "Nonononono, it can't be..."

James. Secretive. Smart. Obsessed with Allie. Hater of Tyler, Flynt and Brock. James with his dead-eyes stare. James, whom she thought she had gotten to know better the last couple months...

It all came crashing into place with a sickening thud. Broad shoulders. Trench coat—she remembered how James had used to wear a trench coat last year. Grey eyes—Allie's notes had said the shooter had grey eyes... Megan talking about how she felt eyes watching her...

It can't be, she thought frantically, looking for any reason why it made sense for this not to be true. *Wait—hasn't Detective Irving looked at every kid in Shady Acres?*

No, he had looked at every kid who went to *Sparrow Hills*. That's what he said: *I pulled the roster from Sparrow Hills and looked at every student that lived in a half-mile...*

James didn't go to Sparrow Hills and wouldn't have shown up on the list. He wouldn't have been on anyone's radar. Except hers, but she hadn't even suspected. She hadn't *wanted* to suspect, because she kind of liked James. He couldn't be a killer! He was more like a big grumpy bear, not a *snake*.

219

Maybe he's a snake disguised as a bear. You don't know. You've never been able to read him—

James played his cards close to the chest. She still didn't know much about him after two years of knowing him. She hadn't even known where he'd lived until today.

And that's why you never suspected him. You didn't know the whole story. You didn't know he lived here. You didn't know that Tyler and Brock and Flynt had done those things to him. There's a reason *he played his cards close to his chest.*

Then why had he revealed so much to her, just now? If he *was* the shooter, wouldn't he be more cautious?

Maybe he hadn't meant to. Maybe the mask had slipped. When he was angry, dwelling on his enemies, maybe he had revealed too much. Maybe he was just now realizing it. Maybe when she came back downstairs…

If that was true, then Liz was in serious danger. If James was smart enough to fool the FBI and the police, he was smart enough to have picked up that Liz had been snooping around. And if she let on that she knew…

Maybe James was down in the basement right now, waiting for her to come back. Maybe waiting with a gun, or a knife. Not that he would need a weapon; he was more than big enough to strangle her to death, and she wasn't going to fool herself about being tough enough to fight him off.

Are you nuts? This is James! He's not dangerous!

She hadn't thought Hank was dangerous either. She had known Hank since she was ten. Hank, her dad's right-hand man, who had come over for dinner and barbeques countless times, who had played football in her backyard with her dad and brother, and who had injected her with drugs and left her to be burned alive in her school. She had kind of liked Hank, too. She hadn't suspected a thing.

And she hadn't thought her boyfriend Rich Rogers was dangerous either. Until he had her alone in the car, and if it wasn't for that spray…

Another wave of nausea rocked her. She felt a little bile in her mouth and swallowed frantically.

She sat on the toilet, gripping her knees. "Okay," she muttered. "Okay."

She took a couple deep breaths, and slowly, she started to calm down. Maybe, just maybe, this was a good thing. If James *was* the shooter— the thought still made her sick—then there was still hope. James hadn't planned for her to come here and be a victim, because they weren't alone in the house—his parents were here. And besides, she had an advantage over his other victims: she knew who he really was. Plus she had a phone. She pulled it out.

But who should I call? J.P.? 911? Why? James hasn't done anything.

Then she thought of Detective Irving, but her panic increased as she remembered that his card was in her bookbag downstairs. Besides, she *still* didn't have any proof, just strong suspicion and a lot of circumstantial evidence.

That brought up another thought. If it *was* James, and she brought the cops right now and they couldn't arrest him, he would be off scot free and know that she was on to him. *Besides, they can't arrest him. They don't even have a search warrant. He'll be free to destroy any evidence. He'll get away with it.*

That thought almost made her sick again—but in a different way. *He will not get away with it.*

She tapped the phone against her palm. "Proof," she muttered, racking her brains. "I need proof." But unless James had a rifle or a bloody knife or something stashed behind this toilet, she wasn't getting any. Not unless she could call someone on this phone who knew something useful about James. She laughed bitterly. *Nobody* knew anything about James; he didn't have any friends except…

It was a long shot, but it was also her *only* shot. She scrolled up to Allie's number, and hit the call button. "C'mon, pick up, pick up. Pickupickupickup."

"Liz? What's up?"

"Hey, Allie." Liz paused. She had to go about this in just the right way, but she couldn't waste time either. "Remember how you said the other day how you, um, knew James better now?"

"Yeah, that's right."

"Well…I was just wondering… what *do* you know about him?"

"Why?" Allie sounded guarded. "Why are you asking?"

"Okay, this is gonna sound funny, but…" Liz turned on the bathroom fan for cover. "Listen," she continued in a near-whisper, "I know you told me to leave the shooting investigation alone—"

"Oh Lord, Liz. What did you do?"

"I'm sorry! I wasn't going to look any more, but I kind of stumbled on something and I really need you to listen right now, OK?"

"Fine," Allie huffed. "What is it?"

"When you were investigating the shooter's victims, did you know that Tyler has been James's next door neighbor since grade school?"

Silence from the other end. Then Allie said, "Are you sure that information's reliable?"

Liz took a quick peek under the door to make sure no one was in the hall. Then, just to be safe, she climbed into the bathtub, the furthest spot from the door, and half whispered, "Oh, trust me, it's pretty stinkin' reliable."

"Why are you whispering? Why are you calling me about this now?"

"I'm at James' house for math tutoring, but never mind about that! Listen. Tyler used to beat the tar out of James as a kid. James has a motive. Did you ever consider James was a suspect?"

"Well, not actually. It couldn't be him!"

"Why couldn't it?"

"Well, I'm pretty sure the shooter is the same guy who fired blanks at me in the hall on the first day at Sparrow Hills last year. James was going to JP2 High at the time."

"Oh," Liz felt almost more disappointment then relief. But then she suddenly felt her thoughts shifting as her memory recalled Allie's first day at JP2. "Oh," she said again. "Oh, oh, oh… Oh no… Ohhhhh nooooo…"

"Oh no what?" said Allie.

"Don't you remember that you and James came to JP2 on the *same day?*"

"The same day?"

"Yeah! They introduced James, and they were going to introduce you with him, but you weren't there for some reason… no! You were in the bathroom cleaning up."

"Oh, wait! I remember! J.P. got me with a shaving cream bomb that day."

"Yes! J.P.'s shaving cream bomb! And so no one ever told you that it was James's first day, too? That we'd never even seen him before?"

"No."

Liz cracked the door and peered down the staircase again. She wondered if she could just sprint out the front door. She hated this trapped feeling. *I've got to go. Now.* Suddenly her phone buzzed: there was another call incoming.

"Liz," Allie was saying, "James *can't* be the shooter, you've got it all wrong, I *know* he's not the shooter—"

"Yeah, whatever, hold on," Liz checked the other number. J.P. was calling! "Allie, I got to go."

She quickly hung up, pressed the button to ignore the call with a text, and sent a quick message to J.P.

23

CAR CHASE

HELP! RT NOW!!!
Meet me Shady Acres entrance across from Dunhollow. GPS it. Bring transportation!!
URGENT!!!

J.P. stared at his phone.

"Is that from the lawyer?" Brad asked hopefully.

"Actually, I was trying to call a friend who would know his number," J.P. said. "Uh… Brad, looks like I've got to go do something. Do you know where Shady Acres is?"

"Yeah," Brad said. "Why?"

"Just my friend Liz; she needs us to pick her up. Sounds like she's in trouble. Liz said she'll meet us at the entrance, the one near Dunhallow. You know where that is?"

"On the other side of town," Brad said, "But we can get there pretty fast." He opened the door to the truck. "If you can open the garage door, I'll drive us out."

J.P. sent Liz a quick return message while he waited for Brad to carefully back the car out of the garage. Then he hopped into the truck's passenger's seat. "Alright. Let's go get her."

Liz hung up. "Okay. Okay," she said softly to herself. *You can do this. You can do this.* She tried to stay calm, and opened the door.

Once she saw no one was around, she tip-toed to the front door, went out, closed it quietly, and crept around the side of the house. Despite the draped front windows, she was afraid of being seen if she ran down the front walkway. So she edged past the bedroom windows to the back of the house where there was tree cover.

Her phone buzzed again and there was a new message from J.P.

HLP ON THE WAY, 15 20 MIN

She saw that there was only one reception bar, but that was OK. She wouldn't need to make any more calls from here. *Okay. Now I just need to get to the entrance sign we passed on the way in.*

She darted towards the trees and instantly she heard a shout. She spun around. James was standing in the back door of the basement. His fists were clenched and he started walking towards her.

Liz dashed into the trees, vaulted over the Kosalinkis' fence, and ran. At least she was wearing her black jacket over her white shirt to hide her in the dark, but her ankle was hurting…

She ran. Pain shot up her leg, getting a little worse with each step, but it still held her weight. *OK. Just a little painful; I should still be able to make it.* A few minutes later, having cut across a couple yards and climbed over a few more fences, she stumbled onto the road, her ankle throbbing now. She stopped to breathe, and for a moment her mind was taken from the pain. The sheer feeling of freedom that washed over her was exhilarating. She came to a cross street and looked right and left…

… and there was James's big black car.

He was chasing her down! She could hear the rumbling of the engine growing in volume as the car slowly made a turn on the street Liz was attempting to cross.

He had seen her. Liz was sure of that. If there had been other cars on the road she might have tried to stop one, but there were none, and even though she felt exposed and in danger, she didn't relish the idea of knocking on some strangers' door and hoping they let her in before James could grab her. The only advantage that she could see was that she could cut through yards, while James had to stay on the street. If she was remembering right, Dunhallow was two streets down and three streets over. *Or was it three streets down and two over? Dammit!*

Recklessly, Liz dashed across the street and up the adjoining road. It wasn't long before she could hear the rumble of an old car engine behind her. Immediately, she turned and ran into someone's side yard, emerging on the next street down. She ran in what she hoped was the right direction, but it was so hard to tell in the dark.

James's car was out ahead of her now, and Liz wondered if he had somehow figured out where she was heading. He obviously knew his own neighborhood better than she did and the moon was nearly full, shedding light on all but the most shadowed areas. All James had to do was patrol some main road or intersection and stay reasonably alert, and he'd see her.

I have to stay off the street. Liz plowed through a holly hedgerow, scraping her hands and face on the way through, busting into someone's side yard and stumbling over a decorative wagon full of flowers she hadn't seen from the other side of the hedge. Pain shot up her leg, but she ignored it as she scrambled to her feet. A light came on in the house and as Liz picked herself up she briefly saw the shadow of a man's head as he peered out of a patio door. "Hey!" the man shouted, cursing. "This is private property! I'm calling the police!"

Liz ran on, heedless, distantly aware that she was in a state of full panic and almost as afraid of angry homeowners as she was of James's car.

Unfortunately, now there were no more yards to cut through, just a small greenbelt leading to the woods. She saw a dark ribbon of road, as well as the reflective paint on an old wooden sign, glinting through the trees in the distance. The neighborhood sign! It wasn't close, but she was sure she could make it. She *had* to make it. Without waiting to see if James's car would appear again Liz booked it for the woods, her ankle screaming at her now and forcing her to a running limp. *Come on, ankle. Just 25 more feet. 20 more. 15… 10… come on, you can do it.*

She fled haphazardly into the treeline. Only when her feet didn't touch solid ground did she realize that between her and the road was a run-off ditch with steep sides running down from the woods and the road, and that what she had taken to be small saplings were actually the upper halves of full-grown trees. Too late, she tried to skid to a stop, but her legs churned in open air for half of one terrifying second that felt like an eternity to Liz, and then she plunged downward and was engulfed in branches. They barely gave way, scratching and scraping as she dropped toward the bottom of the ditch, feeling the vague sense of small impacts without really knowing how many branches she'd hit. She had a quick, hopeful sensation of slowing, which ended abruptly as she slammed, hard, into the ground.

She lay on her back and stared at the moon and stars swimming dizzily through the treetops, caught up in their swirling dance until she blacked out.

Boy, this place is in the sticks," J.P. exclaimed.

"I'll say," Brad said.

The truck bumped over the road and past a sign. J.P. caught a glimpse of it. "Wait! Back up! I think that was it."

Brad pulled over and began to make a three-point turn on the narrow road. J.P. just hoped some other truck wouldn't come along and ram them. It was really dark outside now. No one else seemed to be on the road.

When she came to, Liz was staring at the stars above her and the tops of the trees. It was a cold crystal night, and she had no idea how long she'd been lying there. Then she remembered where she was. In the woods, running away from James.

And like a key turning in a lock, she suddenly remembered where she was at this time, a year ago. In the woods. Not these woods, but woods just like this one. The night she had run away from Rich Rogers at the Sparrow Hills dance. The night she had been making her way home through the woods. Hearing what sounded like a car backfiring. And screams. And rustling in the woods. Just like she was hearing now…

JAMES. He's gotten out of his car and he's come after me. He's hunting me.

She heard the rustling of leaves, and heavy breathing. Someone was coming towards her.

She had to get away. She tried to move, but now her entire body felt the way her ankle had felt before the fall, and her ankle felt like it was literally on fire. She tried to crane her neck to look down at it just to

227

be sure it wasn't, but the movement pushed the pain beyond tolerance and she gasped.

The rustling stopped.

He's heard me. He's coming towards me.

Can't move the ankle. So I can't run. Got to crawl. Fast. Now. Liz gathered all of her strength and rolled over. It hurt like hell. She started crawling up the slope, grabbing from tree to tree.

Up... up... up...

All at once she was at the top and suddenly headlights were glaring into her eyes and she staggered, blinking, unable to shield her eyes.

"Hey, are you crazy? What are you doing there?" someone said.

The voice was vaguely familiar. Liz tried to focus her vision, succeeding enough to make out the figure of Neil Flynt crouched over her.

"What are you doing here?" she asked, blinking stupidly.

Flynt sat down beside her. "I heard my dad shouting at someone outside the house, so I came out to check. I saw you fall down the ravine. What are you doing out here?"

"It's a long story," Liz said. "Hey, uh, I busted my ankle pretty badly."

"I'll say," Flynt said. "Man, that was pretty dumb. You just stay put. You want me to call 911?"

Car doors were slamming, and suddenly J.P. was there, and someone else. "Liz? Are you okay?"

"She fell down the ravine and busted her ankle," Flynt was saying.

"Put her in the front seat," Brad said.

Liz was leaning on J.P., and started to feel fuzzy. "And there was someone following me," she started to say, but then she pitched forward, suddenly exhausted. Flynt moved quickly and caught her.

And then another figure loomed up out of the darkness into the light of the headlights. Pale face. Grey eyes glaring at her.

"You," James breathed.

And he barreled towards her, hands outstretched, eyes squeezed into narrow lines of hate.

Whoa!" J.P. shouted as James flung himself forward at Liz, but he had enough presence of mind to block James and grab him by the shoulder. Brad instinctively lunged, too, and both boys found themselves hanging onto James' arms, while Flynt seized Liz, who had gone limp, and tossed her over his shoulder in a fireman's carry. He ran to Brad's truck and shoved Liz inside.

James' face was contorted into a horrible mask of fear and anger and hatred, followed by a sudden strangled, guttural noise, loud and barking. Flynt had just gotten Liz in the truck when James shook free of Brad and J.P. He shot forward, arms outstretched, as he grabbed Flynt by the throat and throttled him. Flynt tried to get his hands up, tried to pull James' arms away, but his pulling and batting was like a kitten being shaken to death by a Doberman. James kept shouting wordlessly, again and again. J.P. couldn't think, didn't know what to do. Finally, as he saw Flynt's eyes roll back into his head, he jumped on James' back and wrapped his arms around his huge neck, pulling and choking, trying to at least be enough of a distraction to make James let go.

James released Flynt with his bear-like right arm and swung back hard, almost effortlessly throwing J.P. to the side. J.P. went flying, tumbling onto the ground and barely getting his arms in position to absorb some of the fall. He jumped up, relatively unscathed, and saw that his plan had worked, sort of—James swinging his arm back had given Brad the opportunity to come in low, dropping his shoulder and walloping James in the midsection.

The blow forced James to exhale and made him pause, as Flynt staggered toward the passenger door and flopped onto the seat. Brad straightened up, smacking his head into the underside of James' chin, snapping the bigger boy's head back. J.P. heard the clatter of teeth on teeth.

It wasn't enough to stop James. He swung a heavy fist at Brad's unprotected face, clobbering him under the right eye. Brad nearly went down, but had the presence of mind to slip his leg behind James and fall forward onto the larger boy, a knee in James' stomach. Both of

229

them tumbled down, James taking the worst of it as his head hit the asphalt and the air was knocked from his lungs.

J.P. hopped up and grabbed Brad, stumbling and still woozy from the punch, and directed him toward the door Flynt had climbed into. "Keys!" he shouted, and Brad clumsily dug the keys out of his pocket and pushed them into J.P.'s waiting hand. J.P. looked back, worrying that maybe they had killed James. But no, there he was, rising from the pavement, holding the back of his head, no longer shouting but groaning in frustration. "J.P.!" he growled. "Don't you get in that truck, J.P.!"

J.P. didn't wait any longer; he flew into the driver's seat and revved the engine. Liz was sitting white-faced in the seat next to him, gripping the seat tightly in pain or fear or both. Flynt was still half-laying on the back seat, Brad next to him cupping his own squinted, punched eye.

"Go go go!" Liz shouted.

"Hold on!" J.P. said to the others, throwing the truck into reverse.

Right into the Shady Acres sign.

The sound of wood splintering and metal scratching screeched through the air, but J.P. didn't slow down. He plowed the truck through the sign onto the main road, one tire riding up high and coming down hard as it must have run over the broken remains of one of the sign posts still stuck in the ground.

J.P. threw the truck into drive and gunned it as they flew over the twisting country road.

"What. The. *Hell*. IS GOING ON?!" J.P. shouted back. "*You're* all busted up, and James is trying to *kill* us. Why??"

Liz said something, so faint J.P. couldn't make it out.

"What was that?"

"It's James. It was him. All this time."

"What?" J.P. asked, "*What* is James?"

"He's the shooter," Liz said, her eyes closed and tears trickling down her face. "James Kosalinski is the Sparrow Hills shooter."

Athan was waiting by the ornamental iron fence when J.P. carefully backed Brad's dented truck against the curb. "I got your call," he said. "Dad's home. He's waiting for you guys in the study."

"Thanks," J.P. said, helping Liz out of the truck. Brad, his eye still swollen, and Flynt, looking woozy, came out after him. "We're in a mess. We need your dad."

"What's wrong with Liz?" Athan asked.

"Ankle," she said. "Guess I'm off the cheer squad now."

He offered his arm immediately. "Come on, my mom's got all sorts of ankle braces. She's practically a sports medicine pro with all the injuries me and my sibs have gotten." He glanced at J.P. "Just go to the front door and knock. My dad's study is the first door on the left."

Liz looked at J.P. "Don't tell him anything about what I said," she said quietly. "Got to tell Irving first."

J.P. nodded as Liz hobbled off on Athan's shoulder, feeling slightly unreal. He was still trying to process what Liz had told him. *What an odd night this has been*, he thought. *Drug dealers, psychos, the Sparrow Hills Shooter, and now I'm on speaking terms with Athan.*

"This is a lawyer's house?" Flynt asked, gaping at the old stone house with a big trimmed lawn and neatly manicured little bushes. There were pumpkins and little glowing lanterns decoratively scattered on the brick steps leading up to the rounded wooden front door.

"Yeah, I guess so," J.P. said. Athan's house was artistic. Not surprising. There was even a stone fountain with a classical-looking statue of a fish spitting water.

"Come on in," Mr. Courchraine said when he met them at the front door. "I hear you have an interesting story to tell me." He led them down the hall, which was lined with plaques, pictures of Christ, Mary, and the saints with gold backgrounds. Icons. Some of them were new and shiny; others looked old and worn and probably hand-painted. J.P. saw Brad and Flynt both glancing around, looking a little intimidated.

He motioned them into another room, with a desk facing a set of comfortable-looking leather chairs.

"Hello, J.P. And you must be Brad and Neil," Mr. Courchraine said, shaking hands with each of them in turn. "Please, both of you sit. Tell me why you're here."

Hello, Liz. What's going on? Why are you calling so late? Is everything all right?"

Liz leaned forward on the sofa. Mrs. Courchraine had made her comfortable on a sofa in a room just off the kitchen, containing a piano and a few bookcases. She had wrapped Liz's ankle and given her a glass of juice before she agreed to let Liz make a private phone call.

"Hi, Detective Irving." Liz took a deep breath. "I've got something kind of scary to tell you." Then before he could respond, she told him everything that had just happened at James' house, all the evidence she'd pieced together. "So I'm sure it was him," she concluded. "You've got to arrest him tonight."

Irving sighed. "I believe you Liz, but it's not enough. Not for a judge, not for a warrant."

"What!" Liz exclaimed, perturbed. "But for Pete's sake! He chased me through the woods! He attacked me! He nearly throttled the boy who was trying to help me. Can't you get him on, say, assault? Can't you bring him in for that, and then… I don't know, hold him until something comes up?"

"Well," he considered for a moment. "I could probably bring him in for attempted assault…"

"He was trying to kill us!"

"Wait a sec," Irving said. "Wait just a second." He was quiet for a moment, then said, "Liz, can I call you back in a few minutes? I may have something."

"Uh… sure." Liz hung up, bewildered but hopeful, and a few minutes later her phone rang again.

"OK," Irving said, sounding excited, "I'm going to play something for you, and I want you to tell me who's speaking, if you can."

Then Liz heard another voice break in, having a one-sided conversation about an emergency of some kind. The voice sounded a little tinny, but she recognized it unmistakably.

"That's James Kosalinski," she said.

When Irving spoke again, he sounded relieved. "Liz," he said, "we've got him. We've got him. That was the 911 call that was made after Brock's suicide leading us to the body. We've got him!"

"We do?" Liz asked, confused but hopeful.

"Yeah. Listen, I'm going to get the ball rolling on a warrant. I'm going to call in every favor I have, and I'm going to be up all night making this happen. Hopefully we'll have him before morning. Liz, thank you. I couldn't have done this without you."

"Sure. Sure," Liz said, "You're welcome!" But Irving had already hung up.

S o let me understand this," Mr. Courchraine said after the boys had finished telling about the night's events. "J.P., you're saying that you had no idea that you were expected to sell drugs for anyone? That you had no intention to do so? That you didn't know you'd received any, that your parents didn't know, and that a friend whom you don't want to mention both drove you home after you accidentally smoked pot, and then destroyed the evidence for you? That must be some friend."

"I guess so," J.P. mumbled. He hadn't mentioned Flynt, who seemed to appreciate being left out. He sat listening to everything, but keeping his mouth shut while J.P. talked.

"I have to tell you," Mr. Courchraine said, "that's quite a story. If you were me, would you believe it? Would *you* trust you?"

"I would, Dad."

J.P. had forgotten Athan was still in the room; now he turned to see him leaning against the wall by the door.

Athan continued, "I believe him. Besides, even though I haven't exactly seen drugs in the locker room at Sparrow Hills, I've *heard* things when no one knows I'm listening."

Mr. Courchraine sat quietly for a moment, then said, "Well, if Athan trusts you, then I'll trust you, too."

J.P. let out the breath he didn't know he'd been holding and shot a look of thanks to Athan.

"Now Brad," the lawyer continued, "Athan tells me you have something even more important to bring forward. I have to say, I hope it's as big as Athan's made it out to be, because you've already made yourself complicit in some pretty significant crimes. You're seventeen, so you wouldn't be tried as an adult, and I'm glad you're trying to turn over a new leaf, but as things stand I can't promise anything but a fair trial if we move forward."

Brad nodded. "I understand. I..." he stopped, and then plunged forward. "I can prove that Brandon Brock wasn't the Sparrow Hills Shooter. Does that make a difference?"

Silence. For once, the lawyer's confident manner slipped as he leaned forward, a dubious expression on his face. He glanced from Brad to J.P., who nodded in assent, then to Athan, who looked just as shocked as his father. "You're kidding."

"No, sir. I saw him the night of the shooting at a drug pickup. He didn't know I was there, but I definitely saw him. It was the same time as the shooting, so it couldn't have been Brandon."

"And you can prove this?"

"I took some pictures."

Mr. Courchraine sat back.

"And some video. They're kind of grainy," Brad continued, "but they're time-stamped. I held onto it because I thought I might need it later. Figured maybe I could use it if things went sour."

Mr. Courchraine sat staring at Brad, not moving and not saying a word. "Look," Brad said nervously, "I know a lot about the local drug scene. I know who's in charge of selling at Sparrow Hills. Who the grunt sellers are, even at some of the other schools. I know who they buy supply from. Who they sell to. How they distribute. When you know that much, it's a good idea to keep records, because you never know when you're going to need them, you know?"

Mr. Courchraine actually smiled. "I do know. But now I know *you* know, which means I'm in the extraordinarily rare position of being able to take an underage potential informant seriously. Even a little proof goes a long way, but if you have even more than that, we're in business. Do you have more than that?"

"Oh, yes."

The lawyer leaned forward. "Are you willing to tell the police everything you know?"

"No. Not the police."

"Why not?" Mr. Courchraine asked, perplexed.

"Because the Sparrow Hills police already know a lot of it, and they don't care. They look the other way whenever one of the guys on the team does something illegal. That's part of the reason I haven't come forward yet—they're more likely to throw me in jail to keep me quiet than they are to arrest anyone else."

Flynt nodded his head. "That's true."

Mr. Courchraine looked at him. "And what's your part in all this, Mr. Flynt?"

Flynt licked his lips, and stumbled, just as Brad had. "Well, I guess pretty much the same as Brad's. I didn't know about Brock, but well, I've done some pretty bad stuff with drugs, too, but if Brad can come forward and go clean, I guess I can, too." He swallowed and looked at J.P. "And well, I've had my own theories about the shooter: J.P. knows. But no one ever listens to a dumb jock."

"Hey, you're not dumb, Flynt. I know that," Brad said easily. "Maybe they will listen to you now."

"Yeah," said Flynt. "Maybe they will." He looked gratefully at J.P. "None of this would have happened without you, mascot," he said.

"I guess not," J.P. said, and felt cold. He wondered again about what Liz had said, and what the consequences would be.

I guess school tomorrow will be very interesting.

24

HOUR OF TRUTH

When J.P. arrived at school the next day, Tuesday, he half expected the place to be surrounded by flashing cop cars. But instead, there was just the usual straggle of cars and vans, of kids yawning as they made their way through the double doors into the building, or shivering in the cold November air.

"Can't believe it's almost Advent," his mom remarked. "We're heading towards the darkest day of the year."

"Yeah, I guess so," he said. He'd debated telling his parents, but when he found out Liz didn't want to tell hers, he'd agreed reluctantly to keep quiet until the police made their move. Apparently Irving had called back to tell Liz they didn't want to tip off James that anything might be different.

Maybe they showed up at his house first thing this morning and got him, J.P. thought as he took his seat in homeroom. He looked around to see who else was there. Celia, of course, ticking off the attendance. George, working on some trigonometry homework. Brian was looking at his phone and frowning.

"Where's Liz?" he asked J.P.

"Um… she took a fall on her ankle yesterday," J.P. said, which was true. "Not sure if she's going to make it in." He looked around quickly as the door opened, and Liz hobbled in on crutches, looking pale.

There was a flutter of excitement, everyone asking what had happened, and Liz answered questions evasively in a tired voice. Then Mr. Costain came in to start the day, and it was only then that J.P. realized that not only James was missing. Allie was, too.

Please God, let them have arrested James already. Let it all be over, Liz thought when James didn't show up during the opening-of-the-school Rosary.

She hoped that Irving had gotten the warrant and that James was already in a holding cell.

Brian asked about her ankle and she'd told him what she'd told everyone including her mom: that she'd twisted it in the woods—and he'd asked if she needed help carrying her books. She let him for the first class, but they didn't talk much aside from that.

"Just leave my books here," she told Brian when the lunch bell rang. "We can come back and get them after lunch."

"You sure?" he asked.

"I'm sure. See ya," she said, and took a long time with her crutches so that he would leave without her. The weather had warmed up, and she saw out the classroom window that a few kids had taken their lunches outside.

She got her sandwich bag and hobbled out into the nearly-empty hallway. For some reason, she felt like she should go right now and tell her mom the true story of what had happened. But before she could make up her mind, her eyes fixed on a big bulky kid opening his locker. James Kosalinski, the Sparrow Hills Shooter, getting his math and history books out of his locker as though nothing had happened.

He looked at Liz with a sideways glance, almost disdainful. "Hello, Miss Simonelli," he said stiffly. Then he seemed to slump down, defeated. "Elizabeth, there are matters we need to discuss."

"Get away from me," she said, hobbling backwards. "Just go away."

James straightened himself out and stepped away from the lockers, moving toward Liz.

"What I wanted to tell you was that I'm sorry," James said. He paused as though expecting Liz to react. When she didn't, he spoke again. "I'm sorry for trying to chase you down in my car, and for… That must have seemed…" He hesitated a moment. "My behavior must have seemed strange to you." Then he stood straight, his chin jutting out, as though he was trying to prove that his pride could handle the humiliation of this apology.

Liz tried to increase her backward pace. "Whatever James, just please stop. We're…we're gonna miss lunch."

"The truth is," he continued, falteringly, "Well, the truth is that I just wanted to know why you were suddenly leaving in the middle of our session without saying a word. I—I suppose you must have had your reasons, and I should have just let you go. I was only curious, that's all, and I was not trying to scare you. If I made you feel at all *uncomfortable*, I'm very sorry."

Liz was at a loss for words. She felt tiny in that spacious hallway. James seemed to tower over her like a giant. "Um, that's okay," she said weakly. "I just got a phone call from a friend. Said she needed me to come. Had to go right away. Emergency."

James gave her a hard stare. "I am only trying to make amends for my behavior."

Liz took another hobble-step back.

"I think you like this cloak and dagger intrigue," James continued. "Why else do you keep putting yourself in the middle of these things?"

"Um, okay," Liz stammered.

"I'm serious," said James. "You've got Allie's notes. You've been looking into this. I know you *think* you know things."

"I don't know anything!" Liz blurted out defensively. "Allie threw the notes away because they were useless to her, and I haven't done any better with them!"

"Come now," James said, almost pleading. "What have you found out? Please tell me."

For a moment Liz almost felt sorry for him. She did feel terrible about what Tyler, Flynt, and Brock had done to the young James, and she felt another rush of guilt over having gone to the police behind his back. She took a deep breath. Then she said briskly, "You should go. Just go. I'm serious. Go *now*. Get in your car, drive away, just get out of here."

James looked at her with a puzzled expression. "What are you saying?"

"You don't have a lot of time, James," said Liz. "This is the only warning you're gonna get."

"Why are you warning me?" asked James. Then over James's shoulder, Liz could see Mr. Costain emerge down at the other end of the hallway, making a gesture as though motioning for someone to follow him into the hall. "I'm not the one in danger; Allie is. She's the one I'd be concerned with, if I were you."

Allie? What is he talking about? Liz thought. She watched as Mr. Costain was joined by two men, one in a tie and a second man in a police officer's uniform. *Detective Irving and Officer Hichborn! They're here for James!* "You're right!" Liz said, flustered. "Allie! Gotta protect Allie! I'm gonna go tell her right now!" She ducked and tried to go.

"Stop!" James grabbed her arm forcefully. It hurt.

"Ow! Lemme go!" Liz began whapping James's hand with her lunch bag. After the fourth or fifth hit, the bag tore open and the contents of her lunch flew out.

James still had his back to the men down the hall and wasn't aware of them. The two cops, on seeing James grab Liz, began to run down the hall. "James Kosalinski!" Irving shouted. "This is the police! Let her go and come with us! Now!"

James whirled around in surprise. When he turned back toward Liz, his face was furious. "You *knew* about this?"

"I told you to leave! You should have listened to me!" Liz hissed. With a sudden wrench of her arm, Liz twisted free of his grip and began hobbling down the hall, away from James and the cops.

She only got a few steps when she felt someone pass her. It was James. She stood against the lockers watching James run away toward the doors leading outside. She fixated for some reason on the sole of his left shoe. There was a piece of bread and some lunch meat stuck to it. He was leaving a little trail of bread crumbs and turkey meat flecks as his thick legs pumped down the corridor. Dumbly, Liz realized that it was her lunch. James had stepped on her sandwich when he pushed her out of the way.

Seconds later Detective Irving and Officer Hichborn rounded the corner and were pursuing James toward the doors. James ran full force into the exit, pushed it open, and disappeared outside. The two cops followed him.

By the time Liz got to the doors, the two cops were closing in on James, who was swiping at them with his big hands. There were gasps and yells from the students who were eating outside.

No, James, no! Don't fight them! Liz felt like shouting. *You're only making it worse!* It was almost like a dream as Liz watched Officer Hichborn raise his baton in the air and then brought it down against James's leg.

James's leg wobbled and he went down with an anguished cry.

Liz felt Mr. Costain's hands on her shoulders. "Go inside, Liz," he said urgently. She didn't listen, and he didn't force the issue. His attention, like hers, was focused on what was happening.

James was on the ground now in a bulky heap. Officer Hichborn was on top of him a moment later, straddling him and trying to grab one of James's wildly waving arms. His body lurched, as though he was trying to buck the policeman off him, but he was too well pinned.

Detective Irving circled in a crouch around James's prone body and managed to grab one of his wrists and hold it secure. Detective Hichborn caught the other and jerked it forcefully behind James's back. He took a pair of handcuffs from his belt and clapped them to James's wrists. James was writhing on the ground now, but it was clear he was totally helpless. Officer Hichborn got up off him, and James's body went limp. He put his face to the ground in a bodily position of complete and utter defeat.

Officer Hichborn and Detective Irving, each on opposite sides, now helped James to his feet. "Come with us," one instructed, and they began leading James back toward the parking lot while reading him his rights.

"James, what were you thinking?" Mr. Costain said, following along beside them. "They were only here to ask questions. Why did you run?" His voice was strained. Liz could believe he was almost ready to cry.

No one else was talking now. All the students stood or sat motionless, watching everything happen, as though it was a play they had no part in. Again, Liz was conscious that Allie was not there.

240

The cops led James back to a police car and put him in the back, turning his head away as they buckled him into his seat. Irving slammed the door shut on James, who hung his head and slumped down in his seat.

Liz was lying on the family room couch, holding the TV remote in her hand. She didn't want to watch the news. But she had to.

She clicked on the tube and flipped the channel to RCNC, the Reliable Cable News Channel. A police report had just been released stating that "incriminating evidence" had been found in James' locker and there was some discussion of that.

"So what are we to make of this? Is this just a coincidence that this killer, this MURDERER, came from one of these cuckoo-crazy religious zealot nuthouses?"

Liz groaned. The man talking on the TV was Frank Splenetic, the red-faced, shouting host of RCNC's *Frank Talk* news program.

"Now, this place, this so-called 'school,' whatsitcalled, John Paul the Second High. They're grade-A wackos, amirite? So is it fair to say that tiny, cult-like religiously-based schools like this—particularly when they take an extreme form of doctrinal zealotry as John Paul the Second High has—is it fair to say that they bear some responsibility for turning their students into monsters like this James Kosalinski kid turned out to be?"

Liz growled in disgust and clicked the TV off.

Silence ruled the room for several moments, and then curiosity got the better of her and she turned it back on again.

"...here on the scene in Sparrow Hills reporting for RCNC." A field reporter was on the screen now. He was standing in front of the JP2HS building. It was at night, so it must have been live. *"We've been here all day, talking to some of the parents and the students to get a feel for just what kind of school John Paul the Second High is like. Here are some of the responses we got."*

The view changed over to earlier in the day, and Liz was reminded of the earlier chaos all over again. The first interview they played was with Kevin Snyder. He was standing with his parents as he spoke into the reporter's mic. *"After I'd been here awhile, the impression I got was that they're pretty crazy,"* said Kevin. *"Real hard-core with the Catholic stuff."*

241

"What kind of stuff, can you be more specific?" the unseen interviewer asked.

"Well," Kevin said, looking slightly embarrassed, *"my family's… you know, Catholic. But when I'd say things in class, like, that most Catholics today use birth control, for example… I almost got my head bit off. I guess they were kind of… backwards."*

Liz groaned. *Snyder, you worm. I should have stuffed you in that locker and lost the key.*

"We came here because we figured the public schools weren't safe because of the shooting," Mrs. Snyder said, indignant with anger. *"But we were deceived."*

The tape then cut to the next interview. This one was with Mrs. Summers, of all people. She must have heard the news and made a beeline for the school to say her piece.

"I'll tell you this much," Mrs. Summers was speaking somewhat hysterically, *"I decided to pull my daughters out weeks ago. And do you know why? I paid attention. I read the books they were giving the students. I looked at what was being taught and how the students were behaving, and I thought to myself, 'This isn't real Catholic teaching! This isn't what Catholics should be believing and doing!'"*

Liz swung her legs off the back of the couch and sat upright so she could watch the news right side up. That was a very odd place to cut off Mrs. Summer's interview. It made it look as though she was agreeing with Kevin Snyder's family. If they had let her clip run just a bit longer, surely that would have revealed that she didn't believe JP2HS wasn't Catholic *enough*, right?

She stood up on her crutches. Sat down. Stood up again. She had to do something. Suddenly she remembered that her mom had said something about there being a meeting of the staff and parents at the school that evening. *I've got to be there.* She pulled out her phone and called J.P.

25

ATTACK OF THE ZOMBIE MEDIA

The parking lot of JP2HS was lit up that night like nothing J.P. had ever seen. An army of news vans had arrayed themselves across the lot and set up whole banks of Klieg lights to illuminate reporters and establishing shots. It looked like even more news people were there than there had been during the day.

"This is insane," Liz whispered. "This is so bad."

J.P. didn't know how to respond. He wheeled his car to a part of the lot that was free of news vans and parked.

He and Liz walked through the crowds of media trying to look inconspicuous, if you could do that while walking on crutches. At one point, a reporter with a camera guy in tow spotted them and shouted out if she could ask a few questions.

"No comment!" Liz shouted.

To J.P., she said, "We have to get inside."

"Okay," J.P. bounced up the front steps to the school and tried the doors. Locked.

A different cameraman and reporter approached Liz as she leaned on her crutches. "Excuse me, are you students here? And if so, could you tell me your opinion on—"

Liz shoved back at the camera lens and yelled, "Oh, leave us alone!" The other reporters, seeming to sense blood, hurried over. Soon reporters were thronged around the two students, yelling questions and pulling at them.

"They're all over us," J.P. shouted. "Like a zombie apocalypse! What do we do now?!"

Just then he saw a familiar face in the crowd, one that he hadn't expected to see: Neil Flynt. He had appeared out of the crowd of onlookers and was hurrying towards them.

"Hey, get away from them!" he yelled at the reporters, elbowing his way through to Liz. "Need some help?" he asked J.P.

"Can you distract them somehow?" J.P. asked Flynt. "I need to get Liz inside. Please, do something!"

"Uh... like what? Smash their cameras?" Flynt scratched his head.

"No! Just tell them what you know!"

Flynt looked nervous. "I don't know if they'll listen to me..." he said.

"Are you kidding? Talk to them now, buddy! They'll believe everything you say!" J.P. said.

"Really? Ok," Flynn said, and then said loudly, "Yo! Reporter guys! I was with Tyler Getz when he died this past summer!" He swallowed as heads swiveled in his direction, but went on, "I always said it was murder, not an accident, but no one believed me!"

This got the reporters' attention and they clustered around Flynn as he ambled into the parking lot.

"Thanks!" J.P. breathed, and seizing his chance, he hurried Liz around the dark side of the building. He knew there was a door to the cafeteria that was usually locked, but it was worth a try.

Then he saw that the principal's office light was on. Inside, he could see Celia and Brian, talking. J.P. hurriedly tapped on the window.

"Go away!" Celia shouted, clearly annoyed. "I already told you I don't have anything to say to you guys!"

"We're not reporters!" J.P. hissed. "It's me and Liz!" He saw a silhouette of a reporter poking its head around the side of the building. *Not much time to escape.*

Celia looked at the window with a baffled expression. She walked over and cupped her hands to the glass and peered through. J.P. stepped back to give Celia a better view and waved frantically. "Let us in!" J.P. whispered loudly. "We're about to get eaten by zombies!"

Celia disappeared through the office door, and in a moment, the door to the cafeteria cracked open.

Reporters must have seen them. J.P. saw shapes stampeding towards them as he pulled Liz inside the building. Celia slammed it shut just as the crowd reached them.

Now they were standing in the unused back kitchen of the cafeteria, a narrow room with steel equipment and the row of microwaves. J.P.

could hear chattering voices of reporters outside the iron door. The voices were growing louder, gathering round, like vultures.

"What are you guys doing here?" whispered Celia.

J.P. shrugged. "Hey, I'm just trying to escape the horde." He gestured to the now closed, locked and shaded window that was rattling with a score of reporters demanding a sound bite for their respective news channels.

"Yeah, the Walking Dumb," Liz said.

J.P. saw a slender blonde figure standing in the dim light. Allie. She looked pale and anxious.

"Hey, why weren't you at school today?" he asked.

"Detective Irving called my mom and said I should stay home from school," she said. "But when I heard about James and how all the parents were called to the school for an emergency parents meeting, I made her bring me."

Then J.P. became aware that there were people talking in the room beyond, in the cafeteria itself. Loud, angry voices.

Liz leaned on her crutches and tried to see in the dim light. The kitchen smelled of stale air and rust. George was sitting, like a cafeteria lady, on a stool near the service counter, but the shade was pulled down over the serving counter so they couldn't see the crowd of people meeting in the cafeteria. There were cracks in the shade, and Liz and J.P. leaned forward to peer through at the scene beyond.

Mr. Costain had brought in a lectern from one of the classrooms, and he was standing behind it with his back to the kitchen. Beyond them, Liz beheld a sea of faces—the forty-some parents who sent their kids to John Paul 2 High. Of course, the Kosalinskis weren't there, but as Liz looked around, she could see just about everyone else.

"What's going on?" she asked.

"Shhh," George said. "They're trying to figure out whether or not to kick James out."

"Why *wouldn't* they kick James out?" Liz asked, perplexed. "Why is that even an issue?" Of course that was the answer. It seemed so simple to Liz. Just kick him out. Bing bang boom. Problem solved.

She leaned on the counter to better listen to what the adults were saying.

"Look at the scene outside! It's a media circus out there!" It was Mr. Burke's powerful voice. "Do you expect our kids to have to walk through that every day on the way to class?"

"This has been badly handled," Dr. Flynn said. His voice was more rushed than his usual clipped academic tones. Liz knew them well: her mom was always listening to one of Dr. Flynn's tapes on Catholic culture. "As soon as I heard about this situation, I sent an email detailing exactly what should be done regarding the media. They want a statement. We need to give them one."

"They won't be camped out there forever." That was Mr. Costain's voice. "Even if they don't have a statement from us."

"Well, I know a way to make sure they won't." Mr. Burke's voice again. "Take James out of the school and you take away their story. Trust me, they'll pack up and leave after that."

"Precisely!" Dr. Flynn said.

Liz felt a little proud of herself. That had been exactly what she had been thinking. Mr. Burke was an adult she felt awe and respect for, so it was gratifying that he was agreeing with her opinion.

"And if they don't pack up and leave?" Mr. Costain now. "Do we go back to the Kosalinskis and say, 'I'm sorry, we expelled your son thinking it would make our problem go away, but it didn't so I guess we made a mistake'?"

Mr. Burke was almost shouting now, "Expelling a murderer is not a mistake!"

And suddenly all of the parents were shouting, talking over one another. Mr. Costain was trying to make himself heard over the din, "Please! One at a time now, one at a time!" But it was no use.

246

Finally, one man's voice got louder than everyone else and managed to silence them. "James is a *suspect* in a murder case, a *suspect!*" Liz peeked over the lunch counter. It was Mr. Courchraine. *Of course. The lawyer.*

"Being *under suspicion* should not be an expellable offense at this school," he continued after the noise died down. Liz could hear a couple parents snort derisively at him.

"Thank you. Thank you," said Mr. Costain. "That's exactly right. James is a suspect, nothing more as far as any of us knows right now. He has the right to make his case heard before we make any decisions."

"We don't have the time to wait to let a hostile media create a narrative for us!" Dr. Flynn shouted in frustration. "Don't you hear what I'm saying, Daniel? Otherwise, they are going to crucify us. We need to be active here, not having a 'wait and see' policy. That's what's gotten the Catholic bishops in trouble before when it came to the scandals in the church, and I'll be darned if I'm going to let it happen now in this school!"

"This isn't your school, Dr. Flynn," one woman said. Liz thought it might be Athan's mom.

"Excuse me, but I'm chairman of the board, and Mr. Burke is secretary of the board. Our families have put a lot of time, and yes, money, into this school. So I'm sorry, but I think that I—and everyone else here who's donated time, talent, and treasure to this school—has a right to make a decision in this case. And the recommendation of the board is that James Kosalinski be expelled."

There was a silence. Mr. Costain said, "As the principal of this school, I can't agree to that. He has not committed any crime that I know of on the grounds of this school and—"

"You can stand up there behind your podium like you're the head of the class," shrieked one of the mothers. It was Mrs. Andros. "But we aren't your students, Mr. Costain! Dr. Flynn is right! We're the people keeping this school open, with our money and our children. And what? We're supposed to wait until this boy comes to school with a loaded gun and starts shooting our children before we can say he's guilty and finally do something?"

More shouting. "Be reasonable," Mr. Costain tried to calm the crowd of parents. "James isn't shooting anyone. He's in a cell right now and can't hurt a single person at this school—"

"Ah-ha! So you do think he's guilty!" Mr. Fogle said triumphantly. And the discussion disintegrated into more mindless shouting over one another.

"That's not what I said! That's not what I said," Mr. Costain pleaded, but no one seemed interested in listening.

Liz looked around the kitchen to get the reaction from her classmates. J.P. seemed merely fascinated by the spectacle of grownups shouting at each other, including his own dad. George and Brian were scowling at the floor. Allie was looking at Celia intently. And Celia…

Celia had her arms crossed protectively across her chest. Her face was stricken as she watched her dad's bowed shoulders on the podium.

"Celia!" Liz hissed. "Celia! Are you okay?"

Celia lifted her head and look at Liz. She stared at her dumbly for a few seconds and then looked back at her dad.

"Don't you understand what's going on?" Allie whispered.

Liz looked at her and shook her head.

George spoke up. "They've got one chance to get all the parents to agree about what to do with James, or else."

"Or else what?"

"Or else, what Dr. Flynn said would happen is going to happen. JP2 High is going to be blamed as the cause in some way for the shooting. And at least half the parents will take their kids out of JP2 High if they let James stay," said George.

Liz looked at Celia, who was silently crying. Slowly an understanding grew from the back of her mind. *This school can't stay open if half the families leave, especially if those families are big donors,* Liz thought. *And if Mr. Burke and Dr. Flynn are leading the charge to get James thrown out…*

A new thought struck Liz with an icy pang. She looked at Brian, who she realized was gazing at her steadily.

Her emotions descended into a whirl. She always thought she had more time to set things right with Brian. But if he left the school now, they would be parting with unfinished business. He'd go back to homeschooling, she'd go back to St. Lucy's or somewhere else. They'd rarely if ever cross paths again to talk it out. They'd never have a chance to be friends again. She'd basically be losing Brian… *forever.*

"Excuse me! Excuse me!" Liz could not mistake the sound of her mother's voice. "You do know that *if* we kick James Kosalinski out, and then *if* he is acquitted or the charges are dropped, the family would have grounds to sue the school." *Oh yeah,* Liz reflected ruefully. *My mom works in the law office.*

Far from settling the parents down, this announcement redoubled the shouting and crosstalk.

Liz sighed. "I'm sorry about my Mom, guys. Look, isn't there some way we can talk sense into your Dad, Celia?"

Celia's head swiveled in astonishment towards Liz. "Talk… *sense?*" she said.

"Uh, yeah," said Liz, taken aback. "You know, to keep the school together."

"To keep the school together? For what?!" Celia cried. "For *this?*" she gestured at the mob of shouting parents. "Keep the school together for the sake of excluding whoever happens to be inconvenient at the time!?"

Liz was dumbstruck. She turned to J.P. and Brian for help, both of whom shrugged, seemingly unable to decide who was right and who was wrong.

It was George who spoke. "Celia," he said lowly but gently, "If we had caught James corrupting the students, passing out dirty magazines or drugs, we'd have him out of here in a heartbeat. And those situations aren't as serious as this one."

Celia stared hard at George. He met her gaze right back. "No, George, not you, too," Celia said, her voice quavering.

"I'm sorry, Celia," said George, "but it's the right decision to make. It's not our fault if James has to go. James made his own choices. If he was the one who decided to go on a shooting rampage, he's the one who forced this on us."

Liz was going to chime in that James had punched J.P. and attacked Brad and Flynt, but she was silenced by Allie's facial expression. Allie looked from George to Celia. A single tear welled up, and Liz watched as Allie tried, but failed, to keep it from falling. "Please, you two. Please. Please don't fight about it. Leave the fighting to them." She nodded toward the cafeteria. "We all have to stay strong for each other. Please don't do this."

Liz looked at J.P. and Brian. They were both clearly helpless to say or do anything.

"If that boy is able to be identified as a student at John Paul 2 High tomorrow morning, then no one—and I repeat—no one in my family is going to John Paul 2 High ever again!" That was Dr. Flynn shouting.

"That goes for me, too!" yelled another father.

"And our family, too!"

Suddenly, the loudest shout yet from the cafeteria—*"I've heard ENOUGH!"* It was Mr. Burke's booming voice, silencing the squabbling parents.

Mr. Costain took advantage of the silence to say, "Yes, *that is enough.* You folks don't seem to grasp the point of this meeting. I didn't call you here to have a debate over whether or not to expel Mr. Kosalinski. The point of this meeting was for me to explain to you personally *why we will not be expelling Mr. Kosalinski.*"

"I see," said Mr. Burke tersely. "So there it is."

"Yes," said Mr. Costain. "There it is."

"Dan, you and I have been friends for a long time," said Mr. Burke, his voice and manner respectful but with an edge of righteous anger. "But kids *died* up there at Sparrow Hills High School. Gunned down for no reason. It was wrong, and letting James Kosalinski stay here is wrong."

Mr. Costain stared at him for a long pause, and then said, "Not when he is only a suspect—"

"I'm not done yet," Mr. Burke declared. "I propose a vote. All those in favor of allowing James Kosalinski to remain enrolled at John Paul II High, please raise your hands."

Liz, still peeking around the corner, saw her Mom the first to shoot her hand in the air. *Aw, Mom. Stop stirring up trouble.*

Mr. Costain raised his hand. So did his wife. So did the Courchraines, and the Reyes. Mr. Andros half raised his hand, but after a dirty look from Mrs. Andros, he put it back down again.

Mr. Burke continued, "And everyone prepared to quit the school if Kosalinski remains an enrolled student?"

A forest of hands shot up, first and foremost Mr. Burke's and the Flynns'. But also the Vogels, the Snyders, and others. It was mostly new parents, but Liz also saw Allie's mom and step-dad, as well as George's mother, who was crying but held her hand high. Liz knew that hers was perhaps the most crushing blow to the Costain's cause, after Mr. Burke's. Mr. Andros, along with just a small handful of others, didn't vote for either side. They just glanced nervously around, like people looking for the nearest exit. But it didn't matter. Ultimately, it was an overwhelming victory for expelling James.

But still Mr. Costain shook his head. "I am sorry, but I am not expelling..."

"That's it, then," said Dr. Flynn, shoving back his chair. "I'm through." He got up and left the hall in a rage, his face red. Mrs. Flynn, her face also red but seeming to be more embarrassed than angry, followed him out.

After a moment of stunned silence, Mr. Burke spoke up. "Dan," he said in a measured tone, "I supported you when you got fired from St. Lucy's for teaching *Humanae Vitae*. I supported you then, because you were right. But you're wrong now. And I'm so sorry, Dan. You are truly the best of men. But I can't follow you any longer. Not on this."

Mr. Costain stood dignified at his lectern though he seemed to Liz to be visibly deflated now. "I wish I could make you see why this is an issue that I just can't compromise on," he said.

Mr. Burke nodded grimly. "The same," he said.

There was a long awkward silence. Liz heard J.P. groan, and Celia was clearly trying not to bawl. She had her rosary out, and was fingering it nervously. Allie was sitting with her arm around Celia, her face red and blotchy but determined. George and Brian just stood there, stone-

251

faced. Liz waited for something to happen. *Something* had *to happen*. It couldn't just end like this!

But it did.

A few parents coughed self-consciously and stood up out of their chairs. Then more did. They began scooting their chairs toward the lunch tables, signaling they were ready to leave.

Mr. Costain gathered his self-possession and said, "I hope you will all think this over."

But it was already over. The parents were picking up their coats and bags and getting ready to brave the storm through the media circus outside, get in their cars, and go home. Liz saw her mom standing ramrod stiff, defiant, at Mr. Costain's side, glaring at the families as though they were cowardly rats abandoning a sinking ship.

George huffed a sigh as he stood up. "Anyone wanna help me and Brian reset the tables and chairs?" he said.

"Reset them for what?" Allie snapped. She pushed herself off the floor and turned away from everyone. Soon her body was shaking, even though she didn't make a sound.

Liz felt all the energy leave her body as she collapsed against a wall. Allie was right. Most of the students would be looking for a new school and wouldn't need a cafeteria tomorrow. There was no way Mr. Costain could keep paying for everything without Mr. Burke and the other parents.

JP2HS was over.

Suddenly she was aware of a palpable feeling of *déjà vu*. The night of the Sparrow Hills shooting, only half a year ago, the six of them had all sat together in the school like this. Worrying, praying, crying. But that time they were all pulling together. Now they were breaking apart.

She turned to Celia, who was still crossing her arms in front of her, leaning against the wall, fiddling with her rosary. "I'm so sorry," Liz said, and she just couldn't help it—she gave Celia a hug. Celia hugged her back, tightly. Liz just let her hold on, as long as she wanted.

26

END OF SCHOOL

Liz couldn't help with moving the tables on her crutches, so she sat silently watching her classmates pointlessly move the tables and chairs back into their usual spots.

"Well, that's it. I'm off then," George said.

"But you'll be back tomorrow?" asked Allie.

"To be honest, I don't know."

"How did your Mom vote?" Celia asked.

George stared at his shoes for a long time. Finally, he said, "Mom doesn't think James should be allowed back."

"Oh." And Celia was silent for a long time.

After a while, George added, "I don't think he should, either."

"That's understandable," said Celia in a very quiet voice.

"My dad's ready to go," said Brian. "I guess I'll see you guys around."

"Will you?" said Liz.

"Why wouldn't I?" said Brian.

Liz had wanted a few moments of private time with Brian to say all she wanted to say, even though she didn't know exactly what that would be. But it looked like it was now or never, so she just blurted it out.

"I don't know. I got mad and yelled at you. You got mad and yelled at me," said Liz. "I feel like we got issues to work out."

"Issues?" said Brian. "What do you mean issues?"

"What happened in the woods?" she said. She didn't dare say any more, not in front of everyone.

But Brian seemed to know exactly what she meant. His face turned red. "Nothing!" he said. "I told you what happened!"

Liz bit her lip. For a crazy half-second she wanted to call him a liar in front of everyone. But she didn't. She only said, "Are you going to stay with the school?"

"You heard my Dad. We're pulling out."

"I heard your Dad. I agreed with every word he had to say," said Liz. "But I'm going to stick with the school. Why can't you?"

"Your parents are sticking to the school," said Brian. "That makes it easy for you. My parents are leaving. I have to go with them."

Liz opened her mouth. There was so much to say that she couldn't think what to say first.

Brian repeated, "I have to go with them." And he got up from his chair, walked to the doorway where Mr. Burke was waiting, and left without saying goodbye.

"What was that about?" George said, bewildered.

Liz blinked. She couldn't think of how to reply. She really couldn't think of anything except for Brian, and if she would ever see him again...

"Nothing, George," Allie said suddenly, and took a step closer to Liz. "It's nothing. Just a girl thing."

"Yeah," Liz muttered, her eyes on the door that Brian had just walked through. "Just girl stuff. Nothing you guys would understand."

"Yeah, George," J.P. said suddenly. "Just forget about it."

Liz glanced at both Allie and J.P., baffled. Why were they doing this? Did they...

"Um, I gotta go," J.P. said. "I gotta turn off the lights in the... hallway, I guess." And he vanished out the door.

"Um, look. I've gotta go, too, Celia," said George.

"I know you do."

"I'm sorry."

"I know you are."

"I wish it could be different."

"I wish it, too."

"Yeah."

"Yeah."

"Goodbye, Seal."

"Goodbye, George."

And George walked away.

Liz knew herself well enough to know that if she had a major flaw, it would be insensitivity. She was blunt, and she prided herself on that. She presented one mask to the world, and if the world cut too deeply into it, she could discard it on a whim and put on a fresh mask. But tonight every nerve was jangled raw. She had no more masks.

And she agonized for Celia. She knew that Celia's whole world was collapsing around her. John Paul 2 High School was over and done. Celia's father had no job now to support his family. And the boy Celia loved had just walked out the door.

"Come on," Allie said with a sniff as she took Celia's hand. "Let's get you home, girl." And Liz couldn't think of anything better to do, so she watched as Allie hugged a grieving Celia out to the parking lot to the Costain's car.

Click. Lights out in one classroom. Click. Click. Click. Three other classrooms went dark. Click click. The lights in both bathrooms were out. J.P. remembered replacing the fuses and getting these lights to work in the first place over the summer. Now he was turning them off. Maybe for the last time.

He walked up the hallway and listened to the echoes as he went. Slap slap slap went his shoes. He'd never realized how loud he was before.

Miranda's locker was open, and empty. Like she had known they weren't coming back, and had cleared out already. *She's always been the smart one*, he thought idly. He closed the locker gently.

PSSSSSSSSSSSSSSSSSSSSSSSSSSSTTT! He was hit by a spray of water on the back of the neck and yelped in surprise. Spinning around, he found himself face to face with Mr. Costain.

"Sorry, I admit I couldn't resist, J.P.," smiled Mr. Costain. "I found this hidden in the storage room. Yours?"

"Yes, sir," J.P. said. He looked at Mr. Costain, and wished he could think of something to say, some joke to make.

"There's a cell phone in a hidden drawer in my desk that I think you ought to remove," Mr. Costain said, after a minute. "You might want to come up with another use for it. Not that I minded, too much. It helped me to take myself less seriously."

"Really?"

"Yes. Thank you, J.P."

"You're welcome, sir."

With a small sigh, Mr. Costain turned away, as though he knew it was too awkward to continue. As he started up the hallway, briefcase in hand, and the picture of Pope John Paul II under his arm, J.P. realized he was leaving his office for good.

"Hey! Dan!"

Mr. Costain turned around.

"You can't leave! You never gave us that last lecture! Remember? The Four Loves? That last love was about a guppy or something! You know, that last love that you said was the big mystery."

Mr. Costain was silent. In the dark hallway with the light of the cafeteria behind him, J.P. couldn't see his face. "J.P., did you see the meeting tonight?"

"Yes, sir, yes I did."

"Then you did hear the last lecture on Agape."

Mr. Costain turned and locked the front door of the school. "If you all can pull the cafeteria door shut when you leave…" he said.

"Wait!" J.P. said. "I don't get it!"

He hurried up to Mr. Costain, who paused with the front door ajar, and then turned and gave a brief smile to J.P. His eyes behind his glasses were bright.

"I told you it was a mystery," Mr. Costain said.

And then he walked through the door and let it fall shut behind him.

Liz was wiping up the last drops from the cafeteria counter. She didn't want to leave the place a mess: there would be ants. She'd already bagged the trash and left it outside the door. Somehow she didn't want to leave…

"Hey, princess," someone said behind her, and Liz turned and found herself enveloped in a hug. It was her dad.

She rested her head on his leather jacket and smelled his pipe smoke. Her dad rubbed her hair and said, "I just got back into town. Your mom texted me about what happened at the meeting. Lizzie? What's wrong?"

Liz sniffled, and then just hugged her dad and wiped her eyes. How was it that her dad could know when she was upset when no one else could?

After a while she calmed down.

"Lizzie, you and I need to catch up. I had no idea you cared so much for this school," her dad said. "Honest. I thought you'd be glad to see it close down."

When she found her voice, she said, "Yeah. Me too. Surprise."

He shook his head, and Liz thought he looked very unhappy. "Well, sometimes you don't know what you have until you lose it."

"Yeah." That sounded familiar. She wasn't sure where she had heard it before, but she knew she had.

He squeezed her shoulders. "Hey, I'd better go check on your mom. Looks like someone wants to talk to you."

She turned around quickly. But it was just J.P, hands in his pockets, looking embarrassed but not leaving.

"Hey." She walked up to him as her dad walked out, letting the door close behind him.

Now it was just Liz and J.P. in an empty cafeteria. The last two people left at JP2HS. An odd coincidence.

J.P. spoke first. "Whelp. I guess we dunnit."

"Yeah," said Liz bitterly. "We closed down the school. If it weren't for our stupid investigation and wanting to be hotshots, we'd still have a school."

"We said we were going to prank this school so bad it'd be closed down."

"Yeah, some prank. Who's laughing? Not James. Not Celia. Nobody is," Liz said. "Woo hoo. It's our chance to be the Local Heroes. Public service. We Helped Catch the Shooter. Woot."

"Hey! It's not really our fault," J.P. said. "It's a *good* thing we got away from James. It's a *good* thing the police got clued in to him somehow. Even if it wasn't, we had nothing to do with that part! You meant well, Liz. You did!"

"I guess," Liz said, but she didn't believe it. It really felt like her fault. She sat down and muffled her sobs in her hands.

J.P. awkwardly sat down next to her, and began to pat her on the back. J.P.'s standard thing for female breakdowns. Still, she appreciated it. At last she said, "I *didn't* mean well. Everything I did, I did for the wrong reasons."

J.P. stared out the empty cafeteria window at the bright headlights, the former students and their parents heading home, leaving JP2HS for the last time.

"So what should we do about it?"

Liz looked up at him. "I don't think there's anything we *can* do about it. JP2 High is closed for business."

But then she smiled a small, almost mischievous smile. "So we should open it again."

"Huh?" J.P. said. "Seriously?"

"Why not?"

"Well, for one thing, it's a lot easier to knock something down than it is to build it up." J.P. paused thoughtfully. "On the other hand…"

"What?"

"We've proven that we can do the easy thing—we blew it up. Maybe our next goal should be to do the hard thing."

"Bring it back to life," Liz said.

J.P. nodded. "Reopen the school."

"It *would* be the ultimate prank," Liz said.

J.P. grinned. "Well, little lady? Is it a deal?"

Liz smiled, too. "Yeah. Okay. I'm in." She spit on her hand and held it out. J.P. did the same, and shook.

"Now," Liz said, grinning nervously, "how are we gonna do it?"

THE STORY CONTINUES...

"The Mass is ended. Go in peace."

Behind the screen, the tired-looking priest made a quick crossing motion in the vague direction of the inmates, then turned and walked through a door at the left. The congregation, about fifteen inmates, shuffled slightly in their benches. A few of them glanced questioningly back at the guard watching them from the back of the chapel. "Hey, pig," one of them said. "We gonna go, or what?"

"Shut up!" the guard barked. "You got ten minutes left of chapel time."

The inmate who had spoken hunched in his seat, muttering. For a minute or so, nothing happened. Most of the others looked happy for the rest. Most of them were older—lifers, in their sixties and seventies.

The guard grew bored. "Wish I could move them," he muttered to himself. "Still got two more services to sit through—"

"Excuse me."

The guard looked up, suddenly alert. One of the prisoners was standing six feet away—a big, sullen looking kid with a fat face and bushy hair.

"What?" the guard said irritably.

"Can I play the piano?" The kid pointed to where a battered-looking piano stood in the corner.

The guard shrugged and walked over to the piano. He unlocked the padlock on the lid, and gave the instrument a shove to make sure it didn't move. "All right," he said curtly, and went back to his post at the door.

A few catcalls followed the kid as he walked over to the piano. "Look at that lady!" "It's Elton John!"

The prisoner sat down at the piano, and played a loud, ringing chord. The catcalls died away.

The other inmates and guards watched as the kid's fingers ran in a blur over the keys, and a stream of unbelievable music filled the chapel: complex, quick, varied – first angry and frantic, then slow and sad, then dizzyingly fast and desperate...

Then, as suddenly as it had started, the music stopped halfway through, unfinished. The kid sat there for a second, his fingers frozen over the keys, and then stood up, walked back to his pew and sat down, the same sullen look on his face as before.

There was silence for a few moments. There was a scattering of astonished applause. Then a loud buzzer rang.

"Get up!" the guard hollered. The prisoners got to their feet and shuffled to the exit. A few gave the kid curious looks. Some even looked grateful. It didn't seem to matter to the kid. He had the same sullen look as before as he followed the other prisoners out. The only difference was a certain disembodied look in his eyes, as if he was thinking of something far away, or long ago.

READ MORE IN
DARK NIGHT OF THE SCHOOL
John Paul 2 High
Book Six

SEE MORE AT
WWW.CHESTERTONPRESS.COM

ABOUT THE AUTHOR

Christian M. Frank is the pen name for a group of writers known as the John Paul 2 High Team. They developed the series and created the characters, and several of them take turns writing the books. Book 5 was written by Andrew O'Neill and John Doman (with help from Ryan Corrigan).

Andrew O'Neill graduated from Christendom College. He lives in the mountains of northwestern Virginia with his beautiful wife and two excitable children. His Big Boy job is in homeschool education and curriculum, but when he's not doing that you can probably find him playing video games, studying various martial arts, eating Chinese food, or making fun of the other Christian Franks.

John Doman lives somewhere outside Philadelphia with his wife, two sons and his little baby daughter. He's happy to contribute to Book 5. He hopes that you will buy Book 5. He also hopes that you jump up and down, right now. Do it. Jump up and down. Don't you want him to be happy?

CHESTERTON PRESS

is the publisher of fun Catholic fiction that evangelizes the imagination through telling a good story, inspired by the wit and wisdom of the great writer G.K. Chesterton. You can find us on the web at www.chestertonpress.com.

WWW.CHESTERTONPRESS.COM

CPSIA information can be obtained at www.ICGtesting.com
Printed in the USA
BVOW04s1728040315

390251BV00010B/370/P

9 780989 941167